BLACK

To Reality

Russell Blake

First edition.

Books@RussellBlake.com

ISBN: 978-1503048775

Published by

Reprobatio Limited

Chapter 1

Ten months earlier, Los Angeles, California

A spotlight played over the crowd at the Pomona Fairgrounds as the band onstage delivered the last song of their short set to cheers and whoops. The sky was dark, night having fallen an hour earlier, and the assembled throng's eyes glittered as the beam lit them as it passed from section to section.

Four bikers in denim and leather eyed a pair of tipsy sorority girls dancing with each other to the pounding beat. Oblivious to their admirers, they swayed together as the harmonies kicked in on the funky chorus. A trio of Latino youths with tattoos running up their necks pushed by, bandannas tied around shaved heads, eyes darting furtively as they avoided the bikers. The metal detector at the entry gates had discouraged any weapons from entering the venue.

The band hit the final chord, and the singer, Goth ebony ducktails gleaming, held up a black-gloved hand with two fingers extended in a victory sign. He soaked up the applause while pretending to ignore the camera crew filming his practiced stance, adoring his shirt bedecked with ruffles and Victorian frills and his shiny latex pants that left little question about his endowment. Peals of feminine laughter greeted the guitar player's tossing of his soaked T-shirt into the audience, and then the stage went dark in preparation for the set change. The band sauntered off to the side, led by flickering flashlights as the crew took possession of the area and spirited the equipment away so the final act could perform.

The concert was part of the *Rock of Ages* competition, a musical talent show and reality TV show whose goal was to find the "best

1

band of the year," per its much-hyped tagline, centering around the trials and tribulations of the bands as they competed in a series of elimination rounds. On this, the show finale, a roster of name acts had been invited to play for the packed crowd, and each band had worked hard to outdo the others in sheer intensity, if not talent. The earlier song by the first of the two surviving groups had been a showstopper, and the tension was palpable as the final act prepared to deliver the performance of its career.

Backstage was pandemonium as hangers-on, band members, roadies, and film crews contended for limited space. The performers kept to themselves while burly men carried amplifiers to the exit, to be loaded into the U-Hauls that waited like orange sentries on the dirt behind the line of temporary dressing rooms erected that morning. A comedian dabbed his brow by the monitor mixing board, wisecracking with his manager, who'd turned out for his client's first national television appearance, albeit only the entertainment between the main attractions.

Recorded music blared from the PA system as the final band's roadies began the laborious process of readying the equipment for their performance. The comedian got the cue from the stage manager and strode out. A single spotlight followed him to center stage, where a lone microphone awaited his shot at fame and fortune. The canned music faded and he began his shtick. The audience shifted restlessly as he quipped, not being there for a comedy routine but willing to endure it as part of the show.

The upcoming band members exited their dressing room and moved to stage left. The diminutive female singer was visibly agitated as she checked her watch.

"Where is he?" she fumed. "This is a disaster."

Christina's band was the favorite going into the hotly contested final round. Her group, Last Call, a bluesy southern-inspired rock quartet reminiscent of the Black Crowes, was neck and neck with the remaining contender, Nth Degrees, a pop-oriented act in the mold of Maroon 5. Christina's voice, a scratchy croon reminiscent of Janis Joplin, had been a consistent crowd pleaser, and the band's laid-back boogie approach had won many over – but she understood, now more than ever, that none of that would matter if they didn't turn in a heart-stopping final performance.

The bass player shook his head. "He seemed fine earlier at the bar."

"But nobody's seen him since. Which leaves us completely screwed, Peter," she fired back.

"Don't worry. He'll be here," Ed, the drummer, assured her. "Rick wouldn't miss it. He'll be here any second." He twirled a drumstick with pudgy fingers, his perennial grin beaming, offsetting Peter's near-constant frown.

"I swear I'll cut his balls off…" Christina threatened and then spun as loud voices called from the backstage entrance.

"Yo, homeboy. You better check yourself," one of the gargantuan security guards warned Rick, the guitar player, who was clutching the wall for support as he made his way toward them.

Christina's eyes narrowed as she took him in – he looked whacked out of his mind on something. His usually serious expression twisted into a crooked smile as he lit a cigarette and approached unsteadily.

"What the hell is this?" she demanded. "Are you stoned?"

"Just a little something to take the edge off. A few hits of weed. No biggie."

"You ready to rock, wild man?" Ed asked, holding up his beer, trying to lighten the mood.

"Dude. How much did you drink?" Peter muttered to Rick as he scowled at his sister, fearing one of her infamous explosions.

A young woman a head taller than Christina marched up with a clipboard, followed by a camera crew, and Christina choked back her rage, not wanting to air her issues on national TV. By now the cameras were a constant in their lives, and she barely registered their presence, inured to them over the twelve weeks of the show's run. The tension between Christina and Rick had been conspicuously documented as time had worn on, but that was to be expected between boyfriend and girlfriend in a high-stakes proposition like the contest. Still, she wanted to avoid any more dirt being plastered across the websites and tabloids that were following their saga, so Christina fixed a lackluster smile in place as the woman cleared her throat.

"T minus five and counting. Is everyone ready?" she asked, looking Christina dead in the eyes.

"Sarah. What a delightful surprise. I wasn't aware we were going on shortly," Christina said, her tone mild even as each syllable dripped with hate. Christina had cornered Rick several weeks earlier and forced a confession out of him – he'd been having an affair with Sarah for most of the last six weeks, a dirty little secret they'd managed to keep out of the viewers' eyes but not out of Christina's. The obvious source of the friction that had developed between Rick and Christina, it was made worse because Christina couldn't do anything about it. Sarah was the production head and answered to the impresario who ran the show, and if Christina complained, she was afraid her big break would nosedive. Besides, if her boyfriend couldn't keep his dick in his pants, that wasn't anyone's fault but his – and it wasn't like Christina had their trysts on film, so it would be her word against Sarah's.

She turned to watch the comedian build his bit, ignoring Sarah in a deliberately dismissive manner. What Rick saw in her, with her prim slacks and dressed-for-success blouse, escaped Christina, but every time she saw the woman, it was like a slap, and angry as she now was, she didn't want any more interaction than necessary.

"Just doing my job, Christina. Looks like the comedian is finishing up." Sarah glanced at Rick, who was weaving slightly as he smirked at her. "Are you all right?"

"Tip top. Never better. Gonna rock the walls down, baybee!" he declared overly loudly.

Sarah frowned and checked her watch. "When the lights go down, you have two minutes to get on stage and ready to perform. You know the drill by now." She hesitated. "Good luck."

Ed shook his head. "Never say that. You're supposed to say, 'break a leg.'"

"Right," she said, her tone betraying her lack of interest. Sarah turned on her heel and marched away, leaving the band to its last minute preparations.

Rick blew a cloud of smoke over their heads and grabbed a bottle of beer from the cooler strategically positioned near the stage.

"Don't you think you've had enough?" Peter cautioned in a stage whisper.

"Dude. Relax. You're not my dad. I got it covered." Rick chugged two-thirds of the bottle in four swallows and belched loudly, drawing another furious glare from Christina.

The comedian delivered his trademark punch line, and the crowd rewarded him with half-hearted laughter. The lights dimmed and the taped music came back on. A short, wiry man with ebony skin approached, wearing a rainbow-hued three-hundred-dollar silk shirt. "This is it. You gonna kill 'em dead. That's what I'm talkin' about," he assured them, slapping Rick on the back. Rooster was their show mentor, a blues legend who had shepherded the group through a series of successful performances. "Give it everything you got, for real, like at that last rehearsal. This is yours. You own these people."

"Tell Rick," Christina fumed. She strode with catlike grace onto the darkened stage, her trademark black unitard a second skin. The rest of the band trailed her, and the roadies handed Rick and Peter their instruments as Ed climbed behind his drum kit. A buzz of anticipation rose from the audience when Rick flipped on his Marshall amplifier and gave his guitar a quick check, which always infuriated Christina, who felt it was unprofessional and reduced the impact when they began playing.

A disembodied voice emanated from the PA speakers as the host's voice announced them, and then the lights blazed megawattage and Ed launched into the snare roll that started the song. The crowd cheered. Rick and Peter ground out a raucous blues riff, Rick all peacock strut as he did a modified duckwalk, and then Christina let loose, her voice a thing of magic, smoldering soul and bitter lament.

The groove was powerful, and everything was perfect until Rick approached the mike for the chorus and stumbled, his suede boot catching on the edge of one of three oriental rugs that were part of the band's trappings. He saved himself but flubbed one of the chords, shooting Peter a panicked glance as he momentarily lost the notes.

It was a small thing, but enough, and when Rick sang his harmony it was flat, his moxie evaporated. He recovered by the next verse and tried to make up for his glitch with attitude, but when he launched into his solo, it lacked his usual flair, ending on a sour note that elicited winces from the audience.

Christina had tears in her eyes as the song ended, her voice as strong as it had ever been, disappointed realization clear even as she battled her emotions. Rick whipped off his guitar strap, swung his guitar by its neck, and shattered it in a display of rage before storming away, cursing. He tripped again and went down face first at the edge of the stage, drawing a shocked gasp from the audience, and a chorus of boos followed him as a roadie helped him to his feet.

The telephonic votes were tallied, and the results were unambiguous. Last Call had indeed had its last call; Nth Degrees was the winner of the first season.

Within four months their hastily recorded debut album went on to break sales records, and its charismatic front man, Alex Sage, was propelled to the forefront of notable new artists.

Rick and the band parted ways after the show. His departure from Christina's Hollywood apartment followed shortly thereafter. The band soldiered on with a string of guitarists, none of whom lasted for longer than ninety days, as Christina waited for her second chance: the runner-up band would get to return on the second season of *Rock of Ages*, and this time, she intended to win.

Chapter 2

Artemus Black stood next to his Cadillac Eldorado while the gas pump dial blinked as if mocking him, knowing that his meager ten dollars of fuel would be barely enough to get him to his office for the rest of the week. He'd contemplated taking the bus, but nobody except crazies, illegals, and the homeless resorted to public transportation in Los Angeles, and he didn't count himself in their number. Yet.

At the rate things were going, though, he'd soon be sleeping in his car. He hadn't had a case for two months and owed back rent both to his landlady and for the new office he'd leased after solving several high-profile cases that had paid him handsomely. Of course, like most things in his life, that had turned out to be a case of the gods first raising up those they would destroy, and things had taken a nosedive ever since the ink on the rental agreement had dried. Roxie had badgered him into getting the larger suite in a prestigious building against his normally conservative better judgment, which had turned out to be a huge mistake as the bills mounted and his bank balance shrank.

Payday was on Friday, and he had no money for her – a first in their relationship, and one that he'd been racking his brain for ways to avoid, but to no avail. He'd rarely been this broke before, and while he desperately hoped for something to shake loose, nothing had manifested yet. All he was currently holding was the money in his wallet and a depressing future.

The pump clicked off, and he shook the nozzle, trying to eke out every last drop before sliding it back into its socket and twisting the gas cap into place. His head was splitting as he slid behind the wheel and cranked the ignition. The big V8 roared to life, consuming a quarter of his fill-up, he was sure. The fuel gauge barely moved from its position on empty. He sighed as he pulled onto the street and gently eased down on the gas pedal in a futile attempt to stretch the go-juice as far as he could.

Black had recently been moonlighting at a club on the strip for ten bucks an hour under the table, providing security from ten till two – the only reason he had any money at all, but an insult to the value of his PI license and skills, such as they were. After only five hours of sleep, the headache was a constant companion, and he regretted rolling out of bed instead of dozing until noon.

The new building was hardly high-end, but with a granite-tiled lobby and an elevator, it was worlds nicer than his old digs. When he arrived at his floor, he approached the office. He hesitated, debating slinking off and not putting in an appearance, but discarded the idea. Roxie would simply badger him via his cell phone until he answered, and she could be relentless.

He twisted the knob and breezed into the foyer. Roxie was at her desk, on the web. Mugsy's porcine form slumbered at her feet. The faint taint of cat box perfumed the air, and Black's nose wrinkled as he moved toward her. Several weeks ago she'd adopted a bleached white hairdo with orange tips and looked somewhat like a polar bear – although her leather pants and stretch top quickly took his mind off her coif.

"Good morning, Roxie. Any calls?" he asked, choosing to ignore the cat box odor in favor of a diplomatic opening.

"The landlord. Wants to know when you're going to pay the rent."

"Always asks good questions, doesn't he?"

"Speaking of which, we have no money."

"I know."

"And I have to pay my bills. And eat. And buy gas. All that mundane stuff people do with their salaries."

Black sighed. "I'm not going to kid you, Roxie…"

She snorted. "I knew it. I'm screwed. I can't believe I waited around this week to see if you'd pull a rabbit out of your hat and come up with some cash."

"I'm sorry. I really am. I don't know what happened to the business. It's like all my leads just dried up."

"You could always call your parents. They'd have no problem sending you some loot."

He shook his head. "You know better than that."

"Do I? The prospect of starving to death and being evicted must have clouded my judgment." She took in his expression. "You look like shit. I mean more than usual."

"Thanks, Roxie. You look nice too."

"No, I mean it. Are you on the pipe? Is that what happened to all the money?"

"I'm not on crack. We've just had a bad run of it lately."

"Right. Unfortunately I can't tell my landlady that instead of handing her the rent. 'Sorry, Mrs. Tran, my boss swears he's not smoking the hubba rock, but he can't pay me...' You see how that won't solve my problem?"

"At least Mugsy's getting enough to eat. Nice to see he hasn't slowed his onloading," Black countered, changing the subject.

"Right. Pick on a helpless cat instead of doing something productive."

"I'm here, aren't I?"

"That's super."

Black paused before speaking. "Roxie, I hate to say this, but you may need to look for something else."

"No shit. I've been doing that for the last week. This may come as a shock, but these days jobs are really hard to come by. Although I think I've found something that could work. I was just hoping I wouldn't have to do it."

"What's the job?" he asked, edging by her desk, stiff from the two fights he'd had to break up the prior night during his bouncer gig.

"Some old woman who was married to a studio head in the forties. Lives in Beverly Hills. She's a recluse and very demanding,

9

from what I can tell. Mean as a snake, too. I'd be acting as her assistant. 'Girl Friday' is what she called it."

"Does it pay well?"

"She's also cheap. But it does pay better than not getting any money, which is what this has turned into."

"I can't argue with that. When were you thinking about starting?"

"Sounds like I better make the call right now, unless you're holding out on me."

"Maybe she likes cats. Most recluses like cats, right?"

"I already asked. She hates them. Allergic."

"Ah. So what about Mugsy?"

"He'll be staying here until I can convince my landlady to let me have a pet. She's real anti on cats and dogs."

"Tell her he's a long-haired potbellied pig. That's not far from the truth."

"Ha ha, Mister Funny. Very amusing." She returned to playing her video game. "I want this computer as part of my salary, okay?"

"You got it. It'll save me the trouble of hauling it out of here in the dead of night."

"Guess it wasn't such a great idea to move uptown, huh?"

"Might have been premature." Black walked into his office and removed his jacket, taking care to hang it on the coat rack he'd bought. All the furniture and systems were new, and he was kicking himself for squandering ten grand on useless crap when his old stuff had been perfectly serviceable, if slightly worse for wear due to Mugsy's destructive bent. He was just settling in behind his desk when he heard his friend Stan's voice boom from the lobby area.

"Nice digs. How you doing, hot stuff?"

Black moved to the doorway and saw Stan staring at Mugsy while Roxie ignored him, as was her custom.

"Big man. What brings you by?" Black asked.

"Just wanted to see how the other half lives. Sweet. Everything looks expensive. Except for the walrus there," he said, eyeing Mugsy.

"He's not a walrus. He's a hippo."

"I always get those confused."

"Come into my office. Take a load off," Black invited, refusing to acknowledge Roxie's glare.

Stan plopped down on Black's new pride and joy – a two-thousand-dollar black Italian leather sofa that sat at the far end of his office. Black returned to his desk and took a seat in his executive chair.

"So how hangs it? This a social call?" Black asked.

"Nah, I was just in the neighborhood. Had a murder/suicide three blocks from here. Some commune house. The woman who ran it, called herself Sister Mercy, took a golf club to the guy she was sleeping with before slashing her wrists."

"Sounds messy."

"The other nutcases staying at the house say the last thing they heard was her screaming, 'Fore.' That's a joke, by the way."

Black offered a tight smile. "I get it. How you been?"

"Same old. People keep killing each other, so good job security."

"And you still have your health."

"Body of a forty-year-old. German shepherd. But still."

"Could be worse."

Stan nodded. "How about you? Anything interesting?"

"It's been slow, buddy. Really slow." Black recounted his financial woes.

"Damn. What are you going to do?"

"I don't know. I've got calls out to everyone, but nothing's surfaced. I'm kinda up against the wall, to be honest. Roxie's taking another job. It sucks."

"I'll nose around and see if I can find anything. You should have reached out."

"Why burden you with my problems?"

"Misery loves company." Stan ran an approving hand over the surface of the couch. "This is nice."

"Wanna buy it? Special for you, today only."

"I'm surprised that porcupine in the other room hasn't ripped it to shreds. Your last place looked like a holding cell at County Central."

"Roxie's under orders not to let the fat bastard anywhere near my office."

"Since when did that stop him?"

"Fair point."

Stan grinned. "How's the Swedish hottie?"

"Swiss. Sylvia's Swiss."

"Right. So how is she?"

"Good. Selling paintings. She applied for a work permit and got it, so she's here for the duration."

"Do I hear wedding bells?"

"Only if you recently took a blow to the head. We have no plans. We're just taking it slow, enjoying life."

"A sensible man. What's Roxie going to do for work? You never said."

"Play nursemaid to some geriatric."

"You mean other than you, right?"

"Touché."

Stan rose stiffly, his belly hanging over his belt, his sports jacket looking like he'd pulled it off a corpse.

"Remind me not to come by to get a pep talk from you, Black. Now I want to lock myself in my garage with the engine running."

"Your building has a carport."

"Still."

Black escorted his friend to the foyer. Mugsy cracked an eye open and gave them both a truculent stare before resuming his slumber. Roxie didn't acknowledge either of them as they walked past her desk.

"See you around, gorgeous," Stan tried.

She didn't look up from the monitor. "Not if I see you first."

Chapter 3

Black was checking the online help wanted listing of the *Los Angeles Times* when the phone rang. Roxie answered, and after a brief pause, she called out from her desk.

"Boss?"

"Use the intercom, Roxie. These phones cost a fortune so we could speak over it."

"What? I can't hear you."

Black raised his voice. "I said use the intercom."

"Why? Bobby's on line one."

Black looked at the blinking button and was reaching for it when the speaker on his phone crackled to life.

"You have a call," Roxie said.

"I got that."

"On line one. Crap. I hung up when I pushed the wrong button to access this stupid intercom."

"That's really passive-aggressive."

"It was an honest mistake."

"Is Bobby in his office?"

"He sounded like he was on his cell."

Black punched in Bobby's number. When he answered, Black could hear a car radio in the background with the Eagles crooning about tequila sunrises and lost love.

Bobby sounded in typically good spirits. "Babe. That Roxie must not like me. She cut me off."

"She adores you, Bobby. She's just getting used to the new phone system."

"Right. Hey, I think I may have something for you. That is, unless you won the lottery."

"Right now I'm only a night away from turning tricks in rest-stop bathrooms."

"Good visual. I'm headed into the office. Can you meet me here in an hour?"

"I may have to ride the bus. The gas might break the bank. Can't you tell me about it over the phone?"

"Nah. It's…it's sensitive. Just be at my office. Sell blood or something, but make it, okay, buddy?"

"Put that way, how can I refuse?"

"That's the spirit. See you in a few."

Black hung up and stared at the handset before lowering it softly into its expensive cradle. If Bobby was going to drag him across town, he had a client. That was good news. That he needed to break it in person was the bad news – Black knew him well and understood that an in-person pitch meant it was something Black would normally say no to.

Only at this point, no wasn't in his vocabulary.

Black finished applying for two more low-level security jobs that paid only slightly more than minimum wage and shut off his computer, anxious to find out what Bobby had up his sleeve. Roxie was just getting ready to go to lunch when he strode past her. She glared at him like he'd exposed himself.

"I'm headed over to see the dragon lady and cinch the deal. We agreed to terms on the phone," she announced.

"That's great. Bobby says he's got a client, so you may want to hold off for an hour."

"I can always back out if you land something. But I don't want to stall her. I get the feeling I'm the only one she liked out of all the people who applied, and I'd hate to lose it because I ran late for our first official date."

"That's probably wise. Cross your fingers for me."

"Are you going to stop at your place and change first? You look like you slept in that suit."

"I do not. It's just been a little while since I could afford to get it dry cleaned."

"Which is why it looks like the kind you get when you're released from jail."

"I don't think they do that anymore."

"Probably because nobody would hire someone in a jail suit. Which is my point."

"It's only Bobby."

"I'm just trying to save you some embarrassment, that's all."

"I'm going to miss you bagging on my clothes once you're gone."

"Don't get all choked up."

"You going to wish me luck?"

She sighed. "Hope you don't blow it."

"I might cry. That was really touching, Roxie."

Her cell phone vibrated, and she turned her attention to it, Black forgotten as she giggled at a message and rapid-texted in reply.

"Lock up when you leave. I don't know how long this will take," Black said.

"Huh?"

"Roxie, you heard me."

"If it wasn't 'I'll have your two weeks salary by closing time', I'm afraid I didn't catch it."

He sighed and moved to the front door. "Could you clean the cat box, please? The place smells like ass."

"Be happy to, right after I cash my paycheck."

The drive to Bobby's office took half an hour with lunchtime congestion clogging the streets, an endless stream of luxury vehicles on parade in a city where appearances were everything. High streaks of pale clouds stretched across the sky, transitioning from white to beige as they met the horizon, the smog thick after morning rush hour. Black tapped his fingers on the steering wheel as the sun played across his face, the top down, his fedora on the seat beside him, the early spring day delivering just enough snap to be refreshing. An old Yesterday & Today song blared from the car stereo, the guitar wailing over the chorus, and for a moment Black was back in his garage, wailing along with David Meniketti, matching the solos on the album note for note. Had time really flown that fast? It seemed like just yesterday…

A glance at himself in the rearview mirror brought him back to reality, and he switched the stereo off, suddenly maudlin. Here he was, forty-three, with literally nothing to show for it other than an eccentric wardrobe and an old Cadillac, his glory days long faded. He eyed his black hair and noted a few gray strands at the temples and in his sideburns, which depressed him even more. He'd refused to go down the hair dye road, but there was no denying he was getting older. No, scratch that. Getting old. Not older. Women Roxie's age didn't give him a second glance – he was as good as invisible to anyone of the opposite sex under thirty. And in a town where the worst possible sin was being poor, he was doubly forgettable, even to mature eyes. No power to broker, no entourage to command, no bling to flash.

He'd sold the Rolex Nina had given him for his birthday to cover the move and the hefty security deposit on the new office, as well as some unexpected repairs to the Eldorado when the transmission had given up the ghost. Even though he'd felt raped after the jeweler gave him only half its new price, he'd been happy to get the cash. But it had quickly evaporated, and now even that reserve was gone.

When he pulled into the parking area of Bobby's luxury high-rise, the attendant gave him a skeptical glance before handing him a ticket.

"Machine's broken. You going to be long?" the man asked.

"An hour or so."

The attendant took a long look at the Cadillac and nodded, his expression making it obvious that Black didn't belong amidst the Lexuses and Mercedes and BMWs. Black couldn't have agreed more completely. Right now he hated L.A., with its surface glitz and focus on conspicuous consumption.

His mood was glum as he stepped into Bobby's office lobby, where a smoldering Latina in a business suit met his gaze with boredom as he approached the reception desk.

"May I help you?" she asked, white teeth flashing.

"I'm here for Bobby."

"And you are?"

"You must be new. I'm Black."

She blinked twice as she glanced at her console and pressed a button. He noted her eyes were hazel. A good color for her. She murmured into her headset, and her attitude changed to a more interested one.

"Yes, Mr. Black. Er...Bobby says you know the way to his office?"

"I do indeed."

Bobby was at his desk, wearing a banana-colored silk shirt with the collar open, the better to display his Palm Springs tan and a garish gold necklace that would have made an Indian bride blush.

Bobby greeted him with a grin. "There he is. Mr. Fashion. Look at you in that suit. Take a load off, tough guy. It's good to see you."

Black eyed him distrustfully. "I feel like the only blonde at the bar after last call's announced. What've you got up your sleeve, Bobby?"

Bobby came around his desk and offered the cosmetically enhanced smile of a shark. "What I have is your chance to be famous, my lad."

"You start drinking early today?"

"I'm serious. When was the last time you played?"

"Played? Played what? Poker? With myself? What are you talking about?"

"Music. Guitar. You were one of the best."

"What does that have to do with a client?"

"Well, I told you it was complicated. I wasn't kidding."

Black's eyes narrowed. "Uh-huh."

"This one's right up your alley. You're a natural for it. In fact, I'd say there's nobody else who could pull it off."

"Pull what off?"

"I'm gonna make you a star, kid," Bobby said, pretending to flick an imaginary cigar as he waggled his eyebrows.

"You into pills or powder? Or smoking it?"

"I'm serious. This is your big break."

"My big break. Right now I need a paycheck. Tell me what the hell you're talking about, Bobby. I'm not having a great day."

"Fortune has smiled upon you, my friend. Most people never get a second chance. But you just got one. And it pays."

Black perked up. "Go on."

"You ever hear of *Rock of Ages?*"

"Gospel song, right?"

"Reality TV show. A combination of *Jersey Shore* and *American Idol*."

"Oh, yeah, I saw an episode. A bunch of washed-up bands living in some house. It was a freak show. I turned it off when one of the rappers got into a fight with some chick over his banging her trailer-trash roommate."

"A race to the bottom, my friend, but huge ratings. America loves its reality shows, the uglier the better."

"Fine. Where do I come in?"

"Last year the band that looked good to win blew it in the finals. The guitar player showed up whacked out of his skull on something. Cost them the trophy. But they get to come back this year because they were the runner-up."

"And?"

"And they need a guitar player."

Black stared at Bobby like he'd just announced that Jesus was waiting to meet him in the conference room.

"Bobby, I'm not a guitar player. I'm a PI. Remember? A forty-something PI."

"Which is why you're perfect. My client thinks something stinks about what happened last year and wants someone on the inside to root around. If you're in the band, that's the ideal cover."

"Maybe you didn't hear me. I don't play guitar anymore."

"Isn't it like riding a bike? Come on. This is right up your alley. Plus, the money's not bad."

"Really?" Black asked, curiosity getting the better of him.

"Five hundred a week to be on the show, but my client's willing to pay another couple of grand a week for the snooping."

"Who's the client?"

Bobby looked suddenly uncomfortable. "That's confidential."

"Why?"

"Part of the deal."

"Let me get this straight. A mystery client's willing to pay me two grand a week to play in a band and poke my nose where it doesn't belong?"

"That's basically it. Oh, and the grand prize if the band wins is a hundred thousand smackers. Which would be a four-way split. Plus a record contract."

"A record contract," Black repeated.

"Dude. You're a quasi-celebrity. You founded one of the most popular bands of the nineties and penned their best-loved songs. You're a shoe-in for this."

"What kind of music?"

"Who gives a shit? It all sounds the same to me – like alley cats going at it."

"What's the name of the band?"

"Last Call."

"Poetic justice in that, isn't there?"

Bobby paused. "So are you in?"

Black shifted uncomfortably. "I haven't picked up a guitar in twenty years."

"You were a god. Tell me that goes away."

"I honestly don't know if I could do it. Plus, I don't exactly look the part…"

"That's easy. I'll make an appointment with a girl I know who works miracles."

"Does she do cosmetic surgery?"

Bobby ignored him. "I got a CD of the band if you want to hear what they're all about." Bobby returned to his desk, picked up a plastic case, and tossed it to Black, who caught it in midair. He examined the cover, which featured a typical retro-seventies group with a stunningly beautiful female singer lounging on a paisley couch, one leg hanging off the edge, a pouty come-hither expression on her face.

"Wow. Can she sing?"

"Who cares? Look at her! Can any of 'em really sing? It's not about vocal talent, babe, it's about presence. And she's got it in spades."

"Band looks like they're all, what, early thirties? I've got ten years on them, easy."

"Hogwash. You look twenty. And you'll look like a teenager after Monique gets done with you."

"I don't know, Bobby…"

"Check out their tunes. If you think it's something you can relate to, just do it. Don't overthink this. It's a chance to do something you were great at, make some money, and get on national TV. People would kill for the chance."

"How long do I have to think about it?"

"I need an answer by tomorrow. Show starts taping in a week."

"How long does it run?"

"They shoot for twelve weeks. If you make the grade, plan on three months of living at the mansion with the band."

"What? That's insane. I don't have that kind of time to blow."

"I thought you had no clients."

"Not right now. But, Bobby, living in some house with a bunch of musicians, cameras following me around all the time…I mean, that's hell on earth."

"Nonsense. It sounds like a blast. Reliving your youth. Look, I've got a meeting I need to get to, but do me a favor and think it over, would you? I told the client I thought you were perfect, and it's enough money to save your bacon."

"I wish. I already owe three grand in rent, with another three coming due on Friday, plus my apartment, utilities, you name it. Roxie's even going to work somewhere else."

"Then you don't have anything tying you down, am I right? Come on. This is a paid vacation. You'll be out of hock within a month of doing the show, and the rest is gravy. And just think – if you win it, you get a hell of a sweetener, plus another shot at the big time with a record deal. Tell me how any of that sucks."

Black tried to quiet the buzz of unease in his stomach, but the truth was that it *would* get him out of hot water…and the prospect of a record deal was one he'd long ago dismissed as out of reach after the fiasco with his band.

He stood and held up the CD. "No promises. But I'll listen to it and do some thinking. You around tomorrow?"

Bobby approached him again and put an arm around his shoulders. Black noted he smelled of expensive cologne. "Always for you, babe. Now go have a couple of beers or tokes or whatever you do, and listen to your new band. My secretary says they're good. I've got ties older than her, so that means the kids dig it."

"You don't own any ties."

"You know what I mean. Just keep an open mind. Promise me that."

Black exhaled noisily and nodded as Bobby steered him to the door.

"Fine. And thanks, Bobby… I think."

"No, thank you, Mr. Rock God. You and Jimmy Plant, two hall-of-famers in my book. Classics. Old school guitar heroes who can show the youngsters a thing or two."

"Pretty sure that's Jimmy Page, Bobby."

"Whatever."

Chapter 4

Black sat in traffic, listening to Christina's smoky voice wailing over the guitars and bass. The woman could sing, that was obvious, and the tunes were pretty good, he thought – better than he'd expected – and easier to play than some, if you could manage the laid-back boogie style. When the guitar player cut into his solo, it was pure blues, harkening back to a cross between ZZ Top and Stevie Ray Vaughn – a style that Black knew well, although he tended toward more speed. But it was in his league, even if he was rusty.

Rusty being a euphemism for completely clueless after two decades without strumming so much as a chord.

When he made it back to the office, Roxie was still out. Mugsy glared at him with the studied indifference of a feline Buddha from his position on the lobby sofa.

"Look at you, you tubby bastard. I could probably cut steaks off you and live for a week," Black said.

Mugsy, as if sensing his thoughts, leapt off the couch and rubbed against Black's legs, leaving a trail of hair on his trousers. Black stared down at the fur as Mugsy darted into the dark area beneath Roxie's desk. Black debated chasing him down and throttling him but chose the high road, removing most of the hair with some of Roxie's Scotch tape while a pair of beady cat eyes peered at him from relative safety.

When Roxie returned an hour later, she looked about as happy as Black felt.

"How did it go?" he asked.

"I heard this disembodied voice cackling as I shook her hand, and then it said, 'Welcome to hell.' Is that a bad sign?"

"Sounds like a winner to me. You guys should get along swell."

"Tell me you got the client."

"It's not that simple." He filled her in on Bobby's offer.

"Crap. I'm screwed. No way you're going to last more than a week or two unless the other bands suck hard," she offered helpfully.

"I haven't even decided whether I'm going to do it."

"Oh. Right. You're going to turn down national television and having a shot at stardom and a lot of money. I forgot how logical you can be. My bad."

"I don't even remember how to play."

"Start practicing."

"I don't have a guitar."

"That could be a problem."

Black frowned. "I don't suppose you have an extra I could borrow for a few days?"

"Do I look like the local pawn shop or something?"

"That's what I figured."

"Then again, it might be worth it to watch you humiliate yourself. So yes, I do have a guitar. A Gibson SG. Like Angus plays."

"Really?"

"Really. And only because I'm totally bitchin' will I let you borrow it."

"Can we get it now?"

She opened her purse and removed a bottle of black nail polish. "I'm kind of busy."

"Think about how embarrassing it'll be for me."

"You driving?"

On the way to Roxie's apartment she had the bright idea to call one of her friends who played in a cover band and ask if Black could sit in on a few songs. When she hung up, she had an evil smirk of triumph on her face.

"Tonight's your lucky night. He said no sweat."

"Roxie, I'm not sure I'm ready for that…"

"Bullshit. After a few hours of playing this afternoon, it'll all come back. If you're going to be jamming in front of thousands, you need to get used to going out there and putting it on the line."

"You're not just doing this to watch me crater in front of an audience, are you?"

She struggled to keep the delight out of her eyes. "I can't believe you suspect my motives. Of course that's why. I'm bringing popcorn."

"You're going to be there?"

"Absolutely. This will be better than Mel Gibson on a jag. I actually almost peed my pants when Josh agreed to let you sit in."

"Don't you have a show or rehearsal or something?"

"Nope. Wide open. Can't wait."

"You're not really pumping me full of confidence."

"I hope you don't freak out or anything. Like run screaming off the stage. Or freeze. The worst is when they freeze. They say you never get the sound of the jeering out of your head after that. It haunts you forever."

"That's good to know. But remember, I used to play big clubs all the time, so I'm not exactly a virgin."

The guitar was serviceable, the strings fairly new, and Black nodded in approval as he set the case in the back of the Cadillac. Roxie handed him two plastic picks and returned to the passenger seat.

"Come on. Let's get to jamming, wild stone! Woohoo," she said, feigning enthusiasm.

"You really need to work on your bedside manner."

"Is that one of your thinly veiled and super-creepy sexual innuendos? Ew. I should so sue your ass. I would if you had any money."

"You should wait until I'm a rock star again. I hear it pays well."

"Wouldn't know to look at you."

Back at the office he tuned the guitar and began the rusty first runs up the frets. Roxie sat at her desk and listened for a half hour, and then picked Mugsy up and carried him to Black's doorway.

"I can't take it. I'm leaving."

"Come on. It's not that bad."

"It sounds like two chickens fighting."

"But in a good way."

"It's scarring Mugsy for life."

Black brightened. "Are you taking him?"

"Of course not. I'm just debating calling animal protective services and filing a cruelty complaint."

"Which end's his head again?"

She set Mugsy down. "Pick me up at my place at nine."

"You're serious about this."

"I don't have any money to go to a movie with, so this is the cheapest free entertainment I'm going to get. Besides, I'm debating calling your friends and your parents and selling tickets."

"Roxie..."

"Kidding. But have a few bucks available to buy us drinks. You're going to need 'em, and I get thirsty."

Her leather-clad bottom sashayed away, managing to be simultaneously alluring and insulting, and he returned to running scales, trying to get his fingers to obey his brain's commands. So far the fingers were winning, but some of his chops were returning, albeit agonizingly slowly.

At five he took a break and called Sylvia. She sounded busy but happy to hear from him. He told her he'd be occupied until eleven that night and wanted to know if she was in the mood for company.

"Are you sure you'll be up for it?" she asked.

"I'm always up for seeing you, Sylvia. Besides. I have some big news. Or may have."

"That's cryptic."

"I just haven't decided on something yet."

"I'll be up if you want to come by. Or are you thinking your place?"

"Nah, I'll be up on the strip. I'll stop by yours."

"All right, Mr. Black, man of mystery. I'll see you then."

Black hadn't figured out how to break the news to Sylvia about the show, but figured it wouldn't matter if he decided not to do it. Although he had to admit that the thought of standing in front of a crowd, living his dream again, had appeal. Being booted from his band on the eve of their first big tour had festered in his gut like a malignancy for years, and even though he'd thought that was behind him, he realized the burn in his stomach was back, stronger than ever.

Mugsy studied the forbidden leather couch with destructive intent. Black stared him down and called out his name. Mugsy gave him a large cat yawn and, with a final wistful look at the supple black leather, waddled off to wreak havoc elsewhere. Black sat back and began strumming a Rolling Stones song, wincing at the occasional flub or muddled chord. But as he noodled, his confidence returned, and by the time dusk colored the sky with swirls of orange and red, he was feeling slightly less unsure of himself.

But the first real test would be to see how he did with a band.

Which, a glance at his watch informed him, would be in two hours or so.

Wearily he put the guitar back into its case and turned off the lights on his way out of the office. Mugsy was sprawled in his customary position on the lobby sofa, snoring, the oversized food bowl empty, another tough day of lounging around doing nothing having worn him out.

Chapter 5

Roxie led Black into the darkened interior of the Red Pony Saloon, where a small crowd milled around, the flotsam and jetsam that called the strip home – bikers, pimps, blue-collar workers drowning their sorrows, retail clerks dressed up like rockers, everyone participating in the same illusion that enabled them to be whatever they wished away from the harsh light of day.

"Sweet Home Alabama" pumped from the stage as a five-piece band bashed its obligatory way through the standard, followed, no doubt, Black was sure, by "Free Bird". A woman on the wrong side of fifty, looking in her denim vest like she'd been ridden hard and put away wet more times than she could remember, offered a bleary smile to Black as he pushed his way past her.

The club was a reminder of countless similar dives he'd played when his band was struggling to make ends meet. It was at a place much like this one he'd first seen his future wife, belting out a Heart ballad with a set of pipes that Mariah Carey would have envied. The only thing missing was the fog of cigarette smoke, now a thing of the past.

Black watched Roxie – who had exchanged her top for a sleeveless Pantera concert shirt, the better to display her tattoos – as she marched through the quarter-full audience and positioned herself, hip cocked, in front of the small stage. The band hit the final chords to a few inebriated screams of Skynyrd from several sweating, overweight men doing boilermakers as they whooped as if Wednesday in a Hollywood dive was New Year's Eve in Times Square.

The band surprised Black by launching into a Kings of Leon hit instead of another Southern anthem, and he debated the wisdom of a shot of Jaeger with a draft beer chaser. As his nerves jangled with each pop of the snare drum, he decided that this certainly qualified as an emergency, so strong medicine was in order. When the heavily pierced, goateed bartender moved near, he modified his order to a tequila shot and a glass of Red Hook, already feeling guilty at squandering his precious dollars.

The liquid courage warmed him, and when Roxie found him, he was telling a joke to two hard-looking bikers wearing sunglasses long after the sun had set.

"So there's this place in Anchorage, I swear, called Skinny Dick's. The sign by the highway says, and I'm not bullshitting you, 'Liquor in the front, poker in the rear!'"

The men laughed together, and Black waved the bartender over for another shot of tequila. Roxie sidled up to him and elbowed him in the ribs.

"Save some of that for onstage. And yes, I'd love a Grey Goose, straight up."

"Sounds expensive."

"You get what you pay for, Boss," she said and winked in a way that was anything but professional.

Black felt a wholly inappropriate stirring. He shrugged it off as one of his companions described being in the Bakersfield joint for two months pending trial. When the drinks arrived, Black laid a few of his remaining bills on the bar and turned to Roxie, cocktails in hand.

"Mud in your eye."

"Josh said you should head up there whenever you're ready. You guys talk about what songs you know, and they'll figure it out," Roxie said and then knocked back her vodka without blinking. "Now would be a good time, unless you're planning to ride bitch with one of your new boyfriends instead of playing tonight."

"You do know how to frame a persuasive argument, don't you?" Black said and downed his third tequila shot, his nerves now humming. A familiar sense of excitement coursed through him as he prepared to take the stage.

The reality was anticlimactic. Playing in front of maybe forty people, most of whom were there for lack of anywhere else to go, was hardly a substitute for standing in front of a sold-out crowd at the Whiskey. When Black stepped on the stage, he suddenly felt claustrophobic, the area more the size of Mugsy's kitty litter box than a real venue. Josh handed him one of his spare Les Paul guitars and switched on a backup amp and, after a hurried discussion, launched into a Pearl Jam song Black thought he could play in his sleep.

That turned out to be an exaggerated belief. The next song, "Black Dog", went even worse, and by the time they finished an Eagles number, Black was sweating and ready to leave. Josh was courteous, but Black could see in his eyes he was as anxious to be rid of Black as Black was to get off the stage. It hadn't been a complete disaster, but when Josh turned Black's amp down by half in the middle of the second song, it sent an unmistakable message: you suck.

Which the few courtesy claps and occasional muffled boo from the back of the room had underscored.

When he lumbered off the stage, Roxie wouldn't meet his gaze, and all his suspicions were confirmed. If it hadn't been terrible, she would have gleefully given him a supersized ration of shit. As it was, all she did was hand him another tequila shot.

"You can tell me the truth, you know," he said, sweat beading down his face as he tilted his head back and swallowed the harsh liquor in a gulp.

"There's no Santa or Easter Bunny."

He grimaced from the burn in his throat. "I meant about my playing."

"I'd say it speaks for itself."

"Pretty terrible, huh?"

"I'm bored. Let's get out of here."

Black nodded and moved to the exit, Roxie close behind, and when they were outside amidst the cigarette butts and exhaust fumes, she slowed.

"Okay, you asked for it. It was rough. Embarrassing, even. I mean, there were moments where I wanted to gouge my ears out with a jam knife to make it stop."

"Don't sugarcoat it."

"But there were also a few where it was decent. Not good. Decent. And you could see that if you kept practicing, it might get better than decent. Which I'd think you'd know. How many years were you playing before you got good? And how many hours a day did you spend with a guitar in your hands, on average?"

"I was always noodling around…"

"And now, after not playing for twenty years, you expect to spend three or four hours and be any good? Why would you think that?"

Black shook his head and began walking. "Because sometimes I'm a dope."

"No, it's because you have that penis thing going on, where you want to be the dominant one at all times, and it blinds you to reality. Men are competitive, and they forget the negatives in order to blunder forward. What you're guilty of is being male, not a dope. Although you can be a dope, too."

"That's reassuring. I'm not only delusional, but also stupid. I wonder why I never thought about putting that on my dating profile." He grunted. "Thanks for the pep talk."

"My job here is done."

Silence reigned on the way home. When Black dropped Roxie off she turned to him, the car door still open. "What are you going to do?"

"Turn it down. This isn't for me. God's just trying to torture me. It doesn't mean I need to cooperate."

"Sleep on it."

"Good night, Roxie. And thanks. For everything."

The drive to Sylvia's seemed to take forever. Black was lightheaded from the booze, but not so much that he was seeing double – it was always a reliable warning sign he might have overindulged when he had to hold one hand over an eye while clutching the steering wheel to keep from falling.

Sylvia greeted him at the door. Her face changed almost imperceptibly when she smelled the alcohol. She returned to where she'd been sitting on the sofa, reading a book on her Kindle, and Black moved to her postage-stamp kitchen and got a glass of water.

"Rough day?" she asked.

"Yeah, you could say that."

"What were you up to?"

"I spent it trying to remember how to play guitar. Then tonight I jammed with some friends, and it reminded me that there's no rewind on life."

She regarded him curiously. "Why the interest in rekindling your musician days? Not that there's anything wrong with that…"

"It's not important. Just a suggestion from a friend. A well-intentioned friend, but in the end, a bad idea."

"There's no harm in doing something artistic with your free time."

"I know. But I think my playing days are over. I prefer admiring my favorite artists from afar."

"Hopefully not that far. Come over here and let me get a look at those magic musician hands."

"That's the best offer I've had all night."

"It had better be."

Chapter 6

Black awoke to dust motes floating lazily in the sunlight streaming through Sylvia's window. He watched the display as he evaluated whether or not he was going to have a headache, and when the throbbing in his temples started, conceded that he had no reason to expect to get off scot-free after a bunch of rotgut tequila and a few beers. Sylvia was already awake, moving around in the kitchen. He trundled to the bathroom, took two aspirin, and was somewhat relieved that the hangover was no more than a two or a three – not the nine- or ten-alarm blazes he used to have when he was really putting it away. And he hadn't smoked, which always seemed to ratchet up the pain exponentially.

He studied his reflection in the mirror and took in the slight jowls that were developing, the dusting of gray in his morning beard, the bloodshot eyes, and shook his head at the sight. What had he been thinking? What had Bobby? There were too many miles on the chassis. Maybe Bono or Johnny Depp could look like a million as they crossed from forty to fifty, but Black's genes displayed a lifetime of bad decisions on his face like a map of the stars' homes, and it wasn't going in a positive direction. He wondered absently whether, if he had the money, he would go under the knife like Bobby so regularly did, and was glad he didn't have to make that decision. Life had done it for him, and he was going to be spared turning into Mickey Rourke's alter ego.

Sylvia's musical voice called from the kitchen. "Honey? You want some coffee?"

"That would be awesome. I'll be out in a few minutes. I'll rinse off at home."

"Whatever you want. I made eggs."

"Did I mention I'm the luckiest man in the world?"

"Not unless snoring counts."

Black struggled into his clothes and joined Sylvia for breakfast at her dining room table. They discussed dinner plans and her latest battles with the gallery owner over the best way to price and display her art. When he finished with his meal, he checked the time and apologized for having to leave.

"Sorry. I'd love to stick around, but I've got some calls I have to make."

"Potential clients?"

"I wish."

"Still dead on that front, then?"

"It'll turn around. It always does. It's just that my overhead is eating me alive now. I should never have listened to Roxie."

"The old place was a dump."

"No argument. But it was a cheap one."

"So dinner at seven?"

"If you're cooking. I'm so broke I'm panhandling from homeless people."

"I've got some chicken and rice. I'll whip something up."

Black parked down the street from his complex and did his best to avoid Gracie, his landlady, but her unfailing radar was operating perfectly, and she opened her door as he tried to glide soundlessly by.

"Black. Lovely day, isn't it?" she greeted in her whiskey-seasoned voice.

"Gracie, I was just getting ready to come by after I change."

"To bring me the money you owe, I hope."

"That's what I need to talk to you about."

"Sweetheart, last month it was a discussion. This month? I need cash." Gracie was as tenacious as a lamprey when it came to rent, and even though they were friends, she had her limits. Judging by her tone, she'd reached hers.

"I know, Gracie. I'm expecting some shortly, and you're first in line."

"Shortly? What the hell does that mean? And don't try to bullshit me."

"It means that by Saturday I should have the money," Black said with authority he didn't feel, an image of the blood bank flitting through his imagination.

Gracie's squinted at him. "You're not lying, are you, handsome? Because if you don't have the money by then, our beautiful relationship's over. These apartments are a hot commodity. I love you like a son, but I can't carry you forever."

Black sighed. "I know, Gracie, I know. And believe me, I appreciate the extra rope you've given me. I only wish things were going better."

"Don't try to sweet-talk me, boyo. Saturday the fat lady sings, and if you don't have the money, it's going to get ugly." She paused, her message delivered. "Now, you want to join me for an eye opener? Sun's over the yardarm somewhere."

"Love to, but I have to earn my keep." It was eight-thirty in the morning, but Gracie was dedicated.

"That's a shame. The drugstore had the half-gallons on clearance. I cleaned them out."

"Nobody ever said you weren't a smart shopper. Now I've got to go. Stay safe, Gracie."

The shower couldn't rinse the stink of duplicity off him, and as he was toweling his hair dry, he felt lower than ever at having to flat-out lie to his addled landlady. Maybe he'd have to choke down his pride and go whining to Mommy after all...

The phone screeched like a wounded osprey, startling him out of his funk. He answered hoarsely, his hair still sticking up at all angles.

"Black."

"Babe, have I got good news for you!" Bobby's voice was annoyingly cheerful.

"I'm glad you called, Bobby. I did as you asked and checked out the band. They're good. Better than good."

"That's super. Then it's a done deal!"

"No. I tried playing for a few hours yesterday, and it didn't go so well. I don't think I can do this." Black nervously rubbed his left ring finger, the tip of which was still red from bending the steel guitar strings, the calluses he'd had long ago only a memory.

"Come on. You're frigging Jeff Beck. Hendrix. Richards." Bobby paused, his total knowledge of guitar players obviously exhausted.

"Why do I get the feeling you haven't listened to a word I've said?"

"I heard you. I get it. You're playing hard to get."

"No, I'm not. Besides, I'm pretty sure Richards is dead. A zombie or something."

"Stop screwing around. They've got a legend coaching the band, and he's a huge fan of yours. When I told him you were considering stepping in, he just about did a cartwheel."

In spite of his better judgment, Black's curiosity was aroused. He hated how easily Bobby could manipulate him, but had to concede he was good at what he did. "Yeah? Who?"

"Rooster Simms."

The name stopped Black cold.

"*The* Rooster Simms?"

"Do we have a bad connection? Is there more than one? Of course it's *the* Rooster Simms – how many guys do you know named Rooster? Anyway, we've got an appointment over at his recording studio in a couple of hours so you guys can meet, rap, or whatever you call talking shop these days. He's really an admirer, Black. I'm not blowing smoke."

"No, of course you aren't. You'd never do that."

"Come by my office in an hour and a half, and we'll caravan there together, all right?"

"Much as I'd like to meet Rooster, this is a non-starter, Bobby."

"Fine. Just humor me. I'll buy you lunch. That's a free meal just for showing up and playing nice. We got a deal?"

Black knew Bobby wouldn't give up until he'd agreed, and his headache was returning, draining his will to resist. He nodded and closed his eyes.

"Okay, Bobby. But for the record, this is a waste of time."

"Yeah, yeah, and then we all die. I know. Lighten up, buddy. You're going to be a star, and you'd think I just asked you to teabag all of *Duck Dynasty*. I swear, some people…"

Black spent his morning reading about the last season of *Rock of Ages*, and the inevitable mentions of Alex Sands, the hottest thing in the world of pop since Justin Bieber and the narrow winner of the premier season's contest. Alex was handsome, friendly, could sing as well as any, and had an undeniable star quality. A few articles covered the disastrous show by Last Call. A YouTube video of the guitar player's temper tantrum at the end of his performance was one of the most viewed on the site, and Black watched it several times before finding earlier shows, where the band had shone.

Roxie sent him a text message alerting him that she'd be in late – she'd been called to an "emergency" meeting with her new employer that morning – and would be in as soon as she could. She still hadn't arrived when Black had to leave for Bobby's, and he left Mugsy dozing by her desk, feet twitching as he chased slow mice in his dreams.

Bobby was in high spirits when Black got to the office, and after a few minutes of banter, they set out for Rooster's recording studio, on the wrong side of Normandy in a converted industrial building. Black parked on the street behind Bobby's new Tesla. After glancing around the graffiti-tagged neighborhood, they made their way to an unmarked steel door with two deadbolts. The door swung open, and a muscular man wearing a tank top and sweat pants stared at them for a long second.

"We're here to see Rooster," Bobby announced, and the man nodded and pointed down the hall.

Rooster was sitting in a waiting area outside the control booth, smoking a cigarette and drinking a cup of coffee as he read a recording industry magazine with a photo of an SSL console on the cover. He looked up as they entered, and his face broke into a wide smile.

"Well, look at this. If it isn't Jim Black. Man, this is exciting. I remember some of your shows, back in the day. You probably didn't realize it because I was laying low, but I came to several of them – I still remember the last one you played, at the Troubadour. I knew then you were going to be huge," Rooster said, rising. "It's an honor, man."

Black tried to hide his embarrassment at the effusive praise from an industry legend like Rooster as he shook hands. "Well, that's very kind of you. But it was a long time ago."

Bobby slapped Black's back. "The man's modesty is incredible. Did I tell you or did I tell you?"

Black shook his head. "It really was a long time. Twenty years. Lot of water under that bridge."

"Yeah, but it's like anything else," Rooster said. "If you got game, you got game. Look at some of the bands that were big back in the day. They're touring like mad, doing better than ever. And they're exciting to watch. Age is in your mind, man. The Stones are seventy. Mick Jagger is still packing stadiums and running around for two hours plus, showing no signs of slowing. What are you – half that age?"

"I'm forty-three," Black said.

"Hell, man, Jagger and Richards were about that age on *Dirty Work*. That's nothing. You're just getting started. Am I right?"

"Doesn't feel that way."

"Why are you so down, man? I remember you like it was yesterday. I mean, you were good. Had that groove thing going. Ladies eating out of the palm of your hand. And talk about style. Some of the tracks on that first album were like going to school, you know?"

"All ancient history. That's the problem. I picked up a guitar yesterday for the first time in forever…and it wasn't pretty."

"Yeah? Well, lemme tell you a little story. Back in the seventies I had a little tax problem. Wound up spending four years in jail. I didn't play a note the whole time, and when I got out, I was so depressed I didn't want to do anything but climb into a bottle. By the time I was over it, five years had gone by. When I picked up my axe again it was hard, man. For the first week, it was like, whose hands are these, you know? And then it came back, little by little, and within a month I did my first show. I've never looked back." Rooster stubbed out his cigarette and finished his coffee. "If you ask me, a little maturity's never a bad thing for a musician. It gives you perspective, you know? So all you've been doing is a little…seasoning."

"Seasoning," Bobby echoed.

"Let's go into the room. I've got a couple guitars in there, and Luther here knows how to play some drums. Let's see what you remember, all right?" Rooster said, gesturing to the studio door.

Black followed him in, and they filed past the console and into the main recording chamber, which was all polished hardwood. Several amplifiers sat in a corner, along with a rack with six guitars in it. Rooster got two folding chairs and set them up near a drum set behind isolation baffles. Luther slid two of the padded panels aside, revealing a six-piece Tama kit. Black approached the guitars and whistled.

"Nice."

"Yeah, I use different ones for different sounds. What were you playing on last night?"

"A Telecaster."

"Wasn't your old guitar a Gibson?"

"No. A Gretsch. Red double-cutaway."

"That's right. I still remember the tone. Kind of like that one?" Rooster asked, pointing to another rack of instruments behind the drums. Black walked over to the rack and stopped short.

"That looks exactly like my old red Duo Jet. That's…crazy."

"Probably because it *is* your old Duo Jet. When you sold it over at Guitar Barn, the owner called me. I've had it for twenty years, taking good care of it. But I'm thinking maybe it's time it went home."

"That's…" Black couldn't continue, his voice suddenly tight.

"Go on. Pick it up. Not like it bites. I figure maybe you'll play better on familiar frets, you know?"

Black slipped the strap over his head. He adjusted it and strummed a few bars. The semi-hollow body resonated – a magical sound to Black, like nothing else in the world.

Rooster reached over and snagged a Stratocaster from the rack next to him and pointed to one of the amps.

"Try that old Marshall. Good tone. Cords are right there."

Black did as instructed and plugged in. Rooster was right. The tone was rich and warm. Rooster connected his Strat and played several chords through a Twin Reverb that sounded modified, then adjusted a few knobs and did a fluid blues run.

"Well, alrighty, then. What do you wanna play, Mr. Black?"

"Just Black."

"Then you call me just Rooster. You know any Hendrix?"

"Of course."

"Or maybe we should just warm up with some slow blues? Let you get your footing?"

"Whatever. It's all good."

Forty-five minutes later Bobby waved from behind the console and stepped into the room. "I'm going to take off. Black? Call me when you're done, okay?"

"Yeah. Remember you owe me lunch."

"How could I forget?" Bobby walked toward him, digging in his pocket. He fished out a fifty-dollar bill and laid it on the amp. "There you go. Lunch for you and Rooster. Sounds like you're earning it." Bobby gave him a thumbs-up and hurried back to the door, anxious to leave.

When they finally stopped after two hours of jamming, Rooster cracked his trademark toothy smile and shook his head. "See? I told you it would come back. You need some work, but you'll do just fine. Better than that Rick idiot was, that's for sure, even after twenty years."

"You really think so?" Black asked, cradling the Gretsch like a baby.

"No question. You still got it, kid. Now you just need to focus, and you're golden."

"I'm not sure the band will think so."

"Let me handle them. My job's to take them to the finish line. I almost got 'em there last year. This year's ours."

Rooster seemed convinced, and Black had to admit he felt better after playing, his old guitar like an extension of himself. Some of the old magic had slowly come back, and by the end of the session he started to feel a confidence sorely lacking the prior night.

Now all he needed was to have that carry through onstage in front of thousands.

Which was a different story than playing one-on-one with a legend who was throwing soft balls.

Rooster disappeared into the equipment room and returned with the Gretsch's case. Black lovingly tucked the old guitar away and retreated to the lobby to wait for Rooster. When the old bluesman came out of the studio area with Luther, the men were laughing. "Did somebody say lunch?" Rooster asked.

"Yeah. I could eat. And Bobby's buying," Black reminded him.

Rooster waved him off. "Put that money away. No way I'm letting you get our first lunch together. Besides, I have a special place in mind, and fifty bucks won't even cover the cocktails."

Chapter 7

Lunch on Melrose was a lavish affair. The steaks were juicy and well marbled, the wine pricey and delicious. By the time Black returned to Bobby's office, it was four o'clock, and he was considering the merits of a long nap. The parking attendant hadn't grown any fonder of Black's car in the interim, but Black was now simply ignoring him, his mind elsewhere. He locked his guitar in the trunk and raced skyward in the elevator, wondering what a sixties-era Duo Jet was worth. It hadn't been cheap when he'd bought it, and he was guessing that by now one in good condition cost thousands – maybe many thousands.

The receptionist was as gorgeous as she had been that morning, and no warmer at Black's arrival, but he didn't care. Rooster thought he could do this, and if he did, then Black did, too. He wasn't convinced, but he wasn't as pessimistic as he'd been that morning.

Bobby came out to meet him in the lobby, car keys in his hand.

"We'll take my ride. Simon Crisp, the show producer, wants to meet you. He's waiting for us at his office. This won't take long."

"Why would the producer care about the guitar player for one of the six bands in the show?" Black asked.

"Eight bands. But a fair question. He probably wouldn't care, except the last one screwed the pooch on TV. So my sense is he wants to ensure you're not unstable before he green-lights you."

"But I am unstable."

"Compared to this bunch, you're the rock of Gibraltar."

"Wait a minute. Simon Crisp…that name's familiar."

"It should be. He was a record industry maven for years. Then he branched off and started his own production company. This show is his second outing, and it's a smash. So was the last one. About crazy ladies and cat shows. Talk about watching a slow-motion car wreck. But audiences loved it. Now he's one of the go-to guys for reality TV and talent contests."

On the way to Simon's office, Black called Sylvia and tried to explain what was happening. She didn't sound thrilled. When he told her he'd be living at a house for the next twelve weeks, she practically came apart.

"Have you lost your mind? Three months living in some absurd TV show? What are you, nineteen?"

"Honey, it pays really well, and it's an assignment. I'm not just doing it to get back into music."

"Right," she said, skepticism dripping from her voice. "Does this mean I don't see you for three months?"

Bobby had laid out the rules: He would have to live at a mansion in Malibu with three of the other bands, two people to a room, and they could only see girl or boyfriends at contests open to the public, or one day a week when the cameras weren't rolling.

"No. We'll have time together. Just not as much."

"What does that mean? How often?"

Black gritted his teeth and winced. "Sundays."

"That's it?" Sylvia said, her voice now dangerously quiet.

"And at the shows. You can come to those."

"How nice. Along with the rest of the, what do you call them, groupies?"

"It's not like that, Sylvia."

"Right. Because rock bands are well known for their conservative lifestyles."

"I'm a little old for the party-all-night thing, honey."

"Don't honey me. If I'd wanted to date a musician, I could have thrown a rock and hit a dozen from my apartment."

Bobby pointed at a copper-colored glass building. "We're almost there."

"Sylvia, I have to go. We're still on for dinner, right?"

"I'll think about it. I may decide to run off and join the Foreign Legion in the interim."

"Okay, then, I'll call you later."

The phone clicked, and he found himself listening to a dial tone. He glanced at Bobby. "That went well. She was really excited and happy for me."

"I read between the lines."

Bobby parked the Tesla in the underground garage and led the way to the elevator bank. This building made Bobby's look only so-so and Black's like a Detroit tenement. When they arrived at the production company's floor, there was only one door when they stepped out of the elevator – a double teak job that likely cost as much as Bobby's hair plugs.

They were kept waiting the customary Hollywood fifteen minutes, and then a pencil-thin young Vietnamese man with an edgy haircut led them to a palatial corner office. Bobby entered, all energy and sizzle, now in his element. Black trailed him, his sense of misgiving mounting with every step as the door hissed closed on hydraulic hinges at his back.

"Simon, you look like a damn teenager. What the hell's your secret? Tell me. Botox? I want a gallon." Bobby was shaking Simon's hand like the mogul had just posted his bail.

"Just Jesus in my heart and a youthful disposition, my man," Simon said and shifted his attention to Black. "This the guy?"

"I'm the guy," Black said, offering his hand. Simon shook it with considerably less enthusiasm than he had Bobby's.

"Little...long in the tooth, no? I was expecting someone younger."

Black offered a wan smile. "Don't worry. I've had a ton of practice disappointing people."

Simon laughed – a good sign.

"Funny guy. Good. The show could use some funny. Last season the dialogue was as dull as a State of the Union address, am I right? Funny's good."

"He's also a certified rock god, Simon. I gave you his pedigree. How many guys sold that many records?" Bobby chimed in.

Simon looked at Black more closely. "Yeah, but he doesn't really look it, does he?"

Bobby rolled his eyes at the comment. "The man's a frigging stealth fighter. Silent but deadly. And don't worry about the glitz. I've got a girl that's going to make him look like Bon Jovi. Trust me on this. Plus, he can actually play. Anyone else in this office had twenty-nine million people buy his album?"

Simon's door opened, and Alex Sands walked in, dressed in a tight black knit top and cream linen slacks. "Sorry I'm late."

"Gentlemen. Alex. Winner of last year's show, and this year, one of our three judges," Simon announced with the solemn gravitas of a diplomat.

Alex moved to where Black and Bobby sat and shook hands. He leaned against the bookcase on the wall, and all Black could think was that the man was beautiful – dark, thick, curly hair; chiseled tan features; the physique of a gymnast. Black's sense of inadequacy intensified with each passing moment.

"We were just talking about how Mr. Black here sold more records than Elvis," Simon explained.

"Oh, wow, you're him! That's right. Simon said something about that. Cool. Nice to meet you," Alex said, and Black's opinion of him dwindled with each word. Pretty house, but nobody home, Black thought. Figured. Probably had hot and cold running Lamborghinis and a Victoria's Secret girlfriend.

Simon beamed like Black was his new puppy. "And he's funny. A comedian. I don't need to see any more. The man's got my vote. Oh, one thing – you on dope or an alcoholic or anything? We had a problem last year..."

"Nope. Although do you pay more if I am?"

Alex looked Black up and down. "You think you still got what it takes to wow a crowd and win this? No disrespect, but a lot of the audience is going to be young – teens and twenty-somethings."

"My assistant came to a show last night and was literally speechless. Need I say more?" Black figured he might as well get some mileage out of the ordeal.

"Yeah – she's a pistol," Bobby confirmed.

"But what about your…image? No offense, but you look kind of like a movie extra," Alex said.

"I was shooting for mortician."

Simon laughed nervously. "See? Man's a regular Louis CK. Whadda ya think, Alex?"

Alex shrugged. "If he's okay with you, I've got no problems." He gave Black a skeptical look. "You met the band yet?"

"That's next. He just finished jamming with Rooster. I thought the man was going to offer him a production deal on the spot," Bobby said.

"All right. Congratulations, Mr. Black. Or Jim, right?" Simon asked.

"Everyone just calls me Black."

Simon stood and rounded his desk, glancing at his platinum Rolex Masterpiece wristwatch. "Thanks for coming by, Black. A real pleasure. You're going to do great. Bobby, have your friend go to work on him, doll him up. You know the way out, right? Grab some Perrier or something for the road. Me and Alex need to have a talk. You excuse us?"

The Vietnamese assistant materialized just outside the door and led them back to the lobby, his steps silent on the granite floor. Black and Bobby were quiet until they were in the elevator. When the doors hissed shut, Black broached the subject that had been nagging at him.

"Bobby, I hate to bug you, but if I'm going to do this, I need the first week's pay up front. Just like any other job. Two grand. Is that a problem?"

"No problem at all. Can you swing by tomorrow and get a check?"

"Sure. In the morning."

They arrived at the garage level. "Perfect. I called my friend Monique earlier, and she knows all about you. Head over to her place after we get back to my building so she can get to work. Everything's covered by the show, so don't worry about paying for it."

"What did you tell her to do?"

"Make you look like a rock stud. Don't worry, dude. Trust me."

The famous last words were familiar. The same words he'd spoken when he'd had Black sign over all rights to his songs for a lousy hundred grand of hush money.

Back in Bobby's Tesla, Black called Roxie.

"Hey. I'm doing the show. I just met the producer. It's a go."

"Does that mean you have my salary?"

"Not yet. But I'll be making enough so that once I pay for the back rent on the office, three or four weeks from now…"

Roxie's flat tone went even duller. "If you last that long, you mean. Looks like I'm stuck riding herd on the old buzzard."

"I appreciate the vote of confidence."

"It's not that. I mean, not just that. I think I'm already regretting taking this job."

"That bad?"

"You don't know the half. Can you say control freak?"

"Maybe you can kill her by smuggling Mugsy into her house. Although that would be like trying to sneak a medium-sized Kodiak bear in…"

"The other line's ringing."

"No, it isn't. I don't hear anything."

"Ring. Ring."

"You saying 'ring' isn't really the same."

"Gotta go."

"Roxie."

"Ciao, boss. See you tomorrow. Last day, right?"

"I guess so."

The hair salon was on Rodeo Drive, and Black was able to squeeze his car into a parking place a block away. When he entered the shop, house music throbbed from hidden speakers, and an anorexic blonde with black nails greeted him at the reception counter.

"Hello. Welcome to Shear Attraction."

"I'm here to see Monique," Black said.

"I'll page her."

Black wondered whether she had a bat as a pet. The intercom buzzed, and a perky voice chirped, "Tell him I'll be right out."

The blonde shrugged and fixed Black with a dead stare. "She'll be right out."

"You don't say."

"I just did."

The chrome and glass coffee table was covered with cosmetology magazines featuring impossibly beautiful people. A teenage girl sat across from him, texting away on a four-hundred-dollar phone she'd extracted from a five-hundred-dollar purse. Black idly wondered which of the expensive sports cars in front was hers, and decided he didn't want to know – it would only depress him.

Ten minutes later a thirty-something woman with too much makeup and an outfit that would have been at home on a stripper emerged from the rear of the shop and approached him.

"Hi. I'm Monique. Bobby touched base. Oooh, I love your hair. I was expecting something way harder to work with."

"Nice to meet you. Why were you expecting…?"

"Oh, I think Bobby likes to screw with me sometimes. I was expecting old, fat, and bald. Come on back into the magic kingdom. We'll have you fixed up in no time."

They walked through a door into a large, well-lit salon with twenty stations, the area a buzz of activity as the pampered and privileged were primped and snipped. Monique's slot was at the far end, and Black removed his jacket and hung it up before sitting in the chair.

"What did you have in mind?" he asked doubtfully, staring at himself in the harsh light.

"Retired by forty and married to a billionaire," Monique said and laughed, a percussive bray Black instantly disliked. What had Bobby gotten him into?

She played with his hair and nodded as she hummed softly to herself. Black watched her examining him with the clinical precision of a coroner and felt a tickle of trepidation in his gut. Finally, she stepped back and nodded.

"We're going to have to give you some length, do some bangs instead of brushing it back, maybe spike the top a little, and go black – maybe with a midnight orchid cellophane. Something edgy, you know?"

"How are you going to give me length?"

"Extensions."

Black's eyes narrowed. "You aren't going to make me look like a freak, are you?"

"Of course not. I mean, no more than necessary. Part of this is to make you look a little freaky, right? You're in a band. Can't have you looking like Sinatra."

Black sighed and closed his eyes. "I have a feeling I'm going to regret this."

"You want some white wine?"

"Make it a double."

Two hours later he was staring at himself in the mirror in horror and fascination. His hair was now around his collar with a Ron Woods cut, jet black and tousled.

"I look like a transvestite."

"You look hot."

"If you think the guy from Spinal Tap was hot. Nigel? The dumb one?"

Monique stared at him, uncomprehending.

"Never mind. I look like a paunchy Liza Minnelli, so if that's what you were shooting for... How often do I need to get it redone?"

"Once a month." She considered her work and winked. "A goatee would work well with the hair. Might want to consider it. As far as the maintenance goes, I can come to you if the money's right."

"Bill Bobby."

On the way to the restaurant to meet Sylvia, Black's cell jangled in his pocket. He answered, and Bobby's voice boomed at him. "Hey. I hear you look like Marilyn Manson now."

"I hate you."

"No, you don't. Listen, I was going to tell you to pack a bag, but go light. The show will provide a wardrobe for you. They want to pick you up at noon tomorrow."

"What? But I thought I still need to meet the band."

"You do, but they're already getting set up in the house. Rooster told them he'd found a guitar player, so that's already decided."

"That's not how bands operated when I was playing."

"Rooster's responsible for doing whatever it takes to win. He vouched for you. You'll meet them tomorrow and rehearse for the next week in preparation for the first contest."

"Wait. So I'm moving into the house tomorrow? I thought I had till Monday?"

"Rooster thought you needed a head start. And what Rooster wants, Rooster gets."

"Shit. Will they be filming?"

Bobby hesitated. "I don't think so. Not until Monday."

"Do I have any choice?"

"Nope. So enjoy. Look at it this way – twelve weeks of easy living and free beer."

"I'm not seventeen anymore," Black protested.

"Just pretend. They'll be at your office at twelve o'clock. Wear something pretty."

"Did I mention I hate you?"

"You won't when you pick up your check tomorrow morning."

"It'll probably bounce."

"Have a nice night."

When he entered the restaurant and Sylvia saw him, she just about passed out. He'd never seen her mouth actually hang open, so it was a first. He held his arms out to her, and she reluctantly rose from the corner table.

"Oh…my…God…"

"I know. I look like Iggy Pop. And not in a good way."

She hugged him without enthusiasm. "Have you lost your mind?"

"Nice to see you, too."

"No, I mean really. You look like one of those losers on Sunset hanging outside the clubs at two in the morning."

"Those are called musicians. I think that was the general idea."

"I…I'm at a loss for words."

"I got that. Let's order, if you think you can keep food down, and we can talk about it."

Black noticed Sylvia was being more generous about her wine intake than usual. Dinner was strained, and when he broke the news about going to the house the next day, she just about lost it.

"So this whole nightmare starts tomorrow? I thought we had a little time…"

"The thing to remember is that this is a job. I'm undercover."

"Yeah, like *Serpico*. I get it. Only you're not De Niro."

"Pretty sure that was Pacino."

"Don't change the subject. This is a major disruption in our lives, Black. And you didn't even discuss it with me…"

"I know. It all happened so fast. I was going to say no, but then, after I played with Rooster today, everything kind of changed."

She looked at him uncomprehendingly. "You played with a chicken today? What have you become, Black?"

Black smiled sadly. "I'm seriously considering starting. No, that's the manager's name. Rooster. He's famous."

Sylvia took another large gulp of wine. "What's going to happen to us, Black? This is just too way out."

"Everything will be fine. We'll see each other once a week, plus at shows, I'll pay my apartment and office rent and get back on track, and it'll all be over before we know it."

"It's three months of our life. My life. With you in a rock band instead of behaving like a grownup. I…I don't know, Black. I need time to absorb all this."

"What does that mean?"

She cleared her throat. "It means I'm not sure I can deal with this. Not seeing you. This new…look. You being in the rock scene. It's not what I signed up for."

He took her hand, which felt like a dead smelt. "Nothing's going to happen while we're apart. This is all an act. I'm not planning on becoming a musician again. I'm on a job, which pays well at a time when I'm dead broke. I can appreciate this is all a shock, and I'd be lying if I said it wasn't for me too, but we need to make the best of it. I'll do the time, catch the bad guys, and come home. To you. Nobody but you."

Her eyes were welling when she looked at him.

"That's what you say now. Last night you didn't even mention this, and today you're leaving me for three months. I'm not sure your word means much these days."

"I already explained that..."

"Not good enough, Black." She dabbed at her eyes with her napkin, and his heart sank. She was right.

"I know. And I'm sorry."

"You always are."

Chapter 8

Morning arrived too soon, and after a less-than-warm goodbye from Sylvia, Black returned home to pack. He carried the Gretsch upstairs and set it on the coffee table as he scrounged around for any clothes that didn't look conservative, and wondered for the hundredth time since getting his makeover how he was going to pull any of this off. He'd thought playing would be the hard part, but each time he caught a glimpse of himself in a mirror, he realized that he was in unfamiliar territory – what was fun at twenty was horrifying at forty-something.

He selected a few cocktail shirts and a half dozen T-shirts, and ferreted around for his rattiest jeans. Satisfied that he wouldn't be walking around the house half naked, he packed a hygiene kit and some miscellaneous odds and ends, leaving his Glock locked in the safe – he didn't want to have to explain to the crew or his housemates why he was strapped.

Finished, he did a final quick check and remembered to grab his laptop. Once it was stowed in his bag, he hoisted his guitar, shouldered the rucksack and, after a final look around, locked the door, hoping his luck in eluding Gracie would hold.

It wasn't his day. Like a mongoose watching a cobra, she was waiting, her door cracked, a quarter glass of amber fluid in her coffee mug.

"What happened to you? Is it Halloween?" she croaked at him.

"Very funny. I was trying for a new look. More fun."

"You look like a dope fiend. You trying to sneak out?"

"Nah. In fact, I'll have your rent in about an hour."

"Bullshit. You're flying the coop."

"No, I'm not." He told her about the show and explained that he wouldn't be around for a while. "Can you stop in every now and then and make sure nothing's caught fire?"

"Sure thing. But I still don't believe you. I think you've gone and joined the circus or something."

"That's nice, Gracie, but I'm telling the truth. I'm going to be on TV. Look the show up starting next Thursday. It's on one of the cable networks."

"You don't know which one?"

"I haven't watched TV since *ER* went off the air."

"Wow." That shut her up. Gracie had her idiot box on roughly twenty hours a day. "You're really not lying to me?"

"All my stuff's still up in the apartment. And I'll be back with the rent by eleven at the latest. I swear."

"Then leave your guitar with me."

No fool, Gracie.

"I have to take it in to get worked on. Or you know I would." He didn't want her breaking anything, which she well might do while he was gone. Better to keep the guitar out of harm's way.

"Then leave your bag."

Black groaned, but agreed. He placed it on the floor by the entry and winked at her. "Be back soon. Don't go digging around in it. I'll know if you did."

"Relax, tough guy. I have no interest in your dirty underwear. Especially now that you look like something out of *The Rocky Horror Picture Show*."

"I'll be back," he said in his best Schwarzenegger and aimed his finger at her like a gun.

"Don't quit your day job."

Bobby's receptionist practically dialed 911 when she saw him, and it was only when he reassured her that a check was waiting for him that she relaxed. Bobby wasn't in yet, which was just as well, because Black wasn't sure he wouldn't assault him on sight.

The teller at the bank did her best to control her expression when he made it to the window, but he could see the amusement in her eyes as she counted out the hundreds after triple-checking his driver's license photo. When he returned to Gracie's, she was planted on the sofa, remote in one hand, another morning cocktail in the other. He placed the money on the arm of the couch, and she counted it with the dexterity of a three-card Monte hustler before tucking it into the pocket of her housecoat. After declining the obligatory offer of a drink, he slipped away, leaving her to the reruns of *Gilligan's Island* that were part of her daily ritual.

He called a cab on his cell and waited for it at the curb – he'd asked Sylvia to move his Cadillac from its position in front of the complex once a week so it wouldn't get ticketed and towed, to which she'd reluctantly agreed. Ten minutes later a taxi arrived and popped the trunk, and he deposited his things before hopping in the back and giving the driver his office address.

Mugsy stared at him from his spot on the couch as Black shouldered his way through the door. He was lying on his back, all four paws up in the air, looking like a furry basketball with chubby stumps poking out.

"Good morning, tubby. You have a nice night overeating and crapping everywhere?"

Mugsy's tail twitched, but other than that, he could have been dead. Black carried his bag and guitar to his office and placed them safely inside, and then attended to cleaning out the litter box and ensuring the oversized food tray and the water dispenser were full. He cinched the top of the garbage bag with a tie, left it where the cleaning crew couldn't miss it, and returned to his office, where Mugsy was snoring softly on the lobby sofa, as was his custom.

Black checked the time. An hour to go. He spent a few minutes on the web checking for nonexistent messages before calling Stan.

"Yo. Stan. It's yo homey Black in tha house."

"You know how white you sound when you do that?"

"Not convincing, huh?"

"Worse than John Wayne as Genghis Khan."

"Don't be a hatah."

"I'm hanging up."

"No, wait. You busy?"

"Got all the time in the world. We mostly just hang out and take naps around here when we're not watching porn. But don't tell anyone." Stan paused. "Why?"

"I got a gig." Black explained what he was going to be doing for the next three months.

"That's great. What's next? Standing on the street corner warning that the end is nigh?"

"Tough job, that. Too much competition, especially in Hollywood."

"What are the chances you can pull this off and win?"

"I have no idea. But the band's really good. If I come up to speed, we could make it work. Of course, it'll depend on the other groups. There could be a stunner in the bunch."

"Does this mean you're spending your male menopause doing lines of blow off groupies' bare midriffs? I want to be you. I knew I should have gone into the PI game."

"The part where you're waking up at midnight having anxiety attacks over how much you can get selling your blood sort of offsets the highs."

"So you say. All I know is I'm not being asked to play guitar on TV."

"Might be because you can't play, for starters. Just saying."

"Always with the comebacks, smartass. I could always learn."

Black smiled to himself. "If you saw me right now, you'd have second thoughts. They made me look like Alice Cooper after a three-day drunk."

"That's the fashion these days."

"How would you know?"

"All right, I'm just making that up. So you're out of touch for three months?"

"I'm not going to Afghanistan. Only Malibu. And I'll have my phone."

"Well, be careful. You know how I worry. I'd hate to think of you catching something in the hot tub. I've seen those shows. Nonstop orgy. Good for ratings."

"Sylvia's going to love that," Black muttered.

"Sylvia who?"

Black hung up and paced in his office, checking his watch. Turning from the window, he spied his Gretsch. He opened the case, tuned it, and began running scales, hoping to coax his dexterity back. He was in the middle of practicing arpeggios when he heard a knock at the office door.

"Come in. It's open," he called as he packed the guitar away. When he stuck his head out of the doorway, a tall young woman in blue gabardine slacks and a white blouse approached, trailed by a burly man wearing a gray Ozzie tour tank top that did little to cover his hirsute form.

"Mr. Black?" she asked.

"That's me."

"My name's Sarah Miller. I'm the assistant producer with *Rock of Ages*. I help coordinate things for Simon. And this is Lou."

Black stepped from his office, carrying his guitar and his bag. "Nice to meet you, Sarah. Lou."

Sarah's attention drifted away, and her gaze locked on Mugsy, who'd cracked one eye open and was watching her, feet still jutting straight into the air from his bulbous form. "Oh my God. He's beautiful! What's his name?"

"The cat? Mugsy," Black said, amazed at how the porky feline could charm the pants off anything female without even trying.

"Mugsy! Look at you, Mr. Mugs! Aren't you gorgeous! What a handsome boy, aren't you?" Sarah approached Mugsy, whose tail was now swishing slowly, and rubbed his considerable belly. Black could hear the purring from across the room. Another sucker duped by the tubby tabby. She looked up at Black. "Is he yours?"

"Sort of. He's the office cat."

She paused. "Is there anyone else to look after him?"

"Well, I had an assistant, but she…she's on sabbatical during the filming of the show. But she promised to stop in and take care of him."

Sarah's gaze swept the sparse furnishings. "What do you do here? What kind of business is this?"

"Security. That sort of thing."

"Then he's going to be all alone?" The volume of Mugsy's purring increased, now resembling the shifting of tectonic plates. Black should have seen what was coming, but like an out-of-control car skidding toward a gas truck on black ice, he felt powerless to stop the coming calamity.

"Not all the time. I told you, my assistant–"

"He'd be perfect for the show! We've been trying to figure out how to broaden the ratings, and a handsome fellow like this will draw in a whole other crowd. The cat ladies will go insane – he's a natural. Look at that face! That mug! Mugsy! Mr. Muggles. Do you want to be on TV with your daddy?"

"I'm not his–"

"Look at how happy he is! It's like he understands." Mugsy was pawing delightedly at the air with his front paws, probably because he thought he could eat or shred Sarah's blouse. "I absolutely insist. The human interest of you not wanting to abandon your beloved cat will go a long way to making you sympathetic to viewers. And they're the ones who have the final vote after the qualification rounds," Sarah said, her tone ominous. "Anything that makes you more appealing to the audience shouldn't be underrated."

Black sat in the back seat of the gold Suburban, Mugsy and Sarah in the passenger seat next to Lou, as they wended their way down Malibu Canyon. The blue of the Pacific Ocean shimmered in the distance. His misgivings about agreeing to do the show had just trebled with Mugsy, the destroyer of worlds, in the mix, but his protests and warnings had fallen on deaf ears. Sarah was obviously smitten. Black silently cursed the fat bastard and prayed he'd run away once at a strange house, but he suspected that wasn't going to be the way his luck ran.

No, Mugsy was now part of the show, and any mayhem he caused would probably boost the ratings. Black thought about how he was going to explain the cat's involvement to Roxie and decided that he would put that off until later. As the big SUV rolled into the beach town, Black eyed the multimillion dollar mansions on the hills and silently estimated the amount of damage Mugsy could inflict in mere minutes. He dry-swallowed hard.

Even though it was only one thirty, Black realized that he would have traded all the limited money in his pocket for a strong drink. He fought down the impulse, which immediately followed by a craving for a cigarette, and wondered how he was going to make it if this was any indication of how his three-month sentence was likely to go.

Chapter 9

When the Suburban labored up the long circular drive, Black got his first look at the band house. Calling it opulent was like calling Angelina Jolie cute. Drawing its architectural influence from the villas of Spain's Costa Brava, it was easily ten thousand square feet, spread across three rambling stories that climbed up the hill behind it.

"Wow. This is the place?" Black asked, impressed.

"This is it. Home sweet home, until you either win the contest or get booted out," Sarah said. She held Mugsy up so he could see and waved one of his paws at the house. "Say hi to your new home, Mr. Mugsy Man." She turned and looked at Black over her shoulder. "He's a stocky one, isn't he?"

"Stocky would be Mugsy after six months of anorexia."

She returned to Mugsy, who was doing his angel best to appear harmless. "Nonsense. You're just a big, handsome boy, aren't you? You like your cat chow, though, huh?"

"More like his side of beef and dozen doughnuts."

Lou chuckled and then stifled it when he caught Sarah's expression.

They pulled to a stop in front of the mansion's double wood-and-glass entry doors, where a camera crew was filming their approach.

"I thought you said they don't start filming until Monday," Black said.

"Correct. This is just for background. The bands arriving. That sort of thing," Sarah explained. "They've already done a few one-on-one interviews with Christina, your lead singer, who will be doing most of the talking, if last season was any indication. You just need to do a few minutes of canned spiel about who you are, what your background is, that kind of stuff, so the audience can follow along. And then as the season develops, we'll do more interviews to get your reactions to whatever's happening."

"When do I meet my band?"

"After you get settled in. Here. Take Mugsy. It'll be pure gold if you're carrying him as you arrive." She twisted in the seat and handed Mugsy to Black. Mugsy looked like he was going to let go of his bladder, so he held the cat away from him. "Okay. Let me get out of the car, and once I'm clear, the crew will shoot you. Wait until Lou gets your stuff out, and then walk up the steps to the front doors. Holly, one of the hosts, will meet you there. I hope you like cold beer."

"You must be psychic."

Black followed Sarah's instructions and didn't have to pretend to be in awe of the mansion as he approached the entry. Marble, granite, exotic woods, columns…the entire place reeked of money. Big money. Mugsy held off on spraying him, so at least he was spared that indignity, and he hugged the beast to his breast like a newborn, playing for the cameras as he mounted the steps. When he reached the threshold, the doors pulled wide, and a gorgeous blonde woman wearing a baseball cap on backward, a black The Cult T-shirt and ripped jeans, all white teeth and tanned skin and augmented curves, greeted him like he was bringing an alimony check.

"Welcome to the Rock House! Come on in! I'm Holly," she squealed, and Black felt a twinge of alarm at how it would look to Sylvia when Holly hugged him and gave his bottom an on-camera pinch. "Wow. This one's mine. Rrrowrr!" she said, and Black grinned and played along, trying not to think about the fact that she was likely half his age, even if she might have had twice the miles on her.

"Nice to meet you, Holly," Black said as she beamed sex appeal at him.

"Everyone at home, this is Jim Black. He's the original guitar player and songwriter for Gravatar, one of the biggest bands of all time. This is such a thrill. I can't believe you're playing with Last Call. Tell me, Jim…how does it feel?"

"It's a rush. I can't wait," Black said, doing his best to appear enthusiastic. "And it's Black. Just Black. That's what everybody calls me."

"All right. Black. So another question. Is it going to be weird having your old bandmate Nina judging you?" Holly asked.

Black stopped in his tracks and tried to keep his mouth from gaping open. "Say what?"

"Nina. She's one of the judges. Are you afraid she'll be harder on the band, or conversely, might be more willing to vote for you? You were married to her, right?"

Black could hear the sound of his heart hammering in his ears. The hallway he was standing in seemed to elongate as the walls closed in. He was afraid he was going to faint, and then Mugsy saved the day by letting out a long yawn accompanied by a yowl.

"I think I'll let Mugsy have the last word on that," Black said and resumed walking.

"What a beautiful cat! And a husky boy, isn't he?"

"You don't know the half of it. He's actually been the state feline sumo wrestling champion three years running," Black assured Holly without a trace of irony. Her eyes flicked to the side as she tried to decide whether he was kidding, and Black offered no clues. The cameraman shook his head from behind the camera, and she returned to her empty smile.

"Oh, you. I can see you're going to be nothing but trouble," she said, giving Black a playful swat. "Come on. I'll introduce you to the rest of the gang."

Holly led the way into a great room that could have doubled as a hangar, where four impossibly beautiful Asian girls lounged around the breakfast bar that separated it from the kitchen, two in mini-skirts that barely covered their bottoms, the other two in bikinis. Holly did a little bow to them and gestured to Black.

"This is Black, everyone. Black, meet Love Jupiter. From Korea. They're already stars over there, isn't that right?" Holly enthused, and the four girls smiled and waved and made peace signs. Black smiled at each in turn, but he could have been invisible, because everyone's attention was on Mugsy, who seemed to instinctively understand that he was going to be the center of attention as long as he turned on the charm. One of the bikini-clad nymphs moved toward Black, followed by her companion, and soon they were ooing and ahhing as they petted Mugsy, posing as their bandmates took pictures with their phones. Mugsy's purrs resembled a Peterbilt revving, and Black realized that perhaps the truculent cat might be a godsend after all – he was taking all the heat off Black to do much besides pose with him.

Two youths strode through the pocket doors, dressed in full-blown gang attire straight out of South Central, and swaggered to where Black stood.

"Yo, Holly, baby. How you doin', sweetness? What up?" the taller of the pair said, clutching the crotch of his baggy jeans like he was trying to hold his water.

Another blinding smile from Holly. "Good, Lavon. Black, this is Lavon and SnM. They're BrandX."

"Yo, punkass, welcome to da crib. Sorry we gonna stomp yo ass in the contest, you know?"

Black shrugged. "No hard feelings. I'm sure I'll get over it."

"What the hell's that? Look like one a dem koalas or something," SnM said, managing to leer at all four of the Koreans as well as Holly with one glance.

"That's Mugsy. He's the Biggie of cats. Straight up," Black announced.

"Whoa. He do like to eat, don't he?" Lavon commented, hesitantly petting Mugsy's belly.

"Never saw a Twinkie he didn't love," Black said, and the young men laughed.

"Yo, what he weigh?" SnM asked, peering at Mugsy's bloated countenance.

"About the same as a bag of cement right about now, I'd guess," Black joked, earning a titter from Holly. He turned to her. "Nice to meet everyone, but I need to get settled in and tend to Mugsy here. He gets grouchy if he doesn't get a T-bone every hour, on the hour."

More laughs and pictures and squeals, and then Holly escorted him upstairs. The camera crew remained below, the equipment off now that they'd gotten their arrival shot. Black followed her, noting that she must have spent a lot of time in the gym as she moved up the wide marble steps ahead of him, and felt a stab of guilt. He hadn't even been away from Sylvia for half a day and he was already checking out the talent – not to mention being surrounded by Korean hotties who seemed more than friendly.

They arrived at the second floor, which resembled more a resort hotel than a home, and she pointed out the various doors. "There are eight bedrooms in the house, each with its own full bathroom. Four bands, so two rooms for each. We've got you staying with your drummer, Ed."

"That'll work. Which room?"

"This way. Second from the end," Holly said, leading him down the elaborate corridor.

"This is quite a place. Who owns it?"

"Both houses are leased from the same guy. Some bigwig in the car business. Italian name. I wasn't really paying attention when they were talking about it. I'm just on-camera eye candy."

"I'd say you're more than that if you're a host," Black said. "But I have a question. You said Nina was one of the judges?"

Holly slowed and turned to face him. "Didn't you know? I just assumed someone had told you…"

"No, it never came up. They left that out of the briefing."

"I'm sorry. I didn't mean to ambush you or anything," Holly assured him, and he believed her – and not just because she had the bluest eyes he'd ever seen.

"No problem. I'm a big boy. It just took me by surprise."

"I'll bet." She spun and continued down the hall until she stopped at an open doorway. "This is it. Ed's at the pool, so you have it to yourself for now. Lou will be right up with your stuff. We're not going to be shooting anything more until Monday, so you're cool. Peter and Christina will be here this afternoon, and you're slotted time in one of the rehearsal rooms at five, but until then, you're on your own. They explained the rules to you on the way here?"

"Yeah. Community kitchen, no leaving the grounds, no girl or boyfriends. All the food and booze I can drink. And Sarah said something about shopping?"

"I don't know about that. You should ask her. She's going to be here all afternoon, making sure everyone feels at home and doesn't need anything."

"What should I do with Mugsy?"

"You should probably keep him in your room until Sarah figures it out. She's the boss."

He offered Holly a small smile. "Thanks for showing me the way."

"Did you write that one, too?"

Black shook his head. "Pretty sure that was Boston."

"Oh."

Black watched Holly go and then turned to enter the room, which was larger than his apartment and featured marble floors, granite counters, two double beds, and a dresser. Black poked his head into the bathroom and was impressed – it was easily the size of his kitchen. Mugsy was getting heavier by the second, so Black returned to the door, toed it closed, and set the obese feline down. Mugsy tottered several steps and then settled in under the closest bed. The sound of his snoring filled the air within seconds.

Peals of laughter rose from outside the pocket doors that overlooked the ocean. Black pulled them open and was greeted by music and excited feminine squeals. He peered down at the large pool, where two bikini-clad members of Love Jupiter were standing in the shallow end, drinks in hand. A chubby male with disheveled hair stood by the far edge of the deck, dripping water. Without warning, he ran full steam and launched himself into the air, screaming, "Cannonball!" and then hit the surface with his knees tucked under his chin, sending water everywhere, including all over the laughing women. Two dead bottles of champagne sat in ice buckets by the wet bar, and there was a small army of empty beer cans by one of the lounge chairs.

The diver's head exploded out of the water, and he shook it like a wet dog, spraying his surroundings. He glanced at the two Korean singers, and then his eyes locked on Black.

"Jim Black? Is that you?" he cried.

"I think so. Ed?"

"Brutha! Come on down. It's all you can drink, man. Totally hot!"

"Uh, maybe later. I have to get unpacked…"

"Dude. That can wait." Ed turned to the women. "This is Sora, and this is…Yoon Ji."

"Maybe in a little while. Save some cocktails for me."

"You don't know what you're missing, man," Ed advised him. The two bathing beauties smiled and toasted him.

"Looks like it. Hang loose. I think my stuff's here."

Lou entered carrying his guitar and bag and set them on the bed. Mugsy stalked stiff-legged from beneath it, stretched, and fixed Black with his "I want food" glare. Black thanked Lou for bringing his things and asked him for a bowl of water.

"I'm going to the store for a cat food run. Anything in particular?"

"He likes canned. Get the jumbo size, obviously. Oh, and some kitty litter and a box."

"10-4. He definitely looks like he's got an appetite."

"You don't know the half of it. Is Sarah still downstairs?"

"Yeah. She said to come down whenever you're ready, and she'll go through the rest of the schedule with you."

"Tell her I'll be there in ten."

"You got it."

Black sat down on the bed when Lou left and stared at Mugsy, who was eyeing the obviously expensive wooden closet doors. "Don't even think about it," Black warned, and Mugsy, for once, took the hint and retreated. Black gazed around the room and lay back, feeling twice his age. As another volley of laughter echoed from the pool, he closed his eyes, wondering what he'd gotten himself into and how he was ever going to get himself back out.

Chapter 10

Black had just finished unpacking when Ed burst through the door, leaving puddles of water in his wake. Black held out his hand in greeting. Ed ignored it and embraced Black in a bear hug that would have been awkward even if he hadn't been wearing only some soaked swim trunks hanging halfway down his chubby ass crack.

"Dude. It's awesome to finally meet you. Rooster told us all about your history – what can I say? This would be like Sid Vicious joining the band, you know? Bitchin'!" Ed finally released him and stepped back with an idiot grin on his face.

"Nice to meet you, too. I hope he didn't give me too much of a buildup. It's been a while since I was in the saddle."

Ed shrugged. "He warned us you'd be a little rough but said it would get better quickly. I believe him. Rooster's seen 'em all come and go. He's the best. If he says you're what this band needs, I'm all in. Go big or go home. Woohoo!"

Black could smell beer coming off Ed in waves and wondered whether he was always this high on life even when sober. Still, there was something infectious about his smile and childlike joy, and Black decided that he'd rather have a guy like that keeping the beat than a sourpuss. From what he'd seen on YouTube, Ed was a natural showman, and his enthusiasm radiated as he played, making him an audience favorite.

"Well, I'm not here to come in second, so I'll give it everything I've got. Hopefully it gels. I can't wait for our first rehearsal today."

"Crap. I totally spaced on that. I better start drinking mineral water, or Christina's gonna go apeshit on me. She's a little sensitive about booze since Rick…well, you know the story."

"I heard. Was he a big drinker?"

"Not really. I mean, he'd knock 'em back like anyone, but it wasn't like a big problem, you know? And he never smoked dope before a show. That was a total first. And last."

"I wonder why he chose that moment to screw up?"

"He and Christina weren't getting along. Maybe she drove him crazy. Who knows?"

"You weren't that close?"

"Not really. I mean, he and Christina were tight, but he didn't pal around with me or anything. We hung out, but it wasn't like he was calling me to see if I wanted to go to the ball game or whatever. More like friends in the studio and onstage, but separate lives outside. Which was fine by me. Christina's pretty…intense, sometimes. If he could deal with her 24/7, more power to him."

"Singers can be that way."

"Your old lady's one of the judges, right?"

Black sighed. "Nina. My ex. But that was a long time ago."

"What was it like? Being married to the biggest diva of the nineties?"

"She wasn't big yet when we were married – just starting to get there. But I guess you could say she was…intense, too. So I get the whole singer thing."

"Frigging prima donnas, if you ask me. But hey, what are you gonna do? Nobody packs a stadium to see me swat skins."

"Too true." Black checked his watch. "I'm going to go downstairs. You want anything?"

"I'm good. I think I'll take a shower and sober up. Man, oh man, though. Did you see those chicks from Japan? I don't know if they can sing for shit, but talk about bombshells…"

"They're certainly impressive. But I think they're Korean–"

Ed nearly jumped out of his skin when Mugsy rubbed against his leg. "What the hell is that?"

"Oh, that's Mugsy. He's the world's most ungrateful cat. Sarah fell in love with him when she saw him and decided he's just got to be on the show."

Ed bent down and pet Mugsy, scratching behind his ears. "He's a porker, huh? No problemo, boss man. Three's company. I love animals."

"Mugsy might change your mind about that."

Sarah was sitting in the study off the great room studying her clipboard when Black found her. She gave him a courtesy smile and motioned for him to sit on one of the studded burgundy leather chairs.

"Holly got you situated?"

"Yes, thanks. And I just met Ed. Nice guy."

"He's a sweetheart. Doesn't have a mean bone in his body." She eyed a sheet of paper. "I was just going over the itinerary. You've got the band at five; then we'll do a big dinner outside on the pool deck. It's a Hawaiian theme tonight. Then nothing until Monday, when we'll do the whole on-camera orientation thing and lay out the week's challenge."

"Great. I could use a few days to bond with my band before we start on this."

"Now on to the nitty gritty. Every week there's a group activity where you break off into teams and compete, and then there's an elimination round every couple weeks where you play somewhere interesting and different. Then the judges drop the axe. First round, two bands get asked to leave, and then it's a process of elimination, with one each round hitting the road."

"That sounds like pretty standard fare."

"Yes, there shouldn't be any surprises, although last year...well, let's just say when you cram a bunch of performers together in two houses there are bound to be clashes and attractions. That's part of the fascination for people, I think."

"Where's the other house?"

"About a half mile from here."

"Is it anywhere near as gorgeous as this one? This is a palace."

"It is, isn't it? One of Simon's contacts owns it."

"Must be nice."

Sarah took him through the rest of the schedule, including what hours the camera crew would be filming. "The goal is to give the viewers a real taste of what it's like to live and breathe the band lifestyle, so nothing's off limits. We want authentic. If you like to down a bottle of Jack every night, no problem. Drag groupies back, we want it all captured. The more colorful, the better. But nothing fake, and nothing illegal."

"I'm afraid I'm not going to add much to the hard-partying musician reputation. You grow out of that after a certain point. At least, I did. Pretty early, too... But tell me about the judges. Nobody mentioned my ex-wife was sitting on the panel."

"Really? I just assumed Simon had. It's Nina, Alex, and BT Slim, the hip-hip mogul. They judge the first rounds. Then on the last couple their votes count for fifty percent, and the TV audience's votes count for the other. On the finals, it's only the audience, although the judges get to score, comment on the performances, and offer criticism and feedback."

"And you don't think it's a problem that Nina's ex-husband is in the contest?"

Sarah shrugged. "It doesn't matter what I think. Simon's the big cheese. If he doesn't have an issue with it, neither do I."

"Have you ever met Nina?"

"Last year." Sarah leaned forward. "Let's talk about your one-on-one. On Monday, we'll want to do an hour of you commenting on what it's like to be here, the pressure, the competition...you've seen the kind of thing, where they cut away from the action and stick in ten seconds of talk now and then. Everyone does a few, although it's tough with the Koreans. They don't speak much English."

"Seems like their allure doesn't have a lot to do with their language skills."

"Fair point." Sarah glanced at her watch. "Lou should be back shortly with Mugsy's things."

"Okay, but I want to go on record saying having Mugsy around's a bad idea. He's like the Terminator — a one-cat wrecking machine. I can't even begin to imagine the damage he's going to do in a place like this. I want no part of it."

"Don't worry about that. We've got an insurance policy. Besides, how much trouble can he get into?"

"Think demolition crew."

Sarah laughed, which was the first time he'd seen anything that wasn't strictly business out of her. "He struck me as a big butterball."

"That's how he is just before he draws first blood. He's a walking disaster area waiting to happen. You've been warned."

"Well, I appreciate that, but I'm actually thinking of doing a sidebar on Mugsy. Sort of a mini show within a show. Following him around, seeing what he gets up to. Puppies and kitties score big with viewers. I already fired off an email to Simon, and he loves the idea."

"Then get a handler for him. Someone who knows what he's doing. Because it's not a matter of whether he goes berserk, it's a question of how often."

"Noted, Mr. Black. Now, if you have no other questions, just ignore the camera crew and behave as though they aren't there. It'll seem a little strange at first, but after a few days it becomes second nature. Good luck, and if you have any questions, ask Lou. He'll be staying in the service quarters for the duration.

"What about the hosts? Holly and…?"

"Holly and David. They'll only be around at the shows, the competitions, and a few times a week here, most notably when we do the on-camera orientations and the disqualification ceremonies. They're really just here to give the show a coherent voice. If you need anything, ask Lou, or if I'm around, ask for me. Knife Edge will arrive from England on Sunday, so we'll have the usual arrival shots, but other than that, we're done until Monday."

"Okay. Thank her for showing me around."

Sarah peered at him. "She was doing me a favor. But I'll pass it along. Anything else?"

"No, that'll do it. I think I'll make a sandwich. I haven't had lunch and I'm starved."

"Enjoy your stay. Remember, do whatever you want, but no leaving the grounds unless it's on an approved outing. Anything else goes. Within reason."

"I bet that's tough with the rappers. In my experience, they like their funny cigarettes."

"We take no responsibility for contestants choosing to break the law," Sarah said diplomatically. Black had little doubt that the show had a team of lawyers looking at every angle to ensure they were insulated.

"That's good to know if I decide to set up a still or something. Thanks again."

The kitchen was fully stocked with everything he could imagine, and he made a turkey and salami sandwich with Swiss cheese, accompanied by an Anchor Steam beer in a bottle. He sat at the breakfast bar and munched on it, and nodded at Lou when he pushed through the door with several brimming bags of shopping.

"I got all the cat stuff. You want it up in your room?"

"Sure. I'll be up in a few. Throw it on the bed, and I'll set it up when I get there."

Black spent a half hour with Mugsy's new setup while the cat played with his new toys and eyed the food dish every few minutes. Once the kitty litter box was deployed, Black opened a can of food, spooned it into the bowl, and poured a healthy portion of hard food around it. Mugsy moved like Ali, a tabby blur, and was devouring the meal so fast Black was afraid of losing a finger. The bowl was clean within three minutes, and Mugsy trailed Black to his chair by the terrace, sat down next to him, and burped and passed gas simultaneously.

"Jesus, Mugsy. Why? Tell me – why?"

Mugsy burped again, and then his legs seemed to buckle, and he collapsed by Black's side, asleep before his head hit the ground. Black watched him, more than familiar with his post-prandial habits, and grunted. Mugsy would be out for at least a couple of hours. He was far too lazy to try to leap from the terrace down to the ground floor, so leaving the pocket doors open was safe – no way was Black going to let the flatulent mouser gas him out of the room. Ed was back in the pool, splashing around with his new friends, the rappers nowhere to be seen, and Black decided that Mugsy had the right idea – a nap was just the ticket.

He bolted awake when Ed returned an hour and a half later.

"Hey, dude. Rehearsal in ten. I'm just gonna hose off and throw on some clothes. I'll be ready in two shakes. Peter's downstairs, and I guess Christina's already in the rehearsal studio with Rooster."

"I'll go down and introduce myself. See you there."

Black carted his guitar down to the great room, where a tall, thin man in his early thirties sporting two feet of straight dirty-brown hair was sitting on the couch reading the paper, a soda on the table in front of him. He looked up when Black arrived and carefully folded the newspaper before rising – typical anal-retentive bass player behavior, Black thought.

"Peter? I'm Black. Nice to meet you."

Peter was the opposite of Ed, all angles and restraint. His handshake felt dry and crisp, his fingers long and delicate, which matched his birdlike appearance.

"Nice to meet you too. We've all heard a lot about you from Rooster."

"I hope I can live up to his buildup."

"That makes two of us."

Peter obviously wasn't impressed, or if he was, he was doing a stellar job of hiding it.

"How long have you been in the band?" Black asked as he took a seat across from him.

"Last Call? Six years. Christina's my sister, so I've been in pretty much every band she's ever played in."

"Wow. That's a while. You must have a lot of material by now."

"Over forty songs."

"A lot of albums."

"They don't call them that anymore."

"Huh. I missed the memo."

Peter took a sip of his soda. "What about you? What have you been doing?"

Black shifted nervously. "Oh, this and that. I have a little business I run. Haven't played for a long time. After I left the band, I kind of lost my taste for it. I tried producing for a few years, but it wasn't for me." He frowned. "Takes a special kind to sit behind the board sixteen hours a day."

"I have a twenty-four-track recording studio."

Black wondered whether the meeting could go any worse. "That's cool. Must be convenient for songwriting and doing demos."

"It is."

Black asked questions about the kind of equipment he used, what kind of bass guitars, his amps, but Peter wasn't the friendliest, and Black was relieved when Ed came bouncing down the stairs.

"He's here!" Ed said and high-fived Black. Peter made no move to join in the fun.

Black glanced at his watch and stood. "Right on time. Where's the studio?"

"They set up the carriage house on the other end of the grounds," Peter explained.

"Oh, so we're walking. Okay. Lead the way."

Christina was sitting with Rooster when they swung the door open. She gave Black the once-over as Rooster jumped to his feet and made introductions. Christina was friendlier than Peter, but only slightly, and Black guessed it ran in the family – probably not a lot of happy Christmases in their past.

"So you're the guy we've been hearing all about. Nice to meet you, Jim," Christina said. Black was struck by how beautiful she was in person, and how small. If she was more than five feet tall, he'd have been surprised, although she filled out her jeans and tank commendably.

"And you as well. I'm a fan – I've checked out a lot of your stuff on YouTube. You've got a great voice."

"Thanks. But that only goes so far. We need to really rock this season if we're going to win."

"That's why I'm here."

After a few minutes of small talk, Rooster suggested that they play together, warming up on some blues standards. Black took his time setting up his amp to get the sound he wanted, tweaking the gain for just the right amount of distortion when he opened up his guitar for leads.

An hour later they broke for a bathroom visit, and Christina pulled Rooster aside, agitated. Black could hear her whispering, and it was obvious she was concerned.

"He's not going to work, Rooster. Listen to him. He's flailing."

"Sweetheart, give it some time. This is just the first day. Everyone's getting used to things. Trust me – he'll do fine," Rooster said.

Black approached them and addressed Christina. "I know that was rough. It's been a while. But it's getting better as we go along. Ed's a hell of a drummer, and Peter's solid as a rock."

She turned to Black, leveling a dark gaze at him. "That's not going to do us much good if you're not a hundred and ten percent when we hit the stage."

"I know. I'm going to be spending the next two weeks practicing. I know I kind of suck right now. And I don't intend to go on television and suck. I'm not oblivious. I'll do what needs to be done."

"Black was one of the best. An amazing player," Rooster added.

"*Was*," Christina said, refusing to thaw. "What have you done for me lately?"

"Come on, baby, lighten up. We all got to make this work, so hit me with some positive vibes, will you? This is only day one. We've got time," Rooster countered.

"Hey, dude, awesome chops," Ed said, returning from the bathroom. Peter had left the building to have a cigarette outside.

"Thanks, Ed. You keep a mean beat."

"Can you sing any better than you can play?" Christina cut in, eyeing Black.

"Sure. Backgrounds. You heard me all over the record if you ever listened to it."

"The studio can lie."

He nodded. "Yes, it can. But I can sing." Black rubbed his face, now annoyed at Christina's belligerence. She had a right to be worried, but not to be a complete ass, and he wasn't going to let her walk all over him. It was time to draw a line. "Listen, Christina, I know this hasn't gotten off on the right foot. I'm sorry. But in all fairness, I've sold twenty-something million records. That's got to count for something."

"Maybe to some. But that's your career. Mine's hinging on winning this show. Last year, my guitar player cost me everything. I'm not going to let that happen again."

"I totally understand. Come on. Let's give this another try. See if we can make some magic happen," Black said, and Rooster winked at him, nodding.

"You heard the man. Time to earn your fame and fortune. Let's make some noise!"

Chapter 11

True to his word, Black spent most of his time in his room or the rehearsal studio, practicing, running scales, dialing his tone. Rehearsals were getting better every evening, and by the end of the first week the band was hitting its stride. They'd been assigned a standard for their first round, selected at random, but one that Black knew, and it was sounding good – "Chain of Fools" by Aretha Franklin, which gave Christina a chance to show off. Peter had loosened up by the time the second weekend together rolled around, and actually seemed happy with Black now that he was coming up to speed. Ed was just Ed and would have been delighted under any circumstances, Black suspected. He approached life with the wonder of a child, and Black was glad he was rooming with him instead of Peter.

The first team building challenge had been completely stupid – running an obstacle course in a relay race. Black's team had been composed at random with members from all eight bands, and he was hard-pressed to care much about it, but put on a game face for the cameras even though he'd have rather been boiled in oil.

Evenings were spent hanging out with the other bands at the house, which wasn't rough duty. Love Jupiter pranced for the cameras in swimsuits at every turn, and the members of Knife Edge, from Ireland, seemed bound and determined to show the American audience how the rock lifestyle was done across the pond, and were usually inebriated but lively and extremely funny to talk with. Any one of them could have been a comedian, and Black realized as he headed into week two that he was actually enjoying himself, except for the constant intrusive filming.

Sarah had okayed a shopping outing in Los Angeles to get a proper rock wardrobe for the upcoming first show, and Lou had taken him, along with Christina, to several shops that specialized in stage wear. When they emerged from the second store, Black was wearing skinny-legged black pants and a paisley shirt that would have been right at home on Mick Jagger circa 1972, with a bag full of similar gear. He'd gradually gotten more used to his appearance and now didn't cringe whenever he caught sight of himself in a mirror, which he supposed was an improvement, if not much of one.

Black was looking forward to seeing Sylvia tomorrow. Sunday was taking forever to arrive, but the two times he'd called her, she'd sounded distant and annoyed. Despite his hope that she would get over the initial anger that had flared after he'd broken the news, she'd apparently stayed mad, and he was eager to reconnect in case she might thaw once they were back together. Lou had made a dinner reservation for them at an upscale restaurant in Malibu, and Black was counting the minutes until she arrived.

When they got back to the house, Christina changed into a bikini whose bottom was little more than a thong. Black slipped into a pair of baggy surfer shorts and a short-sleeve button-up shirt with ebony skulls – one of his new acquisitions from his shopping spree. When Christina joined him by the pool, where Love Jupiter was frolicking for the cameras, he noted that she could have been a lingerie model, no problem, even given her diminutive stature. Christina, as with all the women on the show, had been encouraged by the producers to show skin on a regular basis, and even though she'd confessed to Black that she hated that aspect of the job, she did so with apparent abandon. If you wanted to win, you had to play the game, and Christina wanted to win more than anything – she'd made that abundantly clear.

Christina stretched like a cat as she applied suntan oil, her lithe body toned and hard as a gymnast's while the cameras soaked in the spectacle. Across the pool the Love Jupiter girls were playing with Mugsy, whom they doted on like their corpulent child. Mugsy adored the constant attention and had even refrained from shredding any of the furniture – a minor miracle to Black, who awoke each morning cringing at what devastation he'd be greeted with. But so far, nothing. Mugsy was on his best behavior, which consisted mainly of overeating and sleeping when not being filmed or fondled.

Ed sidled up poolside in bright red shorts and a cheesy rayon Hawaiian shirt emblazoned with tiki gods, and plopped down next to Black after a glance at Christina. "Hey, dawg. Nice to see you soaking up the rays. I thought you were a vampire or something," he said as he cracked open a tall boy and held it aloft in a cheer.

"Just playing a lot."

Ed gulped a third of the can in a few swallows and sighed appreciatively. "Whoa, Christina, that suit should be illegal. Hubbada hubbada."

"Put your eyes back in your head, smut boy. This is for our ratings, not for you," she murmured without lifting her head.

"I'd give it a solid ten. Just saying," Ed said, winking at Black. "But what do we have here? Korea's in the house. Also contenders, looking at their getups. It's a great time to be alive, isn't it, Black?"

"Never better." Black yawned and sneaked another admiring glance at the Koreans. "You worried about the first round next week?"

Ed shook his head. "Nah. Been there, done that. My guess is the Irish lads get sent packing. They haven't done much rehearsing, and the coach they were assigned looks angry every time they come out of the studio."

"What about our rapper buddies?" Black asked, peering over the tops of his shades at Lavon and SnM sipping champagne and chatting with Yoon Ji and her friends, who appeared puzzled by the conversation.

"Beats me. But rap's usually a tough sell unless they're something really special. I'm not worried. We would have won last year, and the competition was stiff. This ain't no thang."

"And the beer certainly helps."

"That it does. Soothes my delicate nerves, dude."

After a few hours, Black began feeling like a lobster and retired inside, where he had one of three beers he allowed himself each day as he watched the big-screen TV. Lou was in the kitchen, fixing himself a snack, and joined Black when he switched to Animal Planet.

"How's it hanging, Lou?"

"Oh, you know. Just another day in paradise."

"Was it like this last year, too?"

"Nah, different dynamic. I like this group better."

"Did Last Call stay here last season?"

"Yeah. I'll tell you, I never get tired of Christina in a swimsuit."

"What about Rick? Did you know him very well?"

"Yeah. He was all right. Cool dude. Just a regular guy, you know? No attitude."

"Were you surprised when he blew it?"

"Kind of. I mean, he was flawless right up until that last show, and then, bam, he chokes. Nobody could have predicted that. But I got to tell you, talk about fireworks in the house – after that, he couldn't get out of here fast enough. I seriously thought Christina was going to kill him."

"But they were at the hotel…"

"Yeah, but they did the final ceremony here. They wouldn't talk to each other. I wasn't surprised when I read that they'd broken up."

"Did he strike you as having a drinking or drug problem?"

"Not really. Like I said, he was just a normal guy. Drank beer like pretty much everyone, wasn't high that I could tell. It was a total surprise to everyone. Maybe he cracked under the pressure. Who knows?"

"I saw the footage of Alex. He was pretty damned good, too."

"Yeah, he was. It was neck and neck. I'm sure Christina has nightmares about it. She totally believed she'd swept the contest." Lou shook his head. "Tough break, but hey. She's back this year, so you guys have another chance. And if you're able to pull it off like last year…no contest. She's world class."

Black gazed through the pocket doors at where Christina was walking along the pool edge to take a dip and nodded thoughtfully.

"That she is, Lou."

The following afternoon Sylvia pulled up to the mansion in Black's Cadillac. She was getting out of the car when she froze – Black was standing outside the front door, a cameraman next to him, filming her arrival. Black waved to her, and she reluctantly moved to him. He hugged her, but she felt stiff, and the return hug was perfunctory.

"I didn't realize we'd have company," she said, staring into the big lens.

"Oh, that's Stu. He follows us around. You get used to it."

"Maybe you do. Come on. Let's get out of here. I don't want to be on TV."

Black shrugged and took the keys from her. He slipped behind the wheel and dropped the convertible top, then held his hand up in the classic rock sign of the devil's horns before wheeling around and pulling back down the drive. They spent the afternoon wandering on the beach, and Black realized how much he'd missed Sylvia. He told her so, but she seemed unimpressed. "I saw the first episode. Seems like you're living in a party house with a bunch of whores."

"They aren't whores. They wear the swimsuits and skimpy outfits for the cameras."

"Uh-huh. Well, it's convenient that they all have incredible bodies. Black, this really isn't what I'd imagined our life together being like."

Dinner was more of the same, and Sylvia begged off getting a motel room for a few hours, citing a headache. When she dropped him off at the house with a peck on the cheek instead of their usual prolonged kiss, he knew he had a bigger problem on his hands than just a temporary speed bump. He watched her drive away, and when he entered the great room, where his band was hanging out at the dining table, playing cards with the members of Knife Edge, his expression showed his disappointment. Christina's gaze lingered on his face as he went to the refrigerator and got himself a beer, and he felt a stirring again, undeniable, and completely inappropriate.

Thankfully nobody asked him how his evening had gone, and he begged off boozing and gambling in favor of going to his room and taking his frustrations out on his guitar, as he had as a teenager before everything had gotten so crazy and he'd lost his way.

Chapter 12

A bus rolled up to the backstage gates of the Coachella Empire Polo Club and shuddered to a stop. Four members of the security team moved toward it as the door hissed open, and Sarah stepped down, followed by SnM and two members of Love Jupiter. Black blinked as he exited and waited for the rest of his band to get off, his guitar case in hand. He'd developed the habit of always keeping the Gretsch close to him back in his musician days and saw no reason to break the habit now. If the instrument was sitting next to him on the bus, there was no chance of it somehow getting damaged when it was loaded or unloaded, and now that he had it back in his possession, he had no intention of taking chances with it. Cameras recorded everyone's arrival, and the Asian girls flashed mandatory peace signs as they descended and waited near the neatly trimmed grass of the polo field.

The first of the elimination rounds: each band would get to play one song, and the judges would score the performance from one to ten. The two lowest scoring acts would be disqualified, leaving six to go on to the next round. The backstage area was large, set up to accommodate not only the performers but also the film crews, who were shooting each group's preparations as Holly and her male counterpart David worked the crowd in preparation for the first band.

The judges occupied thrones behind backlit podiums that glowed like UFOs in the twilight. Once all the acts had settled in, David introduced each of the judges to applause, and then the bands were herded onto the stage. Performance order was selected out of a hat, with each group's designated representative choosing a number. Last

Call got number five, which Christina seemed irritated about when she left the stage.

"I'd rather be first or last, not stuck in the middle," she complained to Rooster, who nodded understandingly.

"Don't you worry. Doesn't matter what slot you get. None of these other poor clowns stands a chance," he intoned with the conviction of a priest.

"I hope you're right," she said, clearly unconvinced.

First up was BrandX, the rappers. They delivered a spirited performance with all the obligatory strutting and posturing, and received middling marks from the judges, who each took sixty seconds to critique them before announcing their score. The next was a country rock band from the other mansion, Bend in the Creek, which gave an electrifying performance and got all nines and tens from the judges. Peter exchanged glances with his sister – this was the real competition. Next up was a trio of scantily clad women who called themselves Pieces of A**, who'd clearly modeled their act after Destiny's Child. The crowd response was lukewarm, and the judges weren't convinced. That performance was followed by a boy band that featured five smooth-skinned young men, each with a stereotypical look made obvious by their wardrobes. On Top was the brainchild of an obese fifty-something entrepreneur from Louisiana who minted a new boy band every six months, invariably following the same formula: every member could dance and sing, and each group had the lover, the bad boy, the brooding thinker, the nice guy, and the flashy showman. The performance was professional but uninspired, and the live audience's applause was tepid.

Christina received shouts of encouragement and wolf whistles as she took the stage and bowed, a single spotlight on her as the band plugged in. She was clearly an audience favorite even before having sung a note, remembered fondly from the last season. Black felt a buzz of nervousness as he stood facing several thousand people, and then Ed counted off and Peter began with his pulsing bass line, accompanied by Ed's high hat as Christina let loose a show-stopping wail. Black cranked his guitar volume and coaxed feedback out of it that seemed to blend perfectly with her sustained vocal note, and then they were in the song, Black bopping, all attitude and strut, with moves reminiscent of Page in the Yardbirds. Black's solo was professional but plodding, his speed and fast vibrato still not fully returned, and while there was nothing wrong with the performance, Alex commented that the band seemed like three people and the new guy, and expressed hope that things would gel in future performances. Nina tried to be more upbeat, but Black couldn't look her in the eye. BT Slim had nothing but compliments for Christina, but also echoed that he hoped future performances would be "better integrated".

When all the acts had performed, the scores were tallied up, and two groups were asked to leave the show – Pieces of A** and Knife Edge, whose set had been as unlistenable and raw as a Sex Pistols foray. Last Chance was the third lowest, and the mood backstage was glum. Rooster joined them and tried to reassure Christina, but she wasn't having it.

"I told you this wasn't going to work."

"What are you talking about? These first rounds are like going hunting with your buddies and being chased by a bear. You don't need to be faster than the bear, just faster than your slowest friends."

"We need a different guitar player, Rooster," Christina said. "Next time it could be us getting the axe."

"Not with another two weeks of rehearsal under your belts. This was the worst it's ever going to be. Plus the crowd's rooting for you. You're now the underdog, with the new guy trying to come up to speed. It's all good, Christina. Really," Rooster assured her.

Black had heard enough. He was about to respond when he heard Roxie call his name from the backstage entrance. His better judgment told him to prioritize Roxie, so he left Rooster to do damage control and elbowed his way to where she was waiting, her path blocked by two burly bouncers.

"Hey, Roxie. You made it!" he smiled at her. "Fellas, this is my friend. Let her back for a few minutes. Don't worry, she's not dangerous."

The larger of the two shrugged and unhooked the chain, allowing Roxie to slip by. She took in Black's ensemble and hair and shook her head.

"This is horrifying."

"Nice to see you, too. Glad you could make it."

"What's with the pants? Didn't they have anything in your size?"

"It's all part of the act. They dressed me like this."

"You look...well, whatever."

"How did you like the show?" Black asked, changing the subject from his appearance.

"Your singer can really belt it out. She's a star. The rest was...it was rough, but hey, first show and all..."

"Yeah. I was a little nervous."

"You couldn't tell," Roxie lied.

"Did you see Sylvia out there?"

"Not really. But there are a lot of people, and it's dark..."

"Right. Stupid question."

There was a commotion behind Black. Roxie's eyes widened as Alex approached, trailed by Simon and BT Slim. Alex stopped dead when he saw Roxie. Simon muttered something to him about catching him later and continued on with BT, ignoring Black as he brushed past. Alex moved closer to Black and elbowed him.

"Congratulations on making this cut."

"Thanks. It could have been better, I know..."

"Hey, it's over, and you're still in the mix, so all's well. Who's your friend?" Alex asked, his eyes never leaving Roxie's.

"Oh, this is my assistant, Roxie. Roxie, Alex."

Alex stepped forward and kissed Roxie's hand. Black rolled his eyes, but Roxie's full attention was on Alex.

"A pleasure. Did you enjoy yourself?" Alex asked, flashing a smile that was now famous across the country.

"It was interesting," Roxie said, her voice sounding light and feminine – like nothing Black was familiar with.

"You work with Black here?"

"I used to. Kept him honest and cleaned up his messes. Which reminds me – I saw Mugsy on TV! How's he doing? Did you bring him?"

"No, he was too busy wolfing down a twenty-pound box of chow."

"Still bagging on the defenseless cat, I see," Roxie said.

Black was going to continue but spotted Nina moving toward one of the trailers just outside the backstage barricades. "Will you excuse me for a second?" Black asked and, not waiting for an answer, jogged to the barricade and slid it aside just wide enough to fit through. Nina was closing the trailer door when he called out to her.

"Nina!"

The door remained open a crack, light seeping from the sides and bottom, and Black rushed to the trailer. He pulled the door open and heard heavy footsteps pounding on the ground behind him just as he saw Nina, a resigned smile on her face, standing by the small refrigerator.

"You. Freeze. Security. Back off – now," a no-nonsense voice ordered from a few yards behind him. Black slowly turned, his hands raised to show they were empty.

"Relax, guys. I'm in one of the bands."

"That's not a band trailer."

Nina appeared behind Black and waved them off. "It's okay. He's with me," she said. The two brawny security men exchanged a hesitant look.

"Are you sure?" the older of the pair asked.

"Positive." Nina focused on Black. "You going to come in or what?"

"I thought you'd never ask."

The interior was as sumptuous as a trailer could be, and Black momentarily reflected on how different his life was than his ex's. Climate-controlled, a large gift basket of imported snacks on the table, a dozen fresh roses in a vase near the window.

"Want a drink? They've given me everything you can imagine," she asked with a wave of her hand.

"Diet soda, if you've got it."

"Good for you. You'll live to be a million at that rate," she said and fished out two diet colas and handed him one. "Now why are you bellowing my name and scaring the locals?"

"I wanted to talk to you."

"I got that. So talk."

"Why are you a judge on this show?"

"Because I was a judge last year and they invited me back."

Black hadn't paid any attention to who was on the panel the prior year. His bad. He felt like a dolt.

"I...I didn't realize."

"No, you obviously didn't. But that's all right. You can't know everything." She studied his outfit and his hair. "Nice to see you back with a guitar, Black. It suits you."

"Thanks. But after tonight's show, I'm not so sure."

"It wasn't great, but it was good enough to beat out the losers. Next round, though, you've got your work cut out for you," she warned. "How do you feel about being back in the life?"

"Like I said, I'm not sure. I mean, part of me is enjoying it, but the other...let's just say there's been a lot of water under that bridge. I thought I'd gotten all this out of my system."

"You still have some good moves, Black. Shame to have them go to waste," Nina observed dryly. She took a long sip of her soda and sat down. "What's eating at you?"

"I'm on a case here. You wouldn't know anything about that, would you?" he asked, suspicion coloring his words. A light had gone on in his head.

Nina took her time. "What are you asking, Black?"

"Do you know anything about why I was hired to investigate the show?"

Her eyes met his. "Of course. I'm the one who suggested you."

"Damn. I knew it. So this is your idea of charity, along with a chance to publicly embarrass me..."

"Hardly charity. Something about this show stinks, Black. And whether I like it or not, my name's connected to it. It's not like we could have found just anybody to investigate from the inside. It had to be a musician, or they wouldn't get access. So where could I find an experienced investigator who was also big enough back in the day to be known, who would be available to take over the only open slot?"

Black shook his head. "You used me. You should have approached me–"

"Would you have said yes? With that big chip on your shoulder you walk around with and your determination to never let anyone help you – least of all, me?"

He felt his anger building and took several deep breaths. "That's not the point."

"Black, here's how this is going to go down. You'll either succeed or fail with the band based on your own abilities, not for any other reason. In the meantime you're being paid well to figure out what, if anything, is bent about the show, so I'm not involved in a huge scandal and my name tarnished by association. Last year some of the results didn't add up. Now, I'm not saying anyone rigged anything, but it sure was convenient for Alex that Christina's guitar player did a major freak-out at the finals. That left a bad taste in my mouth. Don't get me wrong – Alex is talented, but he's not in the same league as Christina. Which brings us to you. I'm not doing you any favors here. You're working a case I need investigated, and you're the best man for the job. It's strictly business. Nothing more."

Black counted slowly to five as he drank from the can. "I haven't seen anything weird, so you're wasting your money."

"That's fine. It's mine to waste. Maybe there's nothing to all this – in which case, no harm done. But with you nosing around, at least I feel like I'll know if I'm involved in a scam of some kind."

"Then you want me to keep doing what I'm doing."

"Correct. But no contact with me. I'm a judge. You're a performer. I don't want any hint of impropriety from that. This can be our only meeting."

"Okay. I still think it's a waste."

"Just keep your eyes open. And a tip: you might want to talk to the old guitar player and get his side of the story. Something about how he clammed up and disappeared never set well with me. I mentioned it, but nobody seemed to care – the show had a winner, and everyone walked away happy. Except of course, Christina."

Black's eyes narrowed. "What is it with you and her? This almost sounds...personal."

"Maybe it is. She reminds me of when I was starting out. Talented. Hungry. Wanting to take the world by storm on her own terms. It felt like someone punched me in the gut when she lost last year. I want to make sure the same thing doesn't happen again. If something funny's going on, I need to know about it, because I'll blow the whole damned thing wide open. But I can't go off half-cocked. It has to be provable. Which is where you come in."

Black looked at the door. "I've already been here too long, Nina."

"I know. Go back to your band. And work on your solos. You were pretty good except for that."

"Thanks for the tip."

"You can do this, Black. You just have to want it. You weren't playing like you want it."

"Maybe that's because I don't."

She didn't say anything for a few seconds. "You do. You're just afraid to put your all into it. I know you, Black. Remember?"

He pulled the door open and set the empty soda can down on the table next to it. "Thanks for the drink."

"Any time."

Black was returning to the backstage area when he heard Sylvia's voice. "Black!"

"Sylvia? You made it!" He picked up his pace, squinting to make her out in the gloom.

"Maybe I shouldn't have. Whose trailer was that?" she asked as he neared.

Damn.

"Sylvia..."

"I noticed your ex-wife is one of the judges. How cozy. Is that her trailer?"

"Honey…"

"Never mind, Black. You've got your new life, rubbing shoulders with women half your age, your ex on the show with you, behaving like a teenager with no responsibility…I can't believe I actually came here."

He moved to hug her. "Sylvia…"

"Don't touch me, Black. Don't you dare touch me."

"But it's not like it looks," he said, sounding completely lame even as he spoke the words.

"No, I'm sure it isn't. As usual, you're innocent as a lamb, and it's all just a big mistake. Did I miss anything?"

"Sylvia…"

"Good bye, Black. Have a nice life."

He watched as she stalked off, angrier than he'd ever seen, and debated running after her. Christina watched him from one far corner of the backstage area, and Roxie's eyes were tracking him like radar from the other corner, where she was still talking to Alex.

Pride won, and he slowly returned to where the band was waiting, Rooster toasting with Ed, beers in their hands. "Everything okay?" Rooster asked, sizing Black up.

"What? Oh, sure. Just a little drama. My life's way too calm right now."

"The ladies are good for a little excitement, that's for damn sure. You want a beer?" Rooster asked.

"Sure. I see no reason to quit drinking today…"

Alex and Roxie approached as he was finishing his first bottle, Roxie with an odd expression on her face. Alex grinned as he neared, and Black hated him for his youth, success, and good genes.

"I hope you don't mind me stealing Roxie away from you," he began, but Roxie cut him off.

"We're going to grab dinner. Alex knows a cool Italian joint somewhere around here…"

"Dinner?" Black repeated.

"Roxie hasn't eaten, and I'm starved. I'd invite you, but the show rules are pretty strict – plus, you're going to have to do the disqualification ceremony tonight."

"Roxie, can I talk to you for a second?" Black paused, eyeing Alex. "Alone?"

"Sure, boss," she said, and Alex found something else to do, wandering off to congratulate the various band members on making it past the first round.

"Roxie, you don't know this guy. And ten minutes after meeting him you're going on a dinner date?" Black complained.

"Yeah, what was I thinking? I mean, he's totally hot, he's rich and famous, he's a singer – and so am I – and he seems to be into me. I guess I should be hoping the guy over at Jiffy Lube comes on to me or something. Thanks for clearing that up."

"Roxie, he's a huge question mark." A sudden thought occurred to Black. "And he could be mixed up in this investigation."

"Relax. He hasn't asked anything about what you do. If he does, what's your line? Security service? Don't worry about that. He doesn't seem interested in you at all. No offense."

"I don't know, Roxie…"

"I'm a big girl, okay? It's just dinner, a few drinks, a couple of laughs. No biggie. Just me and the hottest pop sensation in America grabbing lasagna, swigging some cheap red. So chill. I can take care of myself."

"I wasn't implying you can't, Roxie."

"I know. You're just worried about me. But don't be. I'll be fine. More than fine. Now, if you don't mind, I kinda want to get back to Alex before he forgets I exist. Those Korean chicks were beaming death at me when I was talking to him."

Black shook his head as Roxie strutted away, her black leather pants hugging her curves. The anger he'd felt in Nina's trailer resurfaced, but with an uglier edge, and he realized as Roxie joined Alex, who seemed enraptured with her, that what he was feeling had nothing to do with the case, or Sylvia, or even Nina.

Plain and simple, he was jealous.

Chapter 13

The disqualification ceremony was depressing, even though Black wasn't one of those getting the boot. But the look of defeat in the eyes of the losers was visceral, and not one of the assembled artists wasn't affected. For those remaining, the second challenge two weeks later would be another gladiator battle to the death, and it could just as easily be anyone there the next time. The Irish lads took it in good stride, mostly half in the bag as far as Black could tell, and Lou and two other security men helped them get their things – they'd have one night in a motel and then catch the next flight back to Ireland.

Black called Sylvia that night at eleven, but she didn't answer. He left a message on her voicemail asking her to call him, but he wasn't holding his breath. That he was innocent of any wrongdoing didn't matter – the innocent were routinely the first to get brutalized, he knew from experience.

As he drifted off to sleep, he thought about his predecessor's gaffe, which reminded him somewhat of his own back in the Nina days: a last minute screw-up that cost him everything. That Black's meltdown had been a bar fight while Rick's had been showing up wasted was more a question of style than anything material. They'd both made poor decisions that had cost them their futures. Black's final thought as his consciousness faded was that he needed to track Rick down and have a heart-to-heart.

The next day was a balmy one, the sky clear and blue, the air fresh from a light breeze blowing off the ocean. Black knew from talking to Ed that Rick worked at a guitar superstore on Sunset. The store wasn't open on Sundays, so Black would have to sneak out of the mansion on a curfew day to grill him. He resolved to duck out that night after dinner, when things were quiet, and see what he could glean from Rick in the hour before closing time. Black tried calling Sylvia twice more during the day, but her line went straight to voicemail.

Dusk brought with it a fog bank and a chill. Black shivered as he waited for the taxi he'd called down the hill from the mansion. His departure had gone unnoticed by Lou or any of the others, Mugsy the house mascot now the constant object of everyone's attention and a useful distraction. Black's hair was slicked straight back under a dark blue baseball cap, his clothes those he'd arrived in instead of his new rock look. He checked his watch and figured he would be able to get to LA before the store closed, talk with Rick, and make it back before his disappearance was noticed – three hours, four, tops.

The cab cost him nearly a hundred dollars, and he made a mental note to bill Bobby for the overage as he paid the driver and climbed out. The shop was located in a large building with a glitzy façade proclaiming a huge spring sale. It had been forever since Black had been in a music store, but not much had changed, and he remembered from his band days that this particular outlet had the reputation of being run like a car lot, replete with haggling over prices and requiring the manager's approval to accept an offer. When he entered the cavernous space, with hundreds of guitars mounted on the walls, he had a momentary sense of claustrophobia accompanied by an overwhelming desire to run from the building.

Black knew what Rick looked like from the footage he'd seen, so he wandered the floor of the mostly empty store until he spotted him drinking a soda with two other salesmen. Black signaled to Rick and pointed at a nearby amplifier, and Rick almost ran to greet him, eager to make a sale.

"Can you tell me about this amp?" Black asked.

"Oh, yeah, that's a great choice. Really versatile. Does well in small clubs, portable, and sounds awesome in the studio, too. Only fifty watts, but a real powerhouse. Two 30-watt Vintage 30 Celestion speakers, so it has that old-school warmth, with a boosted tube preamp. What were you thinking about spending?"

"Price isn't an issue. The sound is."

Rick's interest was piqued. Every salesman dreamed of a customer walking in cold at the end of his shift and announcing that price was no object. Black could practically hear the gears meshing behind Rick's amenable expression. "Well, let's grab an axe and see what it sounds like, then. What do you play?"

"Gretsch."

"Wow, really? That's an awesome-sounding guitar. You have a reissue?"

"No. One of the original Sixties models."

"Sweet. All I've got here is a reissue, but it should get the job done."

"Cool."

Rick returned after a few minutes with a black single-cutaway Gretsch Duo Jet and plugged it in. He strummed a few chords while adjusting the gain, then handed Black the guitar. "What kind of tone are you looking for?"

"I play through a hundred-watt Marshall right now. Kind of a warm, soulful distortion, you know?" Black said.

"I think it'll more than do that. And it beats hauling a stack around, am I right? What's your name, anyway, partner?"

Black held out his hand. "Art."

"Nice to meet you, Art," Rick said, trying to build rapport.

Black noodled around on the guitar for a few minutes and then stopped, as if an idea had occurred to him. "Hey, you look familiar. You're...you're the guitar player from that TV band, right?"

Rick looked embarrassed. "I was."

"I saw that show. You guys were awesome right up until the end."

"Yeah. Well, that's ancient history, you know?"

Black studied his face. "What happened?"

Rick hesitated, obviously tempering his response so as not to lose a sale. "I've made it a policy not to discuss it, if you don't mind. How do you like the tone?"

Black could more than understand, but he needed to get Rick talking. He played for a few minutes, trying his hand at a few Hendrix riffs, then sat back. "I'm going to think about the amp. But if you've got a card, I'll look for you when I come back."

Rick tried to put the hard sell on Black, who was having none of it. They went back and forth, Rick assuring him that it was the best amplifier in the world and that it was the last week before a major price increase from the manufacturer, but Black politely declined. Eventually Rick took the guitar back and returned with his business card and handed it to Black. Black slipped it into his pocket and smiled. "You know, I used to do a lot of studio work around town about a hundred years ago. Worked with some of the biggies. Mutt Lang. Bob Rock. Bud O'Brien. Rooster Simms."

"You worked with Rooster? Small world. I worked with him, too," Rick said, still trying to get Black to warm to him.

"Yeah? On what albums?"

"No, nothing like that. He was the coach for the show."

"Oh, I didn't realize it. You were lucky. He's a good guy."

"Well, if you say so," Rick mumbled.

"Why? He was always straight up with me."

"I don't want to talk shit about anybody, you know?"

"No worries. I won't tell a soul. What did he do?"

"Maybe nothing. Only, that afternoon before the show…we were at the hotel bar, and I was hanging out with Rooster and my bass player, knocking back a few – nothing heavy, just beer and whatnot. The next thing I knew it was show time, I was hammered, and smoking a joint that was frigging rocket fuel. I figured it would just mellow me out a little, and instead it put me into a full-blown tailspin. And the funny thing is I have no idea how I got it. I'm not a big smoker…"

"You don't remember anything after the bar? Not leaving it or anything?"

"Nope. All I know was one minute I was chilling in the bar, and the next I was backstage, shit-faced. How I got there's still a blank. But Rooster should have stopped me if I was boozing that much. I mean, come on, he knew the stakes. Peter, my bass player, should have, too. I'm not saying they're to blame, but still…"

Black appraised him. "You don't seem like a big drinker."

"I'm really not. I'll have a few before and after a show, but I don't get blotto, you know? That was the first…and the last. Great timing, huh?" Rick spat, self-loathing obvious. "Needless to say, Rooster's not on my list of favorite people. Neither's Peter."

"That's heavy, dude. It doesn't sound like you got much support from them. If I'd have been there…well, never mind. I never had anything like that happen with him, but that was years ago. He was a stand-up guy then. And a great guitar player."

Rick's eyes narrowed. "It's funny. I've never seen you in here before. You're obviously local…"

"No, I'm from Vegas – been living there for ten years. I'm just in town and thought I'd look at some gear, you know? Kill some time, maybe get a good buy on something."

"Vegas, huh? What part?"

"Up by Red Rock," Black said, remembering where Nina lived.

That seemed to satisfy Rick, and Black was glad he looked significantly different from on TV – especially with the baseball cap. He'd known there was a small risk of being recognized but had to chance it.

Black made his way to the exit, Rick's attention returned to his soda and the jokes of his co-workers, the big spender having turned into a looky-loo. Black felt a sense of unease – if Rick was telling the truth, it was possible he'd been slipped a Mickey, either by Rooster or Peter, in the bar. That was how it sounded. In which case, it was also possible that Nina's gut feeling was more than a vague doubt and somebody had arranged for Last Call to lose. The question was why either the team's coach, or its bass player, would do that.

His mind turned to Alex. It had been an incredible stroke of luck that his rival had bombed in the finals. That didn't prove anything, but it gave Black something to follow up on now that he'd spoken with Rick. Which left Black with more questions than answers and a nagging sense of unease as he walked down the block, dialing the taxi company as he rounded the corner.

The trip back took longer than he'd hoped, and by the time he made it to the house, the front doors were locked and most of the lights were off. Black cursed himself for not thinking about something as obvious as being locked out, and reconciled himself to having to make his way inside through the great room.

He pulled his baseball cap off and stashed it in the bushes as he crept around the side of the house. Music drifted from the pool area, and Black could hear splashing – which would make it more difficult to slip in without being detected. Three of the Love Jupiter singers were in the pool with SnM, and Black could smell the pungent odor of marijuana drifting from the darkened area. He spotted an ice chest and silently moved to it, extracting a beer and opening it before striding into the great room like he'd just come back from a walk.

It was obvious that his ruse wasn't going to work when he found himself being stared down by Lou and Peter, who were sitting at the breakfast bar.

"Where were you?" Lou demanded, no trace of friendliness in his voice.

"What? I went for a walk. Why? Did Mugsy destroy something?"

"Where did you walk to?" Lou asked.

"Just around. I wanted to think."

"Be specific. Did you leave the grounds?" Peter asked, his tone ugly.

"What's it to you? Are you my mom?"

"You know the rules, Black," Lou warned.

"Shit. I totally spaced on that."

"We have you on the security cameras going down the street, and a taxi comes by a few minutes later. Last time, Black. Where were you?"

Black saw no choice but to tell the truth. If they contacted the taxi company, they'd know his destination by morning.

"I apologize. It's just…I've been trying to fit in, get the band's style right, but I feel like I'm not getting a lot of direction. So I figured I should talk to your old guitar player and see if he could help me out with any tips. I went into town to see him. Nice guy, by the way."

"You what?" Peter sputtered. "Have you lost your mind?"

"Dude. It's not like I went on a killing spree or to buy heroin. I need some help, so I went to find some. You don't do anything but snarl at me, and Christina pretty much ignores me, and Ed's a drummer…so that leaves me with either getting guidance from someone who knows, or continuing to struggle." Black turned his focus to Lou. "I would have asked permission, but it was just building up inside of me…so I took action. I'm really sorry, but no harm done, am I right? And I did it for the show."

Lou shook his head. "I don't make that call. Sarah and Simon do. But if you ask me, it was pretty damned stupid."

"Maybe it's the break we've needed. They'll boot you, and then we'll get a real guitar player," Peter said, his face tight.

"Yeah, because your last one did such a great job for you. Solid, right?"

Peter made to stand, and Lou put a hand the size of a ham on his arm. "Girls. Don't make this any worse than it is. I'll call Sarah and tell her what happened. The rest is up to management."

"Thanks for the support, Peter. Nice to know you've got my back," Black said. "Are we done?"

Lou nodded. "I'll let you know about their decision."

"Do that. In the meantime, I want to try to get another hour or two of practice in before I hit it." Black took the stairs two at a time. When he got to his room, Ed was snoring, Mugsy cradled in his arms, and the atmosphere was redolent of beer and farts. Black retrieved his guitar and tiptoed back out and made for the rehearsal studio, hopeful that his explanation would be good enough to keep him on the show.

Chapter 14

The following morning at breakfast, Black took the opportunity to drill Peter about Rick's story. Peter was sulking over an English muffin when Black came down the stairs. Christina rose and left without saying a word. Black got a cup of coffee and a scoop of eggs from the container by the stove and sat across from Peter.

"I know you don't like me going to talk to Rick, but it's over, and we have to make this work. So lighten up, will you? It's not like I pissed in your Wheaties."

"You endangered the band and our chances of winning. I'm supposed to be delighted about that?"

"I haven't endangered anything, except maybe whether I stay on the show – and you've made your preference more than clear. Christina's an awesome talent and the band rocks. If they shitcan me, you'll get someone else. If not, I'm putting in the hours to do my best. So what's your beef?"

"You're just like Rick. Do whatever you feel like without thinking about how it affects us. I saw how that worked out."

"Rick told me you were drinking with him that day. In the hotel. Is that true?"

"What business is it of yours?"

"I'm interested in how that went down. Rick seems like a stable guy. The official story doesn't make any sense."

"Yeah, I was there. We had a couple of beers. That's it. Not like hammering them, more like time-killing beers to take the edge off. I was surprised as anyone when Rick showed up wasted."

"And Rooster was with you?"

"That's right. Neither of us had any idea that Rick would go berserk."

"How long did you stay with him?"

Peter's eyes narrowed to slits. "What's with the interrogation? I had a few beers. I left. How the hell would I know how long I was there?"

"Was Rooster still there when you left?"

Peter thought about it. "I think so. But…I don't know. Why?"

"I'm just curious, is all. Rick didn't strike me as a drinker. And he seems as puzzled as anybody how he wound up wasted."

"I have a clue: he drank too much and then compounded it by smoking weed."

"He doesn't remember where he got the joint."

"I'm not surprised. You should have seen him after the show. I'm surprised he remembers anything from that day. He was out of it."

"What about you? Seems like there are a lot of hazy memories at work here."

Peter rose, shaking his head. "You're way over the line. I don't answer to you. You're the hired talent, that's it, nothing more. A pair of hands and a guitar. I don't know why you're doing the whole Inspector Clouseau thing. Maybe to divert attention from sneaking out. Whatever. But I don't have to answer your questions. Am I clear?"

"Oh, crystal. You don't want to talk about what role you had in Rick blowing your big chance. Did I miss anything?"

Peter's eyes narrowed. "Who the hell do you think you are?"

Black offered a wan smile. "Like you said. Just a pair of hands." He paused. "Rehearsal's at one, remember?"

Peter stormed off, and Black wondered why he was so angry. It seemed completely out of proportion to Black's transgression, so it had to be something else.

Black was finishing his eggs when Yoon Ji from Love Jupiter came down the stairs wearing her trademarked jean mini-skirt and bikini top. She giggled when she saw Black and approached after getting a cup of coffee.

"Where Mugsy?" she asked, eyebrows arched.

"In the room. Sleeping." Black pantomimed sleeping, and she nodded.

"Love Jupiter…love Mugsy!" she proclaimed.

"Yes, well, there's a lot of him to love, that's for sure."

"You come my room, yes?" Yoon Ji said.

Black did a double take. "Pardon?"

"You. Come my room. Now?" she said, pointing at him, then upstairs, lest he be too dim to grasp her words.

"I…I'm not sure that's a great idea," he tried, but she just tittered her infectious laugh and took his hand to lead him.

"Come."

Black glanced around, hopeful nobody had seen the exchange. He saw Lavon reclining poolside, eyes fixed on Black, and wanted to disappear into the wall when the rapper leered at him and gave him a thumbs-up sign. Black tried a halfhearted smile as he was escorted to paradise. His mind darted to mundanities like condoms and statutory rape laws, and then they were at Yoon Ji's door. She beamed at him and twisted the knob. "You come, yes?"

Black didn't require further coaxing. He was trying to figure out how to lock the door when Yoon Ji moved across the room to a makeshift…altar. There was no other word for it. The top of the writing desk had flowers on it, and the corkboard above it was a collage of color printouts of photos of Mugsy – Mugsy being held by one of the group, Mugsy looking hungry, Mugsy looking sleepy, Mugsy asleep. Dozens of photographs, the area a place of worship to an obese feline with the temperament of a raptor.

"Nice, yes?" Yoon Ji said.

Black felt like a flasher caught outside a preschool. "Yes. Very nice," he said, nodding approval.

"We write song. New song. You say if like?" she asked. A small, ugly part of him quivered, wondering whether this was some sort of exotic foreplay, but he banished the thought and nodded again.

"Sure. I mean, yes."

She went to the closet, retrieved an acoustic guitar, and then sat on the edge of her bed and began plucking the strings, keeping time with her foot. The lyrics didn't make sense to him since they were in Korean, but there was no mistaking the chorus, which featured Mugsy's name every third word. When she finished her performance, he was speechless and could only grin like a buffoon as she set the guitar aside.

"You…like?" she asked, her eyes wide, the irises warm as molten chocolate.

"Yes, I do."

"We love Mugsy."

Me too, he thought, *especially honey-roasted or barbecued*. But he held his tongue, not wanting to spoil Yoon Ji's youthful exuberance.

Christina was coming out of her room when Yoon Ji and Black returned to the corridor, and the look of disgust she gave Black could have peeled paint. He considered trying to explain but thought better of it, knowing that anything he said would just dig him deeper.

Great. Now I'm an aging pervert in addition to a waste of guitar picks. Yoon Ji's voice rang in his head as they descended the stairs, her angelic melody following him like a powerful perfume as he trailed her out to the pool. The refrain would haunt him to his dying day.

Mugsy, oooh-oh-ooooh, Mugsy, MUGSY!

Chapter 15

The second-round competition was one of Black's nightmare gigs – a scenario that every musician dreaded and which most viewed as the bottom of the entertainment barrel: the bands would perform one song each at a wedding in Bel Air. The prospect of playing a wedding made Black's skin crawl. It was a throwback to his musician days, when if you couldn't make ends meet in the club scene, you were reduced to playing covers at some spoiled couple's nuptials.

The wedding party was assembled around three dozen circular white tables while the acts went through their motions. Each had been given a song five days before and instructed to interpret it in their own way. Last Call had gotten The Beatles' "Twist and Shout", which Rooster worked overtime on converting to the band's sound, suggesting novel twists that resulted in a unique take on the standard.

BrandX was finishing up their hip-hop delivery of Michael Jackson's "Billy Jean", and when the song ended, the crowd went wild. Black had to admit the performance had been effective; the pair definitely had talent and their own style. The judges thought so too, and the scores were sevens and eights – more than enough to move them to the next round.

Christina took the stage as Black and Peter plugged in. Holly and David did their back and forth banter in the spotlight as they waited to make the introduction. The judges were seated at their pods at the front of the hall on the far side of the dance floor. Black and Peter flicked their amps on, and after getting the nod from Holly, Black launched into a growling distorted sound effect using his tremolo bar to simulate a motorcycle engine revving. The stage lights strobed in time, and Black's performance culminated in a howl of feedback as

Ed attacked the snare drum in a high-speed roll. Then, as all the lights illuminated, Christina's powerful voice cut through the apparent noise and the song began in earnest.

The background vocals were a tad off, but no more than most live bands trying to replicate the Fab Four's delivery, and when they finished, the applause was spirited. Christina did an elaborate curtsy and blew kisses to the cameras, and then they were standing like prisoners waiting to be sentenced, awaiting the judges' verdict. Alex gave them a seven, Nina a six, and BT Slim a seven, which was at the lower end of the range they'd been handing out all night, but still better than the last performance.

The next contender was Love Jupiter, and Yoon Ji winked at Black as they filed past his position, mouthing the word "Mugsy" as they took their marks. Classical music filled the room, and then a hip-hop drumbeat started. A bass guitar joined it, and the shape of the song became obvious: the Bee Gees' "Staying Alive".

The girls were all dressed in one-piece neon-colored vinyl miniskirts, and while their bumping and grinding was mechanically precise, their harmonies were badly out of tune. When the song was over, the assembly clapped politely, but when the judges weighed in, it was threes and fours, and barring a disaster, it was obvious who would be next to leave.

Yoon Ji was practically in tears when the girls trooped off the stage, and after a hurried discussion with their coach, the woman moved to the soundman and began arguing in English. Black overheard the back and forth – they hadn't been able to hear their voices properly. The soundman insisted that the levels were those he'd marked during rehearsal, but Black wasn't so sure. He'd watched them practice, and their vocals had been dead on every time.

Strobe was up next – a techno-influenced band with an androgynous singer named Terrence who was aloof and distant. Black had hated him on sight, and seeing his performance didn't improve that sentiment, although Black had to concede that the rendition of Hall and Oates' "I Can't Go For That" was as good as any he'd heard. Strobe clocked some of the most impressive numbers of the night, bested only by Bend in the Creek, whose country-tinged rendition of The Rolling Stones' "Mother's Little Helper" brought the house down.

While the judges awarded Strobe their scores, Black drifted to the soundman and glanced at the monitor mixing board. The man stared at Black and went back to shutting down, ignoring him. Black cleared his throat and caught the man's eye.

"The Koreans seemed pretty upset about the mix," he began.

"What are you, Kim Jong-il or something?" the man fired back.

"No, but I heard them saying they got hosed on the mix, and I'm inclined to believe them after hearing rehearsals."

"Oh, yeah? Listen. Every one of these acts blames anyone but themselves when they lose. They did a lousy job. Game over."

"They couldn't hear themselves," Black said.

"Look, buddy, I don't know who you think you are, but I'm just doing my job. Show's over. Move along."

The man seemed nervous, and Black was sure he'd deliberately sabotaged Love Jupiter's performance. The problem was that it was the perfect crime – there was no way to prove after the fact that the levels had been wrong. It was the band's word against the soundman's, and even if the producers were likely to believe the group, the judges had ruled, and their decision was final. It sucked and reminded Black how vulnerable they all were to the whims of the mixing board – even the best delivery could be ruined by lousy sound.

The house band took the stage to provide entertainment for the wedding party as the road crew broke down the last of the gear and trundled it out a side entrance. Black saw Roxie near the backstage entry and was headed toward her when Alex swept in and ushered her through. Black's heart lurched at the look that passed between them, but he fixed a smile on his face and moved to greet her. He was intercepted by Yoon Ji, who tried to communicate with him over the sound of the band's opening song, but all he could do was shrug and shake his head.

She looked extremely young and vulnerable out of the stage lights, and Black's anger rose as she pantomimed and chirped at him. It was a raw deal. Even if they weren't the best of the roster of acts, they deserved a fair shot at winning, just like the rest. Black tried to be polite, but it took him several minutes to disengage, by which time Roxie and Alex were nowhere to be seen amidst the cameramen, crew, techs, and hangers-on.

Black eventually found them outside, talking quietly in a dark corner by the equipment trucks.

"Hey. You made it. What did you think?" Black asked.

"Better than last time. Where's Mugsy? Did you bring him?"

"No, loosing the tabby wrecking ball on the wedding seemed like a bad idea."

"I only get to see him when I tune in. It sucks. I miss him," she complained.

"If it's any consolation, he's even fatter. He hasn't lost his appetite…"

"Who's Mugsy?" Alex asked, and Black realized that he didn't even bother to watch the show. Black couldn't say he blamed him.

"The world's paunchiest cat. Like a furry moon with a tail," Black said.

"Oh," Alex said, obviously confused by the turn the discussion had taken.

Black leaned toward Roxie. "Did you see Sylvia?"

She shook her head.

"Damn. I put her name on the list."

Alex raised his watch and tapped it. "We've got to hurry. They're pretty serious about takeoff times."

Black looked from Roxie to Alex, not understanding. Roxie smiled and took Alex's hand. "We're headed to Vegas on Alex's jet. We've got to get going."

"What?" Black sputtered, almost choking.

"I've got a show tomorrow – one of a series we're doing for the next two weeks, and Roxie tells me she's never been on a private plane, so it seemed only polite…"

"Roxie, could I talk to you for a second?" Black interrupted.

She rolled her eyes. "Here we go again. Yes, Dad."

He walked a few steps away and whispered to her, "Are you serious? You're flying to Las Vegas with him?"

"What? Dinner was great, and I've talked to him on the phone a few times. He even came to one of my shows wearing a disguise so people wouldn't go batshit. He's a really cool guy. And he wants to fly me to Sin City and put me up in a suite. What would you do?"

"I'd take things slow."

"It's been two weeks. This isn't the fifteenth century. And, boss, all due respect, I don't need your permission. I'm going, so get over it already."

"How's your new job?" he asked, changing the subject.

"Imagine terrible, scoop a pile of dog poop on top, and then blend. I can't wait to leave. When are you going to have work for me to do? Or more importantly, when will you be able to pay me?"

"This coming week I'll be even on the office rent, so sometime after that..."

"Great. Then let's talk in a few weeks. My number still works, in case you're wondering."

"I didn't want to bug you."

Roxie turned back to Alex. "Congratulations. Black here has agreed not to chop you into small pieces and spread them around the Valley if you promise not to kill me in Las Vegas."

"Deal," Alex said, with his smarmy million-dollar pop star smile. "Now we really have to get going. The limo's over there." He indicated a dark shape near the edge of the TV crew area.

"All right. Take care, boss. You did good tonight," Roxie said, but to his ear the words were as hollow as the feeling in his stomach, a sensation like a roller coaster's drop right after ascending to the top.

A uniformed chauffeur scrambled to open the rear door for them. Black realized that he was clenching his hands so tight his knuckles were white, his fingernails digging into his palms. He forced himself to relax and focused on his breathing with one of Dr. Kelso's cognitive behavioral tricks, even as he recognized that he felt as low as he could remember. No girlfriend in evidence and his assistant, whom he swore he wasn't enamored with, off to Las Vegas with a man he hated on principle. Throw a band that could barely stand him into the mix, along with a reflection that now looked like something out of a wax museum, and there was no question he was hitting emotional bottom.

Which made Nina's timing perfect as she glided by, holding Simon's arm. "Well, hello, Black," she purred, pausing to look him over. "The playing was better this week."

"Thanks, Nina. Hello, Simon. How are you doing?"

Simon seemed tense and unfriendly. "Sarah needs to have a word with you," he snapped. Black looked around.

"I haven't seen her tonight."

"She's been otherwise occupied, but make time tomorrow morning."

Nina pulled on Simon's arm. "Come on, Simon. Don't you know you aren't supposed to keep a lady waiting to eat?"

They wended their way to another waiting limo, leaving Black to mull over Simon's hostile missive and wonder how, precisely, things could get any worse.

Chapter 16

The disqualification ceremony was depressing, not the least because Black knew in his heart that Love Jupiter didn't deserve its fate. The four beauties stood like stoic soldiers, albeit scantily clad ones, as Holly and David announced their score and resultant banishment from the show. Black felt a very real sense of loss when Yoon Ji tiptoed and kissed him on the cheek as Lou carried their luggage to the Suburban.

When the cameras stopped rolling and the lights went dark, Black found himself on the pool deck with Ed, Lavon, and SnM, downing beer as they listened to traffic in the distance. Their drinking eventually transitioned to Hennessy, and Black was reeling when he finally made it to his bed, where Mugsy was already asleep after a hard day's dozing.

When the sun streamed through the open pocket doors the following morning, it felt to Black like demons were assaulting him, intent on inflicting maximum pain on his tender head. He rolled out of bed and staggered to the shower, accompanied by Ed's snores, and spent a solid twenty minutes under the warm spray trying to revive himself and rinse away the previous night's excesses. When he twisted the shower off and stepped dripping onto the mat, he felt only slightly better than if he'd gone over Niagara Falls in a barrel. He made a mental note to never, ever drink cognac again, and at just the thought of the liquor he felt the sour tang of bile rising in his gorge.

Black decided to let Ed sleep, and after pulling on a pair of sweats and a hoodie, he headed to the kitchen for some resuscitation. The house seemed empty now that the Irish and Korean contingent had vacated the premises. Only Christina and Peter were up, having breakfast together in unhappy communion. Black ignored the kettledrums pounding in his skull as he poured a tall cup of coffee and moved to the eggs, which he peered at for a few seconds before edging to the fridge for milk. He didn't sit with his bandmates, preferring to stand, sipping his dark roast.

"You did better yesterday, I'll give you that," Christina acknowledged. No good morning. No how are you.

Black bit back the possible responses that cascaded through his psyche and confined himself to a polite "Thanks".

Peter shifted in his seat, the habitual frown on his face evidence of his ongoing discomfort. "Not bad."

"It was actually better than not bad," Black said. "It wasn't great, but it was pretty good. With another two weeks of practice, it will be great, and two weeks after that, awesome. After twenty years of not playing, it takes a little time." He thought about leaving it there, but his head was pounding, doing nothing for the buzz of anger he felt. "And while I appreciate both of your condescending attitudes for what they are, this is where I get off that bus. No offense."

They looked like he'd gut-punched them. He decided to spread his misery a little more.

"You had every reason to be doubtful when I first showed up. I was terrible. I knew it, you knew it. That we made it past the first round was a kind of miracle and had mostly to do with Christina's singing. This time, though, we were good. Not blow them out of their seats, but good. That wasn't just you, Christina. That was everyone. If you want to win this, not to mention have a decent career, you need to stop being an asshole and start pulling on the oars with the rest of us. A band's more than the singer, and even though you're an awesome one, if you want to do much besides bang around the local clubs getting older, you need to learn a little humility."

Christina was rising from her seat, the expression on her face ugly. "Who do you—"

"Christina, I've been on the planet ten years longer than you, and by the time you were nine I'd sold over twenty million records. I've tolerated your attitude up until now because I figured you'd mellow out, but it seems like you took that to mean I'm your bathmat, and I'm here to tell you you're wrong." Black sighed and rubbed his eyes. "If you want to work with me, you better park your attitude at the door. That's my message. And frankly, I could give a shit how you react. It's your career, not mine. I already sold my records, proved my point. So let me ask you this: What have you done that allows you to be so high and mighty with me? Because I'm not seeing it."

Christina looked shell-shocked. Black leveled his stare at Peter.

"And you. You play bass. You didn't invent the Internet or cure cancer, or even come up with super glue. You play bass, and you act like your shit doesn't stink. No offense, but in the real world you're just, what was your term, hired hands? You play music. You're lucky if you can make a living doing this, and if you're super lucky, maybe even make some real money. And yet you're walking around like the CEO of Microsoft, treating me like I'm your servant. Guess how much more I'm going to put up with?"

"This is our band. If you don't like it, leave," Peter snarled.

"You know what? If that's your attitude, then I'll do exactly that. And you can scramble to find a replacement, who may or may not tolerate your idiocy. I'll take my fat cat and my old ass and hit the road, and when I see you a decade from now playing some dive on the strip, I'll honk as I drive by. Because that's where you're headed. Blow this season, and there won't be a third one. You'll be old news, and you know it. Again, I don't care. My hopes and dreams aren't dependent on winning this. But yours are. So my advice is to get off the high horse and start figuring out how to win, because otherwise you'll just be two more also-rans in a town that mints 'em like peroxide blondes."

Christina looked like her head was going to explode. Peter actually appeared thoughtful, as though his brain had finally caught up to his mouth. Black's hangover eased as he sipped his coffee, and he realized that he actually didn't care whether he stayed or left. He would find another client. Nina would fend for herself in defending her good name. Life would go on.

They were interrupted by the front doors opening. Sarah appeared, trailed by Lou. Sarah's normally serious expression was even more so as she approached, and Black's stomach did a little somersault.

"Good morning. Black, I'd like a word with you. In private."

Black nodded and indicated the pool deck. "Step into my office."

They walked into the morning sun, leaving Christina and her brother to chew on Black's bombshell. When they reached the barbecue area, Sarah stopped and cleared her throat.

"There's been a lot of discussion about how to handle your breaking the house rules. What you did was intolerable."

"I know. I'm sorry. I explained my reasoning to Lou, and that's my only defense. The guitar store's not open on Sundays, so I had no choice."

"I'm aware of your story. The problem is that even if I believe it, we can't have people breaking rules because they think they've got a good reason."

Black sighed. "Fine. Then I'll make this easy. It'll only take a half hour or so to get all my stuff packed and deal with Mugsy. If you want to film it, have at it, because I don't plan to hang around any longer than necessary. Sorry things didn't work out."

Sarah grabbed his arm. "Let me finish. Simon and I discussed it, and I was in favor of booting you. Simon, on the other hand, felt you should have one more chance. I disagreed, but apparently your wife made a persuasive case in your favor. So you got lucky."

Black studied his shoes. "Ex-wife."

"From here on out you're living on borrowed time. One more violation of the rules and you're out. Oh, and this morning I heard from the head of the sound crew. He said you were hassling one of his men last night."

"Love Jupiter got F-d on their monitor levels. I called him on it."

"Mr. Black, let me make this as clear as I can. You're not to interfere with the crew. You're not to scold people when you feel they didn't do their job. You're to play guitar for Last Call. That's it. Is there any part of that you find confusing?"

"You don't care whether they got screwed?"

"It's not that I don't care – it's that your job isn't to play referee. The producers are satisfied that the performances were legitimate, so case closed. No more disruptions from you, do you read me?"

Black debated pushing it, but decided not to. He'd gotten a reprieve, courtesy of Nina, and he wouldn't waste it.

"Loud and clear."

Sarah appeared to soften. "Good. I hate having to be the hard ass. Just cut me some slack here, would you, and stop making things difficult."

"Put like that, how can I say no?"

"I was hoping you'd play nice. Now, can we go back to making a TV show?"

"You bet."

Sarah went off to her other duties as Black returned to the kitchen for a refill. Peter and Christina had gone to their room, so he was alone, Lou having also made himself scarce. A knock sounded from the front door. Love Jupiter's manager entered and brightened when she saw Black.

"Mr. Black! You are who I need to see," she said.

"Really? Well, today's your lucky day."

They sat at the dining table, and the woman leaned forward with her hands clasped in front of her. "Mr. Black, Love Jupiter asked me to make proposal to you."

"A proposal? About what?"

"They want to buy Mugsy the cat. They love Mugsy."

"Buy Mugsy?" Black's eyebrows raised. "How much?"

"They told me authorize ten thousand US."

"Ten thousand dollars? Are you serious? Where do you expect me to come up with that kind of money to get them to take him?" Black joked. The manager didn't understand.

"We pay ten thousand US for cat."

Black shook his head and looked at his watch. "I have to speak to the other owner, and she's out of town. Do you have a phone number?"

The woman handed him a card with a number written on the back in blue ink. The rest of the card was in Korean. "We leave tomorrow. Flight in morning. You call today at hotel? Ask for Mrs. Kim at Airport Hilton."

Black said his goodbyes and rubbed a hand across the dusting of beard on his chin. The world had gone insane. Someone was willing to pay to take Mugsy. Probably by the pound, based on the price.

He called Roxie, who picked up on the second ring.

"Hey, boss. Vegas rocks, if that's why you're calling."

Black tried to ignore how happy she sounded. "I'm glad to hear it. But no, that's not why." He told her about the offer.

"Absolutely not."

"Now, Roxie, we can go down to the shelter and find another stray, force-feed it marshmallows for the next five years, and it would be almost as big as Mugsy. Think about the ten grand, would you? For a stray cat!"

"He's not a stray. He's mine. I'm just letting you exploit him for your own selfish ends."

"For which I'm endlessly grateful. But, Roxie – with that money, you could quit your job with the dragon lady tomorrow. Think about it. No more endless demands…"

"But no more Mugsy. I'm sorry, boss, no deal."

"I was afraid you'd say that."

"You sound like you have the flu. Did you stay up all night boozing?"

"You know me like the beating of your own heart, don't you?"

"Try to rein in your substance-abuse issues, boss. It's sad once a man reaches a certain age."

"Tell it to Bukowski."

"You seen any pictures of him?"

"Good point."

He could hear Alex in the background, urging her to hurry up. She signed off, leaving Black feeling strangely empty. He was overwhelmed by a sense of fatigue and melancholy – no doubt the alcohol metabolizing out of his bruised system. After debating and rejecting the idea of a Bloody Mary in favor of a few more hours of sleep, he sat back and finished his coffee with a slurp, set it in the sink, and tottered up the stairs to where a gassy cat and his roommate slumbered like innocents.

Chapter 17

Cigar smoke hung over the poker table like a lead-colored fog as the dealer slid chips to the lucky winner. A squat man with a face like a toad sat chewing on the stub of a smoldering stogie, eyes roving over the half-dozen players with good-natured glee. He was cleaning up tonight, winning far more hands than he lost, a tribute to his natural superiority, he knew, and not his subordinates' unwillingness to win too much. "Little" Sal Capelloni's moods were famous for their propensity to change almost instantly, and nobody wanted to be on the receiving end of one of his unpleasant spells.

"Hey, Tommy, why the long face, huh? It's been a good week, no? You can afford to lose a little, am I right or am I right?" Capelloni asked the man next to him, a well-groomed, dignified figure in his late forties who ran many of the legitimate businesses that fronted for the mob's less savory enterprises.

Tommy Greco was a UCLA graduate with a business administration degree who'd become a mover and shaker in the entertainment industry. His stint as the head of a large record label had transitioned into ownership of a dozen production companies, as well as a minority stake in two film studios. He rubbed elbows with Los Angeles' most powerful and influential, and had no police record – not even a parking ticket. He represented the new breed of mob entrepreneurs who'd taken over senior positions as the old guard retired or died, part of a group that had long ago understood that it was cleaner and easier to steal legally than to resort to the sordid tactics of their predecessors.

The mob left the more violent chores to its Mexican and Russian colleagues, whose reach inside the nation's prisons and with the myriad gangs that ran the streets was far more extensive than their own. Over the years it had largely assumed a supervisory and supply role, taxing the respective newer arrivals like a church demanding its tithes, rewarding loyalty with larger territories and punishing dissension with deadly force.

Tommy was first and foremost a fixer, a problem solver in a business that depended upon liquidity and relationships. If you needed a film green-lit with funding in place over the weekend, Tommy was always available to make a deal, and he was equally willing to partner on ventures in television and music – always at favorable terms for his silent backers, of course.

Capelloni was one of the last of the old-school bosses, a street enforcer who had risen through the ranks to become the head of his family by the time he was fifty, a lofty position he'd occupied for over a decade, laundering funds through his underlings as he managed the seedier aspects of the organization's trade – anything to make a buck from civilization's appetites.

Tommy rubbed his eyes, tired after two hours of cards.

"Nah, it's not that. It's just I got a problem. A guy who helped me out with a thing last year has a problem. We were drinking last night over at the casino, and he was betting big and losing bigger, and he told me about the bind he's in."

"Does he want our help?" Capelloni asked, sensing an opportunity.

"No, he was just bitching. But he's a good guy. He's done us a lot of favors over the years, and he's into us for a lot of money from his gambling – guy's kind of a loser with the cards. But I was thinking it would be nice if we could help him. Might come in handy in the future, you know? And I got the feeling his problem could interfere with him paying us back."

"What's in it for us?"

"Not much besides goodwill."

"Ha. Goodwill's for second-hand clothes," Capelloni cackled, using one of his favorite lines.

Tommy nodded, having only heard the joke several hundred times. "Yeah, I know. I was just thinking, it would be a small thing we could do, and it could guarantee we'd get paid. Everybody wins."

"Who is this clown?"

Tommy told Capelloni, reminding him of how the man had assisted them in the past.

Capelloni was silent for several moments and then leaned back. "Well, hell, if that's his only hang-up, it doesn't seem like it would take much to make it go away, am I right?"

"It would seem so. But that's more your call than mine."

"I respect that you don't want to get your hands dirty. You're far too valuable to us to get into a pig-wrestling contest." Capelloni paused. "Just get me the info, and then forget about it. Consider the problem solved, *capisce?*"

"I'm sure he'll be very grateful."

"Which you'll use to our mutual benefit, right?"

"Of course."

Capelloni looked around the table and puffed at his cigar as he held up his empty glass. "What does a guy have to do to get a drink around here?"

A gaunt man with a pencil-thin mustache rose from his position on the sofa at the far end of the room. He took the glass and got a new one, three ice cubes floating in an amber sea of Johnny Walker Blue tinkling against the crystal as he carried it back to the table.

Capelloni took a long, appreciative sip as he studied the faces of his entourage.

"Gentlemen – let's play cards!"

Chapter 18

The following day was the beginning of a new week and, with it, another mindless challenge for team building – although the value of building a team with people you were going to compete against was lost on Black. It seemed like more of an excuse to get the females into swimwear than anything, which Black wasn't opposed to.

This week's event was another obstacle course, this time at a water park, with orientation and rehearsals scheduled for the following day and the big contest on Saturday. Tonight would be a group outing to a rock club, which was in turn an opportunity to have the women dress up in their sluttiest outfits and get drunk for the cameras.

Christina and Peter didn't say a word to him at the orientation, and they couldn't leave fast enough when it was over. They'd avoided him all the prior day, staying to themselves, which was fine by Black. He and Ed had gone to a movie that afternoon, finishing with a dinner of pizza and beer. Sylvia hadn't answered her phone or returned his calls, and Black was inclined to believe that this time she was serious about the relationship being dead. However, there wasn't much he could do from Malibu other than call.

After lunch, he rang Bobby to give him a progress report.

"So how's the rock star doing?" Bobby asked.

"I'm okay, I guess. It's depressing as hell to be around a bunch of kids trying to make it, though. I've been trying to put an exact date on when all my dreams died, but I'm having a hard time. I'm thinking the day the record company axed me."

"And here you are, back again, taking the world by storm."

"You don't watch the show, do you?"

"Who's got time for that crap?"

119

"Here's the rundown. Nothing provable, but I think the last round was rigged." Black told him about Love Jupiter.

"As you say, though, there's no 'there' there. Just suspicion, am I right?"

"Unfortunately, yes." Black shared his meeting with Rick.

"You think he was drugged?"

"It's possible someone slipped him something. Which puts both the bass player and Rooster in the hot seat. Although the drummer told me that Christina was furious with him over banging the assistant producer, so she's not completely above suspicion."

"Why would she sabotage her own career?"

"That's a good question. But I've seen plenty of weirdness since I moved into the house. These are strange people."

"What about the assistant producer?"

"That's also a possibility. She and Christina hate each other. Could have been a nice move to break them up and torpedo Christina in one stroke. But there's another person who won big, too: Alex."

"The kid we met at Simon's? Really?"

"He had plenty of motive. The thing is, Rick can't remember where he got the joint from. So anyone could have given it to him. And judging by the way it hit him, it probably wasn't only weed. Might have been laced with PCP. No way of knowing, of course."

"Great. So basically everyone's a suspect?"

"Welcome to my life."

"Better you than me, buddy. You need anything?"

"Not really. Just auto-deposit this week's money again. I'll call again when I know something. Oh, and by the way, Nina 'fessed up about being the client. You're a real shit sometimes, you know that?"

"Right. The kind who's getting ready to send his secretary to the bank for your deposit."

Rehearsal was at four, and Black was dreading facing Christina and Peter. He didn't want conflict, but he was tired of being treated like crap. No matter what happened, he promised himself, he'd just roll with it.

Ed bounced down the stairs, drumsticks in hand, at 3:50, trailed by Mugsy, who'd imprinted on the chubby drummer since they'd become mattress mates. Black toyed with the idea of convincing him to take the cat, but then remembered that Roxie wouldn't accept a king's ransom for him, so was unlikely to let Ed have him. A pity, because the pair belonged together.

"Hey, Black. How hangs it?"

"Never better. Been practicing. Hopefully I can squeak out some decent notes today."

"No sweat. I think you sound great." Good old Ed.

They walked together to the rehearsal room. When they swung the door open, Rooster was hugging Christina while Peter looked on, his face ashen.

"What happened?" Ed asked.

Christina looked up at them, her mascara running. "It's...Rick. He's dead."

"What? How?" Black asked.

"Overdose," Rooster said. "Christina just got the call a few minutes ago. Damn shame. Boy had a big heart. Hell of a player, too."

"That makes no sense. When I saw him he looked fine. Junkies have a distinctive vibe. I didn't get that from him," Black said.

"Maybe he started experimenting. It's not unheard of," Peter said.

Everyone was in a state of shock, and it was obvious there was no point in rehearsing. Rooster walked Christina back to the house. Peter grabbed Black's arm as he was leaving. "Can we talk?"

Black nodded. "Sure."

Ed squeezed past them. "I'll be hanging by the pool if anyone needs a drum lesson."

Peter cleared his throat as he pulled a pack of cigarettes from his shirt pocket. He stepped outside and lit one before turning to Black.

"You were right yesterday. About what you said. I'm sorry. It's easy to be a jerk when you're nervous and have everything riding on an outcome." He paused, taking a drag. "Christina came around eventually, but she's not that great with people, in case you haven't noticed. But she feels bad, too, and wants things to work out."

"So do I, Peter. But I meant what I said. I think the band's got a great sound and some killer tunes, but to really take this, we've got to be more than just about how we play together. We have to be appealing. And to do that, we have to like each other. If Christina believes she's better than everyone, it'll sour things, and an audience can tell. Rock and roll's about having a blast, and it's hard to pull that off if you're always thinking you could have done better." Black stared at the mansion. "Believe me. I know all about that."

"I hear you, man. So how do we go from here?"

"We're good. Give her a little time to process Rick, and then let's hit this hard. I'd say let's do instrumental-only rehearsals for an hour or two a day before she shows up. The tighter we are as a trio, the better it'll be once she's in the mix. And I think we should focus on originals, not just covers. Some of them are really good, but they could be better, and I have a little experience at that kind of thing."

"That would be really cool."

"The more we're playing your stuff, the more solid the band's sound will be when we have to do a cover for the show."

"Makes sense."

They hashed out some more details, and then Peter went to check on his sister. Black fished his phone out of his back pocket and dialed Stan's number. When Stan answered, he sounded harried.

"Colt."

"Stan. It's Black."

"The prodigal returns. You getting tired of groupies and decided to slum it a little?"

"I wish. I'm afraid you have a completely different idea of my life than reality."

"Liar. I watched the show. You're living in a house with a bunch of babes. Poor you."

"Listen, I just heard that the old guitar player died. Overdose. Is there any way you can look into that for me? Sort of to make sure?"

"Why?"

"I've got a bad feeling about it."

"Oh, well, then sure, I'll drop the triple homicide ticket I picked up this morning and get right on the dope fiend. What's his name?"

"Rick Pearson. Lived in Hollywood."

Stan paused. "Wait a minute. You're not saying a guitar player in Hollywood was taking drugs! No wonder you're suspicious..."

"Ha ha. Just consider it a favor to me."

"Like you aren't running a bigger deficit than the government."

"I can pay it off in beer."

"You make a compelling case. When you need this?"

"Soon."

Chapter 19

Black listened to Dr. Kelso breathe noisily through his nose – a particularly irritating quality he'd never noticed before doing his therapy sessions over the phone. Black had chosen to skip the last few months of visits in favor of luxuries like solid food and toilet paper, but now that money was becoming a nonissue, he was back on the couch, if only telephonically.

"You haven't heard from her in three weeks?" Kelso asked.

"Correct. She was going to try to make it to the second show, but never did. And now she's not answering her phone."

"I see. And how does that make you feel?"

"How do you think it makes me feel?"

"This is more productive if you don't answer my question with another question."

"Crappy. It feels crappy. There. Are you happy?"

"You sound angrier than at our last session."

"Reading between the lines on that, are you?"

"Let's return to your assistant. You said you felt jealousy when she began seeing this singer, hmm?"

"I have no reason to be jealous."

"Yes, but nevertheless, you are."

"*Were*. I've gotten past it."

"Then you accept that you had feelings about your assistant."

"She's like a little sister to me. I didn't want to see her hurt."

"Yes. And the thought of someone else having sex with her…that made you angry, correct?"

"How would you feel if your little sister got picked up by some glamour boy?"

"But you say the anger has passed?"

"Mostly."

"Are you being completely honest that your feelings for Roxie are platonic and brotherly?"

"We've been down this road before, and the answer's still the same. I've got insoles older than her."

"But that doesn't change that you have sexual compulsions involving her, does it?"

"Look, she's cute. Of course there's a physical attraction there. But that doesn't mean I want to have sex with her."

"So you don't want to have sex with her?"

"No."

"If she appeared in front of you right now, and nobody would ever know, and stripped down to just her underwear and danced for you…you wouldn't want to have sex?"

"I'd never be able to forgive myself. Every time she looked at me would be a reminder."

"What if she had amnesia immediately after? So there was no guilt, only pleasure."

"What kind of hypothetical question is that? We're wasting valuable time here, Doc."

"Humor me. If she rubbed warm oil all over her naked young skin and begged you to ravish her…" Kelso's voice was becoming tight, and Black wondered whether he was wearing pants.

"Sure, in that case, who wouldn't?"

"Ah. Finally. The truth is that you want to have sex with your assistant. There's no shame in that. But you'll do better if you admit it to yourself."

"You framed a hypothetical that no man would be able to resist. That doesn't mean I want to actually have sex with her in the real world."

"Because she's ugly?"

"Of course not. Because she's too young, and she's my assistant."

"I see. So if you met a young lady at a show who was the same age, you wouldn't be attracted?"

"That's different."

"How?"

"Can we get back to Sylvia? That's who I'm having problems with."

"Right. If you say so."

"I am. She won't take my calls."

"Because you're living a musician's life, staying in a mansion with young women everywhere, and got caught with your ex-wife."

"I didn't get caught."

"Really? I thought you said Sylvia saw you coming out of her trailer, and that came as quite a surprise. Did I get that wrong?"

Black sighed. "I suppose it looked like that, but it was innocent."

"I see. And if Sylvia was watching you on television, it would appear that you were drinking and mingling with barely dressed nymphs every night?"

"I told her this was all for the cameras."

"Right. But then she spots you with your ex…well, you can see how it looks. And there's the matter of the kiss from the Korean woman. Would you like to explore that some more?"

"I told you, it was just a peck on the cheek. I had no idea they were filming. They're sneaky that way."

"Which brings us to your anger."

"I've been managing it."

"But you've been feeling more of it?"

"What do you think? I'm being treated like an idiot by my band, having to start from square one again while my ex judges me, even my assistant's flying around on private jets, and my girlfriend won't take my calls. Not to mention they've got me looking like the reason KISS wore makeup."

"I'm sorry. I think something broke up. You're saying you want to be kissed while wearing makeup?"

"No—"

Black heard the chime in the background. Kelso sounded disappointed. "There's the bell. You know what that means…"

"Yeah, I just flushed another hundred down the crapper."

"Keep doing your affirmations and breathing exercises, and let's take this up next week."

"It'll just be another big fat waste of time," Black grumbled. "Besides, I can only afford every other week."

"We're making progress."

"I'm still angry."

"But you can talk about it. That's a big step."

"If you say so."

"Give your credit card information to my receptionist and make another appointment. It's good to hear from you again."

"Yeah. Right."

Chapter 20

Lake Havasu City, Arizona

A jet contrail streamed in the late afternoon sky, a white horsetail splashed against the pale blue. Black looked off in the distance at the lake, where clusters of boats were tied together, cinched into floating party islands for the mating rituals of Spring Break. Last-minute preparations were being finalized by the crew on the mammoth stage, where bands had been playing throughout the day for the entertainment of privileged inebriates courting sunstroke and alcohol poisoning. The crowd numbered over two thousand, and the security detail had their hands full confiscating bottles and bongs while checking for weapons.

The judges' podium was cordoned off near center stage, where camera dollies rolled on rails to nowhere in preparation for the shoot. The acts had arrived midday and were given fifteen minutes each to acclimate themselves to the stage and the heat. The third round would result in another band being disqualified, and the contestants' nerves stretched taut.

Black roomed with Ed at the hotel for the night, Mugsy again left at the mansion. Black had gotten permission for Roxie to come over and visit with her beloved cat while they were gone. He was reassured that Sarah seemed to be warming up to him as time passed – she could easily have fought him on it, but when he'd explained that Roxie's visit was a condition of Mugsy remaining at the house, she'd made a call and gotten the go-ahead.

Mugsy's segments were among the most popular, and he now had his own Wiki page and fan club as well as a cult following. One of

Roxie's friends had set up an online Mugsy store and was selling shirts, cups, and assorted knickknacks at a dizzying clip, surprising Black more than anything to date: his third of the proceeds were now enough to pay the office rent.

The cat's stardom hadn't surprised Sarah, who'd made sure that every week featured another Mugsy spot: with Love Jupiter erecting their shrine; basking in the sunshine by the pool with SnM and Lavon with little cat sunglasses wedged in place; going crazy in the great room when the stereo was turned on and running in manic circles. The latest absurdity had come when a prominent publisher had approached them about doing a book of cat memoirs featuring Mugsy. Roxie was handling the negotiations, although several agents had indicated strong interest in taking him on.

Black, on the other hand, was just another member of the band, who kept to the shadows as much as possible except when required to mingle for the cameras. The entire thing amused him, even as Roxie had become more communicative as they discussed Mugsy's career moves and the merits of signing for his own TV show versus holding out for a motion picture deal.

Black tried not to dig too much into Roxie and Alex, but it was obvious the star had won her over and that she was in lust, if not love. He knew the signs from her stint with Eric, her tattoo artist boyfriend, and they were as unmistakable as they were annoying. Black pretended interest in the progress reports on Alex's tour – he was currently in the Midwest but was trying to get back to Los Angeles for a few days of R&R, which of course would include lots of Roxie. Black's romantic life was now officially nonexistent; Sylvia had been dark for a month. He'd tried everything, including having Roxie send flowers to her apartment, but they'd been returned as undeliverable. He'd braved the trip into L.A. on his last Sunday to plead his case, but when he got to her place, there was no sign of life and his key no longer fit the lock.

That night he'd overindulged in tequila while in the hot tub with Ed and Christina. The resultant footage had been prominently featured on the next segment as Christina, wearing a thong and the most microscopic bikini top Black had ever seen, had done an impromptu wiggle dance for the cameras that would have been the envy of any stripper. Ratings had surged, as had her fan mail, although Mugsy was still more popular. Black could only imagine what Sylvia thought upon seeing the spectacle, and he'd stopped calling her after that episode, his protestations of chastity laughable, even if they were true.

Christina moved to where Black was standing, watching the gear being loaded onto the stage. She was carrying a small bottle of water, her black Harley Davidson top molded to her breasts, a pair of distressed, torn jeans struggling to contain a walk that would have been at home at the Playboy mansion.

"How're you feeling?" she asked.

"Good. I feel like this is the first real chance we have to show what we're made of. Not you. You're always spot on. I mean as a band – as a unit, not four separate personalities stuck on a stage together."

"I know what you mean. Rehearsals have been really good lately, haven't they?"

"Better than good. I'd say we're ready for prime time."

The song they'd been assigned was Aerosmith's "Walk This Way", a tune Black had grown up on and could nail in his sleep. But his approach to the solo was more Stevie Ray Vaughn than Joe Perry, making for a hypnotic juxtaposition over Christina's rhythm guitar – something she hadn't felt comfortable playing live, but which Black had helped her gain confidence with. He'd shown her a few moves that she could use the guitar for that would accentuate her persona for the song, and even Rooster had been impressed when he'd watched the band play the night before.

"We better be. Bend in the Creek's a big favorite right now, and they have their act down pat. We'll need to be amazing to give them a run for their money," she said.

"They're really good, but they don't have our secret weapon."

"What's that?"

"You."

She looked at him with a small smile. "Why, Black, if I didn't know better, I'd almost believe you've forgiven me for being such an insufferable ass those first weeks."

"Well, I'm all about forgiveness. And frankly, this is starting to get fun again. I'd forgotten how cool it is to be onstage in front of thousands of people." He eyed her. "You nervous?"

"I don't get nervous anymore. I get psyched."

"That's the way to be. This is your show. You own the crowd."

"Let's not get carried away."

"Hey, at least we drew the last slot for the night. That'll leave the audience with a good impression leading into the next round."

"One in five chance. But I'll take it as a win."

Rooster swaggered over, looking fresh in a mint green silk shirt and cream linen slacks. They shot the breeze as they watched the final preparations, and Black noted that the soundman running the monitor system was a different one from the last show. For all Sarah's faults, perhaps she'd taken his observations to heart and arranged for someone new?

Shooting wouldn't start until dusk so that the elaborate light show would have maximum impact on camera. When the show began, Holly and David did their customary routine, recapping the last week's performances for the audience, shots from that show to splice in during post-production the following day, and then the first band took the stage: On Top, the boy band from Louisiana.

The five youths bumped and ground their way through a rendition of "Papa Was a Rolling Stone" that had Black's teeth on edge, but the audience response was good, and he couldn't fault either the vocals or the choreography. Next came their nemesis, Bend in the Creek, with a blistering version of ZZ Top's "Sharp Dressed Man" that brought cheers when the last note died. Black and Christina exchanged glances as Simon smiled and nodded from his seat next to the judges.

"We should have gotten that song. You would have torn the lead up," she said.

He nodded. "It was good. But it doesn't stand a chance against Aerosmith."

Their housemates BrandX followed the country-tinged band and seemed shoe-ins to win because of the rowdy youth of the audience, but when they were ready to start, their DJ signaled to the rappers, frantic. Black struggled to hear and could make out hurried back and forth about their samples not triggering.

"What? They were fine at sound check," Lavon growled.

"That was then. Memory says they ain't here no more," shot back the DJ, a lanky street tough with two gold front teeth and a baseball cap on sideways.

A bead of sweat rolled down SnM's face. He wiped it away with a swipe of his NY Yankees jersey. "Well, do something, man."

"Nuthin' to be done. The sounds ain't here."

Their coach had a terse discussion with Holly and David. Sarah got on her radio as the crowd began booing. When the word came back, it wasn't good.

"I don't know what to tell you guys. Figure something out. You've got five minutes. You'll have to do it without the samples if you can't make them work. Just like breaking a guitar string. The show must go on."

"That's bullshit. This is equipment failure. It isn't our fault."

"Not my call. Five minutes." She turned away from the rappers and held her two-way to her mouth. "Doug, crank the house music," she ordered the soundman.

Black and Christina remained where they were, every performer's worst nightmare unfolding for the rappers – having to wing a show with no preparation. To their credit, they gave it a game try, choosing to tackle their rendition of "Heard it Through The Grapevine" a cappella, but it was no good, and by the time they were done, the booing had sealed their fate.

Strobe delivered a typically effete performance that got commendable scores, and then it was time for Last Call. Peter and Black exchanged glances after Holly announced them, and Black played the famous riff, putting a unique spin on it by using a wah-

wah pedal to coax a new slant from the standard. Christina was in her element, shucking and jiving while playing her black Les Paul and giving the vocals her all, but it was Black's solo that was the highlight of the song. When it was over, the roar of the crowd sounded like an avalanche, and Christina and Black held their guitars up next to each other, sharing the spotlight. The judges took a minute to gather their thoughts, and then Alex led off with his critique and score – a ten. Nina followed suit with a ten of her own, and BT Slim rounded it out with another ten – the first perfect score of the season.

Rooster was waiting offstage as the cheering died down. He hugged everyone multiple times, congratulating them on an incredible performance – which it was, and which everyone in the band knew. Black enjoyed his moment of attention, but excused himself when he saw Lavon arguing with his coach. Black sympathized with him – it was a horrible way to end a great run, and over the six weeks they'd been together at the house, he'd grown to like the young rapper, who was wickedly funny in a self-deprecating way.

"Lousy break, Lavon," Black said, extending his hand.

Lavon took it and shook. "Yeah, well, every show got to have a loser, you know?"

"What do you think happened?"

"Some equipment shit. Nothing's where it's supposed to be except the beat. The music, the samples…gone."

"How?"

"Nobody knows. Just one of them things. Can't let it get you down. It's cool," Lavon said in a tone that made it clear it was anything but.

"Who was watching your stuff after rehearsal?"

"House security and the sound crew. You was up here. You see anything?"

Black tried to remember. With all the crew hurrying around to get things set up, nothing sprang to mind. Except…

"There was a guy. Latino looking. Skinny dude. Goatee, like a vato. I thought I remembered him hanging around and thought it was weird he wasn't busy," Black said, his words carefully chosen as he tried to clarify the image that was in his head.

"Yeah? You see that punkass here?"

Black watched the road crew breaking down the gear and rolling it off stage for several minutes, scanning the faces, and shook his head. "No, I don't. Maybe he's outside loading."

"I got to tell our people about this. This ain't right," Lavon said, returning to his dejected coach.

Black moved to the new soundman and thanked him for a great job. The man grinned behind his bushy red beard. "That's nice of you, man. Nobody ever says anything to me unless it's to complain they didn't like their sound."

Black described the crew member he'd seen. "Is that anyone you know?"

The soundman shook his head. "No. But there are a lot of new guys here. On a big production like this, there'll be dozens of local talent to lug stuff."

Lavon was asking the stage manager the same sort of questions, and Black left him to his task, cringing when Lavon pointed at Black and continued talking, obviously agitated. The last thing he wanted to be accused of was instigating another disturbance, and he couldn't get back to his band's dressing room fast enough. The incident receded in his mind as celebratory beers were cracked and swigged, and within an hour it was just a hazy blur as another round of cold brews were consumed to keep the desert heat at bay.

Chapter 21

Dinner was at one of the restaurants on the lake that jutted on pilings over the water, whose surface was inky black except for where the spring moon glinted off the small waves stirred by the eastern wind. Everyone was in a festive mood, the performance's perfect score validation of the many hours they'd invested practicing. Heaping platters of pork ribs and barbecued chicken, along with an ocean of beer and Jack Daniel's, seemed a fitting reward.

By the time they finished eating, Black's head was beginning to spin, and against his better judgment he asked Peter for a cigarette. After all, he was a guitar hero, and a lousy smoke or two wasn't going to put him into an early grave. Peter slid his pack across the table, and Black removed one, along with the matches stuck in the cellophane wrapping. He stood somewhat unsteadily as Rooster held another shot of Jack in the air and toasted. Black waved the drink off – Ed could knock back enough for them both without any help from Black.

The waitress waggled a cautionary finger at him as he looked around for someplace to smoke and pointed at the deck over the water. He nodded his thanks and slid the door open, taking in the dry air like it was his last breath, and fumbled to light his cigarette, his fingers clumsy from the booze. He cursed under his breath as the match fizzled out and was striking a second one when a voice spoke from behind him.

"Hey, pal, you need help with that?"

Black was turning around when two pairs of powerful hands gripped him under his arms and hurled him over the wooden railing into the water fifteen feet below. Black struck the surface with his

135

back, and the impact knocked the wind out of him. The assault had been so sudden he hadn't had time to register what was happening – one moment he was on the deck, the next doing an ungainly swan dive.

Water rushed into his nose and mouth as he went under. Tiny pinpoints of light danced behind his eyes, and then instinct took over and he kicked to the surface, his lungs burning for air. His head broke the surface, and he sputtered out a coughing blast as he struggled to breathe. He was finally able to draw air as he treaded water, his boots pulling at him, and he glared up at the restaurant lights above him. The same voice that had asked whether he wanted a light echoed off the water.

"You like asking questions, huh, tough guy? Sticking your nose where it don't belong? This is your only warning. Knock it off, or next time we'll start off with breaking all your fingers. How does that sound?"

Black was mustering a response in his alcohol-addled brain when he heard the footsteps departing on the plank deck. He listened intently, but didn't hear anything else. The smoking area was empty.

He peered into the gloom at the side of the restaurant and resigned himself to having to swim to shore – no small feat when drunk and wearing skinny jeans and cowboy boots. As he paddled around the pilings, another, darker thought occurred to him: what if his attackers were waiting for him in the dark?

The idea stayed with him as he stroked for the bank, huffing like he'd run a marathon, water in his eyes and nose, a vague odor of petroleum in his hair. Off in the distance a line of boats was lit up like a parade float. Music boomed across the lake, accompanied by female squeals and male whoops that reverberated like sirens.

When he finally reached the water's edge, there were no goons lying in wait. Black pulled himself onto a flat area of the gravel beach and lay staring at the moon peeking through the clouds, wondering how he'd gotten himself attacked in the middle of a restaurant. Even for him, that was a record – in a night of them, he thought grimly. Obviously whoever had tossed him in had followed him and waited for their opportunity. His probing about the mystery roadie had triggered a response he hadn't expected, and the only lucky thing about it had been that they'd only thrown him in the water and not tailed him to the hotel and worked him over with pipes.

The voice had sounded East Coast. Not Latino at all. No, more like New Jersey or New York – he wasn't great with accents, but it wasn't L.A., that was for sure. As his heart rate returned to normal, he wondered just what he'd tripped onto. It was one thing to try to nudge bands out of the running, and another to assault someone overtly.

He retrieved his wallet and shook a stream from it, tilting his head to clear the water from his ears. From here on out he'd have to be much more stealthy about his behavior and play the part of the oblivious guitar player better.

Black pulled his boots off and dumped them out before removing his socks and wringing them. He was cold from the nocturnal bath, but stayed where he was for ten minutes before standing and moving back to the restaurant. Inside, the party was in full roar, and nobody had noticed his absence. Peter saw him first, followed almost immediately by Ed, who put his beer down and shook his head.

"Dude. What happened to you?"

Black tried a smirk. "I thought it would be a good idea to sit on the rail and have a smoke. Turns out that's not the best thing to do after you've had a few. And the worst part is, I didn't even get to smoke my cigarette."

"You fell in?" Christina asked in disbelief.

"I prefer to think I slipped."

The table exploded with laughter as Peter stood. "I didn't know you'd need a chaperone to have a smoke. Come on. I'll make sure you don't go over again."

"Thanks," Black said, eyes roving over the tables, searching for anyone who visually matched the voice on the terrace. He wasn't sure whether it was a good thing or a bad thing that he didn't see anyone suspicious, but from now on he'd have to carefully monitor his alcohol intake and stay alert. One swim per case was more than enough, and he suspected that the next time he wouldn't be so lucky.

Chapter 22

The following day the bus home left early, and by the time it pulled into Malibu, Black was ready to get off. Sarah had announced that the bands would be consolidated in the one mansion since only four remained, and that the new arrivals would arrive that evening.

The afternoon went by quickly by the pool, and Lavon and SnM took their last dips before being officially booted on TV at seven. They were bitter about how they'd lost but were putting a brave face on it, shrugging it off as just another pothole on the road to stardom. The roadie had never surfaced, and after spending hours with the sampler, the DJ had concluded that wiping the memory had to have been premeditated – and the user interface wasn't intuitive.

"They had to know what they were doing, which means they knew what gear we was using and studied up on it," Lavon said.

"Have you spoken with Sarah?"

"Yeah, yesterday after the show. But she just gave me that honky bitch look and ignored me. Said what was done was done, and if we didn't have anything solid, there wasn't anything to investigate."

"You could go to the papers."

"Yeah, we thinking about that. Only how do we prove it? Don't wanna get our ass sued."

"You can probably tell them what happened and make it clear enough so even an idiot could figure it out."

"Our manager said it would look like sour grapes. Best to just move on. Besides, we talkin' to a label that liked what they saw. So it may be no biggie in the end. Although I'll miss the free booze and that big boy," he said, pointing at Mugsy.

At six o'clock the other bands showed up, and everyone did a meet and greet for the cameras. Sarah escorted the new arrivals to their rooms. Terrence, the lead singer of Strobe, stopped when he saw Mugsy.

"There's going to be a problem. I'm horribly allergic to cats. Have been all my life," he announced. "Sarah, you're going to need to have the housekeepers clean the whole house if I'm going to stay here."

Sarah made a call and nodded. "They can be here tomorrow. Will you be okay for one night?"

Terrence sneezed. "I'd prefer a hotel, just in case." He turned to Black. "You need to keep him in your room from now on. I hope that's not a problem."

"Not at all. I know it can't be helped."

Terrence rubbed his nose and pursed his lips in displeasure. "I have to get out of here."

Sarah nodded. "Okay, Terrence. I'll ask one of the cars to take you back to the other house for the night. Just go outside until we do the ceremony, and they'll take you immediately after. Will that work?"

"I suppose it'll have to, won't it?" he said and moved to the pool deck. Sarah turned to Black. "I didn't see that coming."

"Man's got a medical condition. What can you do?"

"Thanks for being understanding."

"As long as Mugsy's getting regular meals and is allowed to sleep twenty-three hours a day, he'll be fine." Black scooped Mugsy up and hauled him upstairs, followed by Ed. They changed into their more formal rock clothes for the ceremony, to be held on the beach by tiki torchlight, followed by a group dinner. Black's cell phone rang just as he was getting ready to join everyone downstairs. It was Stan.

"I took over your boy Rick's case," he said.

Black considered Stan's words. "Then it's a homicide?"

"I'm treating it as one. There's just too much that looks odd on it for my liking."

"Such as?"

"No other track marks, for starters. And conflicting reports from a neighbor who says she thought she heard something, like a scuffle outside his door."

"Damn. Well, I've got something else for you, too." Black told Stan about being thrown into the lake and warned off.

"You think it's related?"

"That's my bet. I'd take a hard look at Rick's bank records and see whether he got a big slug of money after he blew the competition, or went on a buying spree. The story never hit the press other than the party line that made him look like a screw-up, so my guess is he was paid off to stay quiet."

"Or threatened," Stan said.

"Right. Or both. Carrot and stick. He'd already broken up with Christina and been thrown out of the band, so maybe a slug of cash looked pretty good."

"I'll have someone go through his accounts. Good idea."

"You might also want to look hard at who benefitted. Obviously Alex. His band. His manager. Peter and Rooster…and Christina and Sarah, too. The motive could be as simple as either one of the women getting back at him. I'd turn over rocks and see what you find."

"Whoa. That's way outside of the scope of the investigation. I don't have time. I still need to establish whether it's actually a homicide or not. It's not clear." Stan paused. "That sounds like a job for Black Investigations."

"I was afraid you'd say that."

"Sorry. Tough love."

"My problem is that I'm stuck at this house six days a week, and Roxie's not available to do research right now."

"So there's nobody to do your work for you. I get it. A shame."

"Thanks for nothing."

Stan grunted. "Hey, one word of advice. If there is a connection between Rick and the mugs who tossed you into the drink, I'd be careful. This is the big leagues."

"That occurred to me."

"Then you're not just a pretty face wearing a wig."

"I wish it was a wig."

The ceremony went by quickly, and dinner was livened up by a dozen Playboy bunnies whom the producers had lined up for visual appeal. Now that it was down to four bands, the only female was Christina, and the ratings clearly indicated that skin brought in the viewers. Black wondered how Simon was going to contrive to have a stream of swimsuit models at the house, and decided that being a TV producer was only one step below being a Greek god. The bunnies were fun, if professional, and Black took care not to overdo it on beer, Stan's warning still fresh in his ear.

When they made it back to the mansion, Christina invited Black to have a nightcap with her in the hot tub, sans cameras. He debated saying no and then realized that there wasn't any reason not to join her. He trotted to his room and changed into swimming trunks. The noise of a card game drifted up the stairs from the great room, where Ed and Peter were preparing to fleece the new arrivals out of some money. As he listened to the banter, he wondered at Christina's change since their chat. She'd been positively warm of late, and suddenly their age difference didn't seem like that wide a gap.

He padded down the stairs, a towel draped over his shoulders, and studiously ignored Ed's raised eyebrows as he slipped past the game table. Christina was already in the Jacuzzi, warm bubbles frothing around her, a fresh bottle of champagne in an ice bucket next to the tub.

"I thought a little bubbly would be nice," she said. Black eased himself into the water and sighed. She poured him a drink and they toasted. "To a big win."

Black smiled. "And many more."

Christina downed half her glass in a swallow and set it down as she glanced at the house. "What did you think of the hired talent?" she asked.

"The girls? Cute. But that's kind of what they do for a living, isn't it?"

"Aren't you temped by all that flesh? I never see you with anyone."

"I…I'm sort of in a relationship."

"Sort of?" She smirked.

"That sounds lame, I know. The truth is, I don't know whether I am or not." He took another swallow of champagne and felt the effervescent warmth flow to his stomach.

"As a woman, I hate to break it to you, but if you don't know whether you are, you're not." She finished her glass, poured herself another, and topped off Black's.

"You're probably right."

"Sounds like there's a story. I've got time." She smiled again and lifted her hair off her neck. "Mmm, this is nice."

"Relaxing."

"So what's the deal, Black?"

"It's complicated." He took her through it and realized as he described what had happened that it seemed like a year ago. When he was finished, she looked at him for a long time.

"Thank God. For a while there I was afraid you batted for the other team."

Black laughed. "Being married to Nina could do that to you." He closed his eyes.

They finished their second glass, and Black split the last of the bottle between them before sticking it upside down in the steel bucket.

"So what kind of women do you like? What's your type?" Christina asked.

"I…I'm not sure I have a type."

Her foot touched his calf, and an electric charge seemed to course through him from the connection. He didn't know whether he was misinterpreting what had just happened, so he stayed still. Christina's eyes met his, and she moved to him and kissed him, taking her time, her breath sweet, her lips full. After what seemed like an hour, he pulled away. She regarded him curiously.

"What? You no like?" she asked.

He shook his head. "It's not that. It's just…we're in a band, working together. This isn't a great idea."

"I'm an adult."

"I know. But it's…the timing's wrong."

She smirked. "You're going to let that stop you?"

"I have to. I don't want to blow this."

Christina sighed and nodded. "We aren't going to be in this contest forever. Only six more weeks."

"Six long weeks, at this rate."

She laughed. "Very long. But there's always week seven to look forward to." The invitation was unmistakable.

They finished their drinks, the moment over, and Black said goodnight when Ed left the game and came out to socialize. His mind was racing as he climbed the stairs, wondering whether he'd done the right thing or was being a complete dolt, turning down a willing, available, extremely hot woman who seemed into him. Mugsy lifted his head as he entered the room and then returned to his catnap.

Black changed into sweats and was about to brush his teeth when his phone rang. He did a double take when he saw the number and punched the line to life.

"Sylvia! You…you called."

"About time, wasn't it?"

"I've been trying to get hold of you for a month. No, longer."

"I left town."

"What? Where did you go?"

"Home. Switzerland. My parents bought me a ticket. Said they missed me, so I thought I'd take them up on the offer of free food and drink for a while."

"I miss you too," Black said quietly, relief at having declined Christina's overture flooding him.

"Oh, Black…" she said, her voice closing down on her as she tried to speak. She cleared her throat and tried again. "It's Sunday tomorrow."

"Yes, it is."

"I was thinking about your car. I wonder if it'll start?"

"If not, you can always get a jump."

"Seems like nice weather for a trip to Malibu," she said.

"With the top down."

"Maybe a picnic on the beach? Unless you're busy…"

"I have the whole day."

The silence was uncomfortable, and when Sylvia asked her question, there was no mistaking her meaning. "Is there anything you want to tell me? About…while I was gone?"

He was glad he didn't have to lie. Much. "No. Just that I really miss you."

The relief in her voice was clear. "That's nice to hear. I'll call you in the morning when I'm ready to head out."

"If you can't get the car moving, take a cab. I'll pay for it."

"Sounds like a deal."

Black was grinning ear to ear when he lay down, and even tolerated Mugsy waddling over and hopping onto the bed. As Black drifted off to sleep, whiffs of cat gas rolling over him like waves of pungent surf, an image of Sylvia played in his imagination, and for the first time in weeks he felt homesick for his old, uneventful life.

Chapter 23

Black spent Sunday with Sylvia ambling by the water's edge while they exchanged stories about Switzerland and life on a reality TV show. They checked into a motel near the beach after an early dinner and spent four hours in each other's arms before Black's curfew pulled him back into his chaotic make-believe world of round-the-clock filming and arrested development.

The next two weeks went by quickly, with another vapid team activity out of the way before hearing about their fourth musical competition: a charity event in Northern California, near the wine country. For that concert they would be only one of the draws, with several major acts playing to raise money for Native American scholarships. It was already sold out, limited to a thousand lucky attendees in general admission, with an additional ten dinner tables in a VIP area running five hundred dollars a seat.

Last Call drew Wilson Pickett's "Mustang Sally" as their song and spent the week making it their own. Christina's vocals shined on it, and by the time they loaded onto the bus for the eight-hour drive north, everyone in the band was pumped. Rooster would fly in, as would Holly, David, and the judges. The plan was to arrive, have an early dinner while the headline bands played, and then close the concert with the four performances by the *Rock of Ages* contenders.

Black dozed most of the way, the luxury coach's suspension softening the ride as it droned toward San Francisco. The concert location turned out to be in the middle of nowhere, surrounded by redwood forest, with a newly constructed lodge boasting twenty guest rooms on the perimeter and the stage erected in the center of a large clearing. It was three o'clock when he stepped off the bus and stretched. Lunch in San Jose sat like a lead brick in his stomach, and the sun felt good on his skin as he waited for Sarah to arrive and tell them what to do.

He counted fifteen semi-rigs parked near the stage, along with a bank of industrial generators to supply power. The audience wouldn't be allowed on the grounds until five, with the concert starting at six and ending at nine with the *Rock of Ages* performances. He closed his eyes and tried to imagine what the darkened area would look like, under the stars with a thousand people, when a voice like nails on a chalkboard called out from behind him.

"Artemus! You're here!"

Black's stomach did a flip as he turned slowly. His parents, Spring and Chakra, approached wearing their usual tie-dyed hippy outfits, Spring with flowers in her gray hair.

"Mom. Dad. What are you doing here?" he asked, his voice several pitches higher than normal.

"I thought you knew! This is our retreat. Remember we told you we were going to buy it? What do you think? It's beautiful, isn't it? And it's Spring, not Mom."

"You own this?"

"That's what I just said, didn't I?"

"How did the show wind up choosing this, of all places...?"

"Nina put the producer in touch with us. She's a doll. She's supposed to be here in a few hours." Spring looked him up and down. "Have you put on a few pounds, Artemus?"

"No, it must be this outfit. And everybody calls me Black. Just Black."

"It's not really your color, is it?"

"Nice to see you," Black lied.

Sarah, who was standing by the bus, clapped her hands together and called for everyone's attention. Black excused himself and went to her, grateful for the reprieve. He loved his parents, but it was an adoration he preferred to appreciate at a distance – the greater the better.

Sarah gave a typically efficient orientation. They'd be staying in the lodge overnight, two to a room, and dinner would be in the main building – a towering A-frame next to the guest facility. Sound check would be in two hours, at 4:00, with each group allocated fifteen minutes to get familiar with the setup. The two headliner acts would each get an hour. As she was speaking, a squeal of feedback shrieked from the tower of speakers on both sides of the stage.

The band members followed her to the rooms as Black returned to his parents.

"This is quite a spread. It's…bigger than I thought it would be. How many acres is it?" he asked.

His mother looked at his dad, who had a typically tuned-out expression on his face, his eyes veiled behind a pair of cheap sunglasses. "Oh, I can never remember. Do you know, Chakra?" she asked.

"Not really. Something like…twenty, maybe? Or two hundred. Whatever the number, it's got a two in it, I'm pretty sure."

Black bit back his annoyed response. "Wow. And what are you doing with it? Besides the concert, I mean?"

"We have retreats here," Spring said. "We just started a few weeks ago, and we're already booked up for most of the year. Meditation. Yoga. Drum circles, modern dance and movement…whatever interests us. There's a whole roster of guest speakers and instructors scheduled. And of course, corporate events. You'd be surprised at how many big companies want to send their managers somewhere to get in touch with their spirit guides in a peaceful environment."

"Nothing would surprise me," Black agreed. The irony was lost on his parents.

"Well, honey, it's just so good to see you. And it's so exciting that you're back in the music thing. You always seemed to like that."

"It's a culture shock after being out for twenty years."

"Has it been that long? Where does the time go?"

A blare of guitar sounded from the stage, followed by the beginning of the drum check, starting with the kick. The thudding sounded like the gods themselves were hammering on an anvil, each boom more explosive than the last, which thankfully cut short their discussion.

"All right. Well, nice to see you. I've got to get to my room and get ready for the show. I'll see you after, okay?" he yelled as both his parents held their fingers in their ears. His mother nodded, and he seized the opportunity to make his escape.

Ed waved to him from the doorway of an upstairs room, and Black mounted the steps to join him, toting the Gretsch. The drum check ended and the bass guitar began playing as Black set the guitar case down inside the simple room and eyed the narrow beds.

"Not exactly the mansion, is it?" Ed said.

"I've seen surfboards wider than that."

"Hey, they may not be wide, but at least they're uncomfortable," Ed said, bouncing on the one nearest the bathroom. "Who were you talking to?"

"It's a long story. My parents."

Ed's eyes widened. "Whoa. That's cool. They came all the way out to see you? They live around here?"

"Sort of."

"My parents don't even watch the show. I haven't talked to them in forever. They hate me being a musician. They're both schoolteachers. Total tight-asses."

"When you're rich and famous, it won't matter much."

"That seems a long way away. Or it did until you started playing with us."

They approached the stage at 4:00 and watched as Bend in the Creek did a blistering version of Bon Jovi's "Wanted Dead or Alive". Last Call was up next, and they deliberately kept their playing low key, not wanting to give the competition any hint of what they were up against – on Black's advice. When they finished, Black glanced at the round tables set up around the judges' pods, where a hundred privileged diners would enjoy the show untroubled by the throng on the other side of the barricades. Black approached Sarah, who was standing by the monitor board, and pointed to an adjacent area with folding chairs.

"Who's that for?"

"Oh, the Native Americans. They're bussing in a bunch from Southern California."

"They don't get tables?"

Sarah smiled. "They didn't pay five Benjamins apiece to be here, did they?"

"Well, we did sort of take their whole country away."

She shrugged. "Those are padded folding chairs. Could be worse."

Sarah turned back to the soundman, the same from the prior show. Black nodded at him, and he returned the gesture, his face impassive.

Dinner was a variety of organic dishes and curries prepared by a rotund chef, served by a variety of sixties throwbacks typical of those his parents surrounded themselves with. Black leaned in to Christina as a waitress set a plate of unidentifiable sludge in front of him and whispered, "I haven't seen this much underarm hair in a long time."

"And that's just the women." She smiled. "Ed tells me your parents are here? You have to introduce me."

"I'd rather not."

"Oh, come on. How bad could it be?"

"Imagine the worst thing ever, cube it, and that's not even close."

"Everyone feels that way about their parents. I bet they're cute."

"The way a pit viper's cute."

"Well, I still want to meet them after we win tonight."

"Which we will." He gave her a high five.

"I know. Although Menudo over there sounded pretty good at rehearsal," she said, indicating On Top with a nod of her head.

Black made a face. "We've got the strength of ten boy bands."

"Yeah, but they've got shiny pants and dance moves."

"Good point."

After dinner the bands went their separate ways. The field was packed with concert-goers waiting in anticipation of the first headliner. When the first band took the stage, guitars held aloft, the clearing broke out in cheers, and then the first thundering riff of the group's signature tune thundered from the speakers while the lead singer let loose a sustained shriek that could have broken glass.

Black watched from his position backstage, noting that the monitor system seemed to be working flawlessly. He caught a glimpse of the VIP tables filled with well-fed Silicon Valley CEOs and Napa winemakers drinking champagne and enjoying the show next to the Native American contingent, who sat drinking beer with unreadable expressions as they watched the band gyrate and bop. For a brief moment Black was struck by the absurdity, but he decided not to let it bother him – he had more important matters to occupy his limited mental bandwidth.

There was a brief intermission between the first band and the second: one of the most beloved country rock groups from the seventies, still going strong with its geriatric members the worse for wear from their epic battles with the bottle and drugs. When it opened its set with a song that had been a number one hit in 1976, the genteel crowd went wild, and even the bussed-in tribe seemed to be enjoying it.

Then it was time for the contest. Holly and David had appeared in a rented black SUV an hour before the camera crews started filming, and Black watched as three Humvee limousines rolled down the long dirt drive toward the backstage area. Nina emerged from the lead car accompanied by Simon and a curvy platinum blonde half his age, and Black considered again how much he'd missed in life by not being a record mogul. Nina cheek-kissed the members of the legendary band who had just finished their set, obviously friends. Black noticed none had given him even a second glance.

Last Call had drawn third slot, with Bend in the Creek opening, followed by Strobe. On Top got the final position, which was fine by Black. Following Last Call's performance would be a tough act if things went as they had in rehearsals.

Bend in the Creek delivered a scorching rendition of Falco's "Der Kommissar", which surprised Black given its origins, but the country-infused approach actually worked, and Black wasn't shocked by the two tens and a nine awarded by the panel. Strobe did its usual standoffish but polished techno rendition of Robert Palmer's "Simply Irresistible", which garnered nines across the board, and then it was Last Call's turn at bat. Peter's bass rumbled like a chained dog and Black's guitar wailed distorted torture for several seconds before fading off and cleaning up, cutting into the main chords as Christina's voice transfixed the crowd. By the final chorus of "Mustang Sally", the audience was singing along and cheering, and it looked like a clean win, barring the unexpected from On Top. Two tens and a nine tied them with Bend in the Creek for the night.

They bounded off stage, adrenaline coursing through their systems, and Rooster high-fived everyone while woo-hooing and slapping them on the back.

"Another incredible jam, people. Taking names. That's what I'm talking about!" he exclaimed, and Black grinned as the veteran bluesman hugged Christina. Black was having a hard time believing Rooster could have been involved in anything to bring down the band the prior season, but he knew appearances could be deceiving.

The high from the performance was still with him when On Top took the stage, but even so he sensed something was off from the onset. Two of the members looked green, their faces strained, and their performances were wooden. That was enough to cause them to lose points, but when Jimmy, the putative tough guy, stopped during the last third of the song and ran to the side of the stage to vomit, it cinched the deal. When they finished, the scores were terrible, although Nina awarded a few mercy points, congratulating them for going on with the show even though some of the members were sick. That was slim consolation on a night of brilliant performances, though, and it didn't require Holly's summation to calculate who would be leaving the mansion the next day.

Black approached On Top's coach, who was commiserating with the band members, to express his condolences.

"I'm so sorry," he started, and he could see the hurt in her eyes.

"They got food poisoning. It couldn't have happened at a worse time."

"That's odd. I mean, we all ate the same stuff. Maybe it was lunch?"

"Who knows? Although nobody started feeling bad until three hours after dinner, so I doubt it."

"That's a tough break."

"Yeah. Great performance, by the way. You've come a long way since the first round."

"Thanks. We've all worked very hard."

The show doctor arrived, and Black left the dour group, their hopes crushed by a random pathogen, and then stopped in his tracks. Had it been completely random? Could somebody have planted bad food or some kind of agent in the group's meals to throw them off?

The idea didn't seem so farfetched after his nocturnal swim.

Once the field had been cleared and the audience sent home, the disqualification ceremony took place on stage, two of the members of On Top still looking shaky from whatever bug they'd caught. When it was over, Black's parents greeted him backstage, where they were chatting with Nina, Simon, and his date.

"You were wonderful, Artemus. Like Hendrix or something," Spring enthused.

Simon looked at him strangely, and Black corrected her. "Black. And thank you. That means a lot."

"Seems like you've got your swagger back. Congratulations. It was really impressive. You guys look good to go neck and neck with Bend in the Creek," Nina said.

"I wouldn't count Strobe out. They're an audience favorite. Not my cuppa, but still," Black said.

"Yeah, they're cool, but you guys rock!" Simon's date chirped, drawing a pained smile from Simon.

Black shrugged. "Thanks."

"Good to see you pulled it together, Mr. Black," Simon added, glancing around, clearly ready to leave now that the cameras were off.

"Black! There you are!" Christina bounced up. Even next to Simon's companion, she was a standout. "Are these your parents?"

"Um, yeah. Christina, meet Spring and Chakra."

She shook hands with them, and Black noted that his father seemed suddenly more interested in the proceedings.

"Did you hear about those poor boys? Food poisoning. What a shame," Christina said, shaking her head.

"I can't understand that. I buy all the vegetables and fish from organic suppliers. And Jacques is one of the best chefs in Napa," Spring said.

"It does seem weird that only some of them got sick, doesn't it?" Black asked.

"Sometimes that's how it happens. Different immune systems," Simon countered. "I've been to Mexico with friends, and one guy gets sick and everyone else is fine. Just the way it goes. But I agree it's a pity. They were audience favorites."

"It's just so…nobody's ever gotten ill eating our food."

Nina shrugged. "There's no telling what caused it. Maybe they had a snack that had turned. Or a drink that had gone south. I wouldn't worry about it, Spring."

Black watched as the line of limos departed with the judges and VIPs, his parents at his side chatting with Christina, the moonlight bathing the surrounding trees in its otherworldly light. The same unease he'd felt after the last two disqualifications churned in his stomach. He now had little doubt someone was methodically disqualifying the acts, but the suspect list was still too long. He made a mental note to call Roxie the next day and beg her to dig around in everyone's backgrounds and see if anything jumped out as a possible clue, and then began the long process of extricating himself from the discussion with his parents, which he knew would go on for hours. A stab of guilt twinged when he saw the look of disappointment in his mother's eyes, but that only lasted until the next time she called him Artemus.

That night, he and Ed sat on the terrace outside their room and drank Heineken as they watched the security teams roaming the grounds, safeguarding the stage until the riggers could tear it down tomorrow. Black moderated his intake and begged off a card game with Ed and the others in the lodge, preferring to keep to himself, fatigued now that another round had come and gone. His eyes scanned the parking area near the rooms a final time, and then he trudged inside, taking care to ensure the door was securely locked before hitting the shower and preparing for a hard night on the uncomfortable bed.

Chapter 24

The bus ride back seemed to take twice as long. Somewhere around the rolling hills of Coalinga, Black's phone trilled at him. He pulled it from the breast pocket of his Western-style shirt and held it to his ear.

"Hello?"

"Hey. Saw you on TV last night. Look at you – Mr. Rock Star. I'm surprised you answer your own phone."

"Stan. You watch that garbage?"

"What can I say? My Internet's down, so no porn."

"Should have paid the bill."

"I think it's the NSA. Spying on me to protect the children. Or stop terrorism."

"I think it was the war on drugs."

"I get so confused sometimes."

"Lack of dirty movies will do that to you."

"Speaking from experience, I see."

Black gazed through the window at the seemingly endless tall grass yellowing in the sun. "So you resorted to reality TV? The horror."

"Yeah. And who do I see but my old buddy burning up the frets in front of a crowd of thousands?"

"Did they show the Indians? They didn't look impressed."

"Negative. Just all you, baby. And the bombshell singer, who I'd love to take out for a twelve pack of tall boys and a Carl's burger. Hell, I'd even be willing to supersize it."

"Sounds like love."

"She's something else."

Black peered at where Christina was sitting two seats forward. "Yup."

"You tapping that?"

"Stan, I'm with Sylvia."

"Didn't answer the question. Damn it. I so knew I should have become a PI. I hate you. I really do."

"Must be a slow day at work, huh? Not too many butcherings?"

"Exactly. Haven't seen a stiff in forty-eight hours. It's got me worried. Maybe everyone's given up murder?"

"Don't sweat it. Someone's plotting to kill their mother-in-law or slaughter a rival gang member as we speak. Cheer up."

"You're just saying that."

"Okay, I am." Black paused. "What's up? I'm kind of busy on my all-day bus ride here."

"Your buddy Rick. It's definitely a homicide. Forensics finally got off their ass and confirmed it. But the problem is the case is cold. I did some interviews with the neighbors and checked the nearest traffic cams, but nothing. So it's looking like a dead end. No pun intended."

"You use that all the time, don't you?"

"One of my favorites."

Black considered the new information. "Does that make investigating the suspects I can name more of a priority?"

"Yes, it does. Shoot me something with a brief synopsis of why you think they're possibles and I'll take a look."

"It'll have to be this evening. I really am on a bus."

"I can't believe you don't have your own plane yet. Slacker."

"I have no comeback. It's on my list, right after a new liver."

"At least you've got your priorities straight."

The big tires thrummed against the asphalt as the bus began its ascent up the Grapevine, the big diesel laboring as it slowed to a crawl on the steep grade. Black was dozing off when his phone rang again. Sylvia's voice sounded so distorted he had to struggle to hear her.

"Congratulations. I saw the show."

"Seems like half the world did."

"You were wonderful. I mean that," she said.

"If you're trying to flatter me so I'll sleep with you, it worked."

"Are we still on for Sunday?"

"Absolutely." The line beeped, signaling another inbound call. "Hang on for a second." He put her on hold.

Roxie's voice sounded typically deadpan. "I guess I'm still going to be working for the old badger for another two weeks, huh?"

"You heard about the latest round?"

"Duh. She forced me to watch it. She's developed a fixation on you since I told her I knew you."

"Great. At least I can still get the cougars interested. I've got that to fall back on."

"She's been bugging me for an introduction. I'm serious."

"Too bad I'm confined to the house."

"I told her you like boys. Ever since prison."

"I can always count on you. You should do public relations. You're a natural."

"She said that wasn't a problem. She thinks you look a little like Liberace. Her words, not mine."

"That's super. Was there some other reason you called?"

"I miss Mugsy. When can I take him home?"

"By home I presume you mean the office."

"Don't deflect."

"I agreed he could stay in Malibu as long as I was on the show. How's the merchandising going?"

"Mugsy mania is sweeping the country. It's off the hook."

"Why it took me so long to think of pimping the cat, I'll never know. If this keeps up, I might even be able to recover my outlay on cat chow and furniture he's destroyed."

A long silence. "I want to come out there on Sunday."

"That shouldn't be a problem. I'll clear it with Sarah and Lou." Black paused. "How are things with your new boyfriend?"

"Good. He's really romantic. Something you could learn from."

"Seems like I've got the cougars wrapped around my little finger as it is."

"I'm serious. He texts me at least twice a day, even though he's crazy busy with his tour."

"Wow. Texting. If I knew what that meant, I'd do it, too."

"Don't be a hatah, boss. He's way different than he seems at first. A good Italian boy."

"Italian? With a name like Sands?"

"That's his stage name. It's short for Sandri."

"Aren't you part Italian?" Black guessed, having no idea what her heritage was.

"Nice try. German and Spanish."

"Which are both way closer to Italy than, say, Inglewood."

"Your knowledge of geography is impressive."

"What did you think of the performance?"

"I shouldn't say this, because your head'll swell bigger than it already is, but you were really good. And I'm not just saying that so you'll start paying me again."

"That reminds me. I have a little favor to ask you..."

"Sorry. You're breaking up."

"Roxie, come on. Help out. I'll remember this." He told her what he needed. "Stan's waiting for it, and I could really use some help digging around in everyone's backgrounds."

"Thirty bucks an hour."

"Roxie..."

"Girl's got to get paid. Yes or no?"

Black sighed. "Deal."

"Minimum ten hours."

"Roxie."

"I'll take that as a yes." She paused. "Cash."

Black groaned. "Of course. It's not like you can trust me or anything."

"Small bills."

"Do you have a pen? I'll give you the names."

"Shoot."

When Black hung up, he remembered that Sylvia was on hold. He looked at the call indicator and saw he'd lost her four minutes into the discussion with Roxie. After peering at the signal bar, which showed no service, he resigned himself to yet more apologies when they got to the other side of the mountain range and closed his eyes, hoping for more sleep before they hit Malibu and the filming started again upon their arrival.

Chapter 25

The next week went by quickly, and when Monday morning arrived and the bands had to begin their practice for the elimination round, Black was more than ready for serious rehearsals.

The challenge involved three hours at a top tier recording studio for a film score. Each band would perform the same song, and then the audience at home would vote for its favorite. The group receiving the least votes would be invited to leave. There were no rules, and the bands broke off after the announcement to listen to the demo each was given. Rooster joined Last Call in the rehearsal studio and began brainstorming how to best perform the song, branding it with their signature sound.

Black felt confident after hearing what they were expected to do. He, out of everyone involved, had spent countless hours in the studio recording his album, so he had a better than fair idea of what worked and what didn't. Things might have changed over the two decades he'd been out of the loop, but recording a live band hadn't, and he felt uniquely qualified to help his group win the round.

By the time rehearsal was over, they'd agreed on an approach. Black and Christina were walking back to the house with Rooster when Black's phone interrupted them. He glanced at the number and excused himself.

"Roxie, what have you got?"

"I sent your buddy Stan the list three days ago, along with the preliminary info. Didn't he call you?"

"No, and I sort of forgot."

"I've come up with a lot more since then."

"Really? Like what?"

"I already sent it to your email."

"Give me the highlights."

"Everyone's got baggage. Some more than others."

"Can you be more specific?"

"Rooster. He's got an axe to grind with Simon, the producer."

"He does?"

"Yes. Back in the day, Simon signed him to his label and basically took him to the cleaners. Rooster had to declare bankruptcy in the nineties. So he could be holding a grudge against Simon."

"Then why would Simon have him on the show?" Black asked, thinking out loud.

"Could be he feels guilty? Or maybe they reconciled and it's all ancient history. But it's out there, and if Rooster was feeling pissy…"

"Good find. Who else?"

"Simon himself. He might be trying to influence the outcome. He's got a management company in addition to the production company, and Alex is signed to it."

"Yeah, but I bet if you look back at the timing, Alex signed after he won the show. The prize this year is a recording contract, but what do you want to bet Simon puts the full court press on the winners to have him guide their career?"

"Could be. I didn't think of that."

"Who else?"

"Well, I hate saying this, but you've probably already thought of it. Alex benefitted pretty significantly."

"He did. But why would he be trying to game it this year? That part makes no sense."

"No, but I wanted to be impartial, so I included it. Although I can state pretty categorically that he wouldn't do something like that," Roxie said.

"Anyone else?"

"I haven't turned up anything on Christina, Peter, or Sarah. Why do you have them down as suspicious?"

"Christina was angry and hurt over Rick and Sarah last year. That could have driven her to mess with him."

"Weak. No way would she throw the contest to get back at a boyfriend."

"Agreed. But I don't want to assume anything. And she could be messing with bands this year to improve her odds of a win."

"Same with Peter?"

Black grunted. "Basically."

"I don't know. Sounds like science fiction from here."

"I know it does. But they could also be working together. Peter does the sabotage part, and she's the mastermind. He was with Rick at the bar last year."

"Right, but so was Rooster," Roxie said.

"I know. Which brings us to Sarah."

"And why would she be sabotaging anyone?"

"Maybe she did it last year to get even with Rick for calling it off?"

"Why this year?"

"I've been watching her. She's pretty friendly with the lead singer for Bend in the Creek."

"He's a hunk. If you go in for that redneck charm thing," Roxie agreed. "So your theory is she could be edging the odds in their favor?"

"I know. Doesn't sound convincing, does it?"

"Not really."

"That's what I was afraid you'd say."

"It's all in your email. Now I have to get back to driving Miss Daisy. She's like that wicked witch in *The Wizard of Oz*, and I'm Toto."

"They were a great band. Little saccharine, but a lot of hits."

"You don't get out much, do you?"

"What?"

"Nothing. Is there anything else?"

"Not right now. I appreciate you doing this."

"I appreciate the three hundred smackers."

"Ah. Yes. How could I forget? I get paid on Friday. I'll go to an ATM, and whenever you come by to see Mugsy…"

"I already wrote a company check and cashed it."

"How?"

"I forged your signature, of course."

"Of course."

"I should have never told you – you'd never have known. I do the books. It's the perfect plan."

"I'm glad you're more honest than that."

"Next time I'll give myself a little bonus. See you later, boss."

Black stared at the phone and then slid it back into his shirt pocket. Overhead, a stippling of stars glimmered in the night sky as a dark fog crept in from the coast. The vista was idyllic, and he took a moment to absorb the tranquility before heading back into the house, where the camera crew would be filming the bickering that had become the norm between the competing band members at dinner as the stakes increased with each round. A part of him couldn't wait to get clear of the show, but another had awakened and was commanding an increasing share of his attention: the part that wanted to win and be on stage, touring, the stuff of teenage dreams.

The real question in his mind was whether that was a good thing or bad. He figured he'd take it up with Kelso on the next call, and whatever the quack recommended, he'd do the opposite. Assuming he could tie the slippery therapist down. Kelso could avoid a direct answer more effectively than a politician, which Black supposed they taught first year in shrink school.

He pushed the front doors open, and Ed greeted him with a whoop. The party was already starting, and Black would have to pull his weight and take one for the band. Fortunately he was thirsty. Especially since Roxie had managed to do nothing but muddy the already murky waters, leaving him with even less direction than he'd had before talking to her.

Christina appeared wearing leggings and a purple tube top that would have gotten attention from a corpse. The camera caressed her like a lover, and Black acknowledged that she knew how to play the TV game as well as anyone.

"Come on, big boy. I'll buy you a cocktail," she said, mischief twinkling in her eyes.

"It seems rude to turn down a scantily clad woman bearing drinks," Black conceded. "Let me go check on Mugsy, and I'll be right down."

"It's a date, Sensei."

Black hoped against hope that the exchange would get left on the cutting-room floor; otherwise he could expect more difficulty from Sylvia. But he had a part to play, and as they were nearing the finish line, it wasn't the time to go conservative on the viewers. If he had to down some brews with a gorgeous nubile as a concession to ratings, what could he say?

After all. The show must go on.

Chapter 26

The morning of the recording session, Black was awakened by Terrence barging into the bedroom, a look of rage etched on his petulant face. Ed sat up, groggy, even as Black tried to assimilate what was happening.

"Where is he? I'll kill him," Terrence hissed.

"Who?" Ed asked.

"Yeah, Terrence. What's up?" Black echoed.

"That damned cat."

"Mugsy?" Black asked, looking around. Ed shifted the covers, and there was Mugsy, looking innocent as a lamb. "Why? What did he do?"

"I can't breathe. He must have gotten into my room. I told you to keep him in here," Terrence said.

"I have. He's been confined to this room ever since you threw your hissy fit," Black countered.

"He got in. Somehow. And now my eyes are swollen shut and my throat's on fire. Listen to me!"

Black had to admit he sounded hoarse and raspy.

"Take a pill. If it's an allergy, won't that knock it out?"

"It's not that simple," Terrence whimpered. "You did this so you could win the round. You knew today was the big day."

Black threw the covers off and stood. Terrence was about as threatening as the baristas Black jousted with routinely, all attitude and snark. "That's a pretty ugly accusation, Terrence. Do you have any proof?"

"Listen to me. That's the proof."

"Maybe you caught a cold," Ed said helpfully.

"Or maybe something else triggered it," Black added. "But storming in here and throwing around wild accusations...Terrence, I think you'd better leave."

"Make me," Terrence said, his hands on his hips.

Black moved to Ed's bed and hoisted Mugsy, holding the bloated feline in front of him like kryptonite. An expression of horror flashed across Terrence's face and he fled. Black shrugged as he moved to the door, kicked it shut, and then tossed the cat back onto Ed's bed. Mugsy, no worse for wear, promptly burrowed into the covers with an annoyed grunt and resumed sleeping.

"What's with Sybil there? He can't really believe we'd put Mugsy in his room to screw him over," Ed said.

"Who knows? Maybe it's that time of the month."

"He did sound terrible."

"I know. But that doesn't mean we slipped him cat dander."

"Cat dander?"

"Never mind. Although...I mean, it's theoretically possible that someone let Mugsy out, maybe when the cleaning crew was here, and he got into Terrence's room..."

"But if so, that has nothing to do with us," Ed said.

"Right. Which is why I'm not going to worry about it. We've got a big day ahead of us. Terrence can deal with his issues. We've got our own," Black said, although privately he was wondering whether Terrence's incapacitation couldn't be the latest act of sabotage.

The ride to the studio took an hour, and when Last Call arrived, they were shown into the waiting room as two heavyset men unloaded their amplifiers and instruments. Rooster was already there, joking with the engineers, and again Black had a hard time envisioning him involved in anything underhanded. He seemed as excited by their wins as they did, and Black couldn't reconcile the aging bluesman with the picture Roxie's financial data had painted.

The cameraman recorded their arrival and setup, to be spliced into a montage for the show that afternoon once everyone's sessions were over. Each band was in a different studio, but all were state-of-the-art, so there would be no difference in the finished product other than the abilities and performance of the artists.

It took thirty minutes to get tones on the bass and guitar. Ed announced he was happy with the house drum kit, which was already isolated, microphones in place. They ran a couple of practice tries at the song, instruments only, and cut the basic track in one take. Next, Black laid down the lead and a second rhythm guitar, which after three tries he was satisfied with, and then it was Christina's turn. Black watched from the control room as she knocked out the vocals like a pro, requiring very few punch-ins to correct any inconsistencies. They finished with the background harmonies, which for expedience they blew through in two takes per chorus.

Rooster did a rough mix, with the final version that would be judged by the audience to be finished by the engineers as Rooster acted as producer. When the final tones had faded, Rooster gave Black a high five.

"Yeah. That's what I'm talking about! You guys are magic. Really. That's a solid ten performance. You should be proud." He stood and moved to Christina. He hugged her and whispered in her ear, "You're a star, baby. You watch. Audience is going to go berserk for this."

That evening, all three bands gathered at a televised ceremony where they performed their renditions live. Terrence was still struggling, and Strobe's performance didn't come close to Bend in the Creek's or Last Call's. Even before the studio version of each band's take was aired, it was obvious to everyone that Strobe was the night's loser. Black felt sorry for Terrence as he wept quietly into his hands when the results were announced, but more than that, the niggling conviction that Strobe's demise had been preordained had Black on edge.

The judges gave their obligatory pep talk once Strobe had been shown the exit, but it rang hollow in Black's ears. They were now down to two bands, and Black suspected that whoever was rigging things didn't have his best interests in mind. On the ride back to Malibu, Christina nudged Black with her elbow.

"What's wrong? We did great."

"I don't know. It just seems like something fishy's going on. Botched mixes, lost samples, food poisoning, now this...don't you get the feeling we're just pawns?" Black asked.

"What are you talking about? We won that last round fair and square."

"True, but Strobe was taken out of the running. Terrence couldn't compete. Don't get me wrong – I'm not saying that he would have done better than us. I'm saying that he never got the chance."

Christina frowned and shook her head. "I don't get you. We're down to the finals. Months of hard work are paying off. Why are you stressing over Terrence? You hated him. I could tell."

"It's not so much Terrence. It's that if we're not winning fair and square, the whole thing could be called into question at some point, and that'll diminish everyone who's participating. I want to win. But I don't want to feel like I did because somebody fiddled the game."

"I don't know what's eating at you, but I'm not going to let it affect me. We need to give a hundred ten percent for this last round, Black. That means everyone."

He nodded. "I know. I intend to. Trust me on that. Maybe I'm just paranoid. They're...the police are treating Rick's death as a homicide."

Christina's eyes widened. "How do you know that?"

"I have a buddy who knows somebody. Point is, the cops don't think it was an accident." Black watched her face for ticks or other giveaways, but got nothing but shock in return.

"You're joking."

"I wish I was."

The rest of the ride went by in silence as Christina absorbed Black's news. When the van arrived at the iron gates at the bottom of the drive, Black wasn't sure whether the bars were to protect the mansion or to imprison the residents.

But with the finals only two weeks away, he wouldn't have to wait long to find out.

The cameraman filmed them as they filed through the door, their mood glum, completely out of keeping with a group that had just gotten its second perfect ten score of the show. Christina took the stairs two at a time as Black, Ed, and Peter moved into the kitchen for celebratory beers. After two bottles, Black went out on the pool deck and called Sylvia. The sound of her voice had a calming effect on him, and when Ed joined him, carrying an ice bucket with four more beers in it, he felt relaxed for the first time since he'd awakened that morning.

The beers came and went, and by the time Black mounted the stairs, Christina having never put in an appearance, his head was spinning, his best intentions trumped by Ed's coaxing and a desire to numb his racing thoughts. When he opened the bedroom door, his movements clumsy, Mugsy eyed him with disapproval.

"Screw you, Mugsy. Don't you dare judge me."

Mugsy snorted and laid his head back on the pillow as though deeming any response unfit, and as Black brushed his teeth, the cat was already snoring, his conscience clear as a mountain stream. Black returned to his bed and studied the corpulent feline's furry face before crawling under the covers, envying him the simplicity of his existence. Ed remained downstairs, youth working its miracle even as the soporific effect of the beer had its way with Black. The last thing he registered before he was out cold were Mugsy's jowls puffing from breathing, the rumble of his emanations oddly comforting to Black as he drifted into oblivion, free for a brief while from his earthly concerns.

Chapter 27

The second season, the final elimination round would feature both acts playing two songs apiece – a concession to the prior year's criticisms that one song was inadequate to crown a new champion. Each band would perform a song of its choosing along with one selected at random. Much discussion and strategy had gone into the choice, and after considerable back and forth, Christina's unusual preference of a Gloria Gaynor classic made the cut: "I Will Survive". Black was familiar with several versions that had taken the familiar tune and twisted it to serve new masters, and the band rose to the challenge over the next two weeks, imbuing it with new life. Christina's logic in lobbying for the standard was that it was so far from a rock band's comfort zone it would demonstrate the group's versatility.

When they received their mandatory selection, everyone was agape at how to best pull it off. Madonna's "Like a Virgin" was not exactly the stuff from which rock dreams were made, and it took several days of experimentation before they settled on a rendition that didn't sound like a bag of cats.

Midweek before the finals, they were scheduled for a night out at a Los Angeles rock club, presumably so the cameras could catch the local wildlife in full roar. The group hit town at 11:00, and Black's sense of dislocation grew stronger as the night progressed. The crowd was at least ten years younger than he was, and the few old timers looked worse for wear. Three beers into it, the headlining band was grinding away, and Black's head had started to hurt. A shapely young woman in denim and leather had been flirting with him for half an hour, and when she suggested he follow her outside for a cigarette, his headache screamed yes even as his conscience said no.

Cigarettes won, although at the last minute guilt made him decline her offer of one. She lit hers with a dented steel flip-top lighter, and Black asked the obligatory questions. Stacy was a cosmetologist from the Valley, single, and loved to party. She had gorgeous eyes, Black thought, as he wondered whether it was the beer talking. He was musing that the band thing wasn't so terrible after all when two youths in oversized basketball jerseys and baggy pants approached from down the sidewalk.

"Yo. Sweetness. You got a smoke for a playah?" the taller of the two said, eyeing her up and down.

"Um, no. Not really."

"Come on, baby doll. Break loose for me."

Stacy looked to Black, her eyes nervous. Black stepped forward. "She said she doesn't have a cigarette."

"What you lookin' at, grandpa? I talkin' to you?" the tough snarled.

"Hey, guys. We don't want any trouble, okay?" Black said, hands raised in front of him, trying to defuse the tension. He barely registered the shorter youth swing a pipe at him, cracking one of his ribs as he went down. Both punks began kicking him, their construction boots thumping into his torso as he folded his arms to shield his face with his elbows. The smaller one hit him with the pipe again, but because of the angle it glanced off his forearm, instantly rendering it numb. He was waiting for Stacy to scream, but instead all he heard was her heels snicking against the sidewalk as she ran back to the club entrance. After sustaining a dozen well-placed kicks, one of the club bouncers cried out from the front doors, and the two assailants ran back down the street.

"You okay, buddy?" the heavyset bouncer asked as he approached. Black heard a motor rev and looked up just in time to see an old Chrysler K car peel away from the curb. He blinked, trying to focus as it rounded the corner and disappeared. Another vehicle pulled from a slot across the street – a Buick, Black thought, noting its lights were off until halfway down the block. He raised a hand to his mouth, and his fingers came away with blood. He flexed them to ensure he hadn't broken one, and they worked, although he felt like his ribs and back had been run over by a truck.

"Yeah. I think so. Just give me a minute," Black said, trying to clear his head. He couldn't be sure, but he thought he'd recognized the Buick driver's profile when the man had turned to ensure he wasn't going to get hit by oncoming traffic. Although nothing made any sense.

Another bouncer arrived. Stacy was nowhere to be found as he struggled to his feet, assisted by the two security men.

"You better get to a hospital, buddy," the second bouncer advised.

Black shrugged them off. He'd been through worse.

But now he needed to figure out why Rooster would be parked outside of a club in an old Buick while Black was beaten senseless.

Chapter 28

"You sure you're all right?" Ed asked, watching Black tape his ribs, Mugsy's eyes boring into him from the bed.

"Yeah. There's nothing a doctor can do besides charge me a thousand dollars to confirm the rib's broken."

"What about filing a police report?"

Black shook his head. "Is my face bad?"

"You've got a fat lip, but it looks like they missed it. Mostly. You're lucky you were wearing that heavy leather jacket. That probably saved your arms and back from the worst of it."

"Sounds like you're speaking from experience."

"I've been in a scrap or two."

Black nodded. "Me too. Back in the day. But it's been a while."

"How are your hands?"

"I kept them balled up. The right one hurts, but that's my picking hand. Left one's fine. The ice took down the swelling, so I should be good to go by tomorrow."

"That was close."

"Tell me about it. It was a broken hand that lost me the world tour with my band. I don't have to tell you how that would feel if it happened again." As he spoke, a thought occurred to him: Rooster knew his history. Regardless of what Black said, the media would assume he'd lost it in a fit of rage, just like he had before. It wasn't a bad setup. Assuming it was Rooster behind the wheel and not one of ten thousand men in Los Angeles who looked like him.

"You'll probably have a bruise on your face."

"Nothing a little makeup and no shaving for three days won't cure."

"What about the cameras?"

"I told Sarah that I was coming down with the flu, which is why I took a taxi home. It was so dark in the club she didn't notice anything. I figure I'll make a miraculous recovery just in time to play. They're never around when we rehearse these days, so all I have to do is get to and from the rehearsal studio and I'm golden."

"Man. What a crummy break."

"Yeah. I know. But you play the hand you're dealt." Black finished with the tape and tossed it to Ed. "Is there any way you can get me a shot of Jack and a brew? For medicinal purposes, of course."

"You bet. Give me two minutes."

Ed left, and Black dialed Stan's cell. When he answered, he sounded out of it.

"Hell – hello?"

"Stan. Black. Sorry to call so late."

Stan groaned. "It's not late. It's two in the frigging morning. Have you lost your mind?"

"I presume that's a rhetorical question. Listen. I don't have much time. I was attacked outside a club tonight. I think it was Rooster who organized it." Black told him what had happened.

A long pause greeted Black's disclosure.

"You called me at two in the morning to tell me that you think your coach perpetrated assault and battery? You do realize I work homicide, right?"

"I think he's got something to do with Rick's death. The only thing that makes sense is that he was trying to injure me badly enough that I can't play on Saturday."

"Did you file a police report?"

"What good would it do? You know it'll just be filed and forgotten."

"They could check traffic cams."

Black paused. "Damn. I didn't think about that."

"Have you been drinking?"

"Not enough. Is it too late to file one, you think?" Black asked.

"Where are you?"

"Malibu."

"So you're going to drive back to L.A. and file a report that two punks beat you up? You should have done it while you were at the scene. It would have been taken a lot more seriously."

"But will it do any good if I file one now?"

"I should tell you yes, just so you stay up all night doing it. But the truth is, not a chance."

"That's what I was afraid of. What about the traffic cameras?"

"I was kidding. No way will the department devote that kind of manpower to a beating. Unless you're in the ICU. Is that too much to hope for?" Stan asked.

"Just a broken rib and some bruises."

"Then you're hosed."

"Back to Rooster. I think it was him."

"*Think*. As in, you aren't a hundred percent sure."

"It was dark, and I just had the shit kicked out of me."

"I'll take a hard look at this Rooster character tomorrow, okay? That's all I can promise. Hate to say it, pal, but right now you don't have squat."

Ed returned, a highball glass with two inches of bourbon in one hand and two Heinekens in the other. Black gave him a feeble wave.

"Sorry to call so late. We can talk tomorrow," Black said.

"Not if my caller ID's working."

Black hung up and tossed the phone on his bed before gratefully taking the drinks from Ed. He polished the bourbon in three swallows and winced as it burned going down, and then drained half his beer before holding the bottle up in a toast.

"Thanks, man. That hits the spot," Black said.

Ed clinked his beer against Black's. "Damn. The man was thirsty."

"I get that way."

Ed yawned, and Mugsy joined him, his mouth open, any feline amusement from watching the show now over as he lost valuable beauty rest. Black shuffled to the bathroom and gulped the remainder of his beer. He set it on the vanity as he studied his reflection in the mirror. The area around his mouth was discoloring, but it wasn't terrible, and would fade to amber by Saturday, with any luck. Worst case he would come up with a story about tripping and falling for Sarah and the crew. Ed would keep his secret.

As his red eyes looked back at him, he wondered why the band's coach would be setting him up for failure, and no matter how he turned the problem over, none of the answers made sense.

Chapter 29

Black remained in bed the following day. Ed brought him a cinnamon roll for breakfast and a sandwich for lunch. Christina ducked her head in that afternoon, and Black reassured her that he'd make rehearsal at the usual time.

"Why all the secrecy about being in a fight, Black?" she asked. "I don't get it."

"It's a long story."

"Try me."

He told her about his aborted musical career's abrupt end, and when he was done, she nodded. "Oh. Yeah, I could see why you wouldn't want all that dredged up again."

"The flu seems a lot better."

"Now it does."

Black tried a smile, but his lip protested. "Have you heard from Rooster?"

"No. Should I?"

"He's going to be at rehearsal tonight, isn't he?"

"Should be. He hasn't missed one yet. Why?"

"Nothing special. I just want to hear how he thinks the tunes sound."

She looked at him, her brow furrowed. "You sure you didn't hit your head? Why would anything be different than it was yesterday?"

"Maybe I'm just feeling clingy and need some reassurance."

She shook her head. "Get some rest, Black. Don't worry, I'll keep quiet about your adventure. You're sick as a dog if anyone asks."

"I appreciate it."

"Just make sure you play like Hendrix and we're square."

He winked at her. "That's my middle name."

"Hendrix?"

"Square."

When Black made it to the rehearsal studio at five, Rooster was already there. He looked up as Black entered and gave him his usual shuck and jive smile, then finished making his point to Peter, underscoring it with jabs of his pen. Black walked slowly to the cooler containing a twelve-pack of beer and cracked a can open. Rooster turned to him.

"I hear you're under the weather."

"Nothing clean living and the Lord's love won't fix."

"What's wrong with you?"

"I tripped and fell off a curb. I'm fine," Black said, trying to keep it light.

"Oh. Christina told me you had the flu. I was worried about you getting everyone sick," Rooster said uncertainly.

Christina cleared her throat. "I must have gotten my wires crossed."

"Just some aches and pains. Nothing life-threatening," Black assured him, making his way to his amp. Peter watched him move stiffly.

"You going to be okay for Saturday? You look kind of worked," Peter commented.

"Never better. It's just old age creeping into my bones."

Peter's eyes narrowed. "Nice bruise on your face. That from the curb?"

"No, that was a door knob. I was trying to catch Mugsy and wasn't watching what I was doing."

"Seems like we're going to have to pack you in bubble wrap for the next couple of days," Rooster said. Black tried to detect any unusual tension in Rooster's voice, but couldn't be sure. If Rooster had tried to have him taken down, he was a good actor. Then again, having been in the music business for half a century, he'd have to be.

Rehearsal went well, and Black was pleased to note that even though his right hand hurt like a bitch, it hadn't interfered with his picking technique. After two hours of drilling the music, they switched to working out how they would move during the performance, leaving nothing to chance as they agreed on who would run where, whose microphone Peter and Black would use when they paired up on a single mic for the second chorus, and when Black would stand back to back with Christina while she leaned against him on the final coda. Rooster seemed his usual self, and by the end of the practice Black was undecided about him. Maybe he'd gotten it wrong, and whoever was in the car was someone unrelated.

After wiping down his guitar and putting it back into the case, Black stood and approached the bluesman.

"What do you think?"

"Magic, is what I think. Bend in the Creek's going to have a tough time, that's for sure."

Black nodded. "I hope you're right. By the way, I thought I saw you the other day in town. What kind of car do you drive?"

Rooster glanced at the door – a momentary darting of the eyes that he quickly corrected, but not before Black noticed it.

"BMW. Germans know a thing or two about making a car."

"I've always preferred American. You know. Cadillac. Buick."

Rooster glanced away again. "It takes all kinds. Give me a Benz or a Beemer any day."

Christina looked at Black with a flicker of hesitation. "It's sounding pretty damned good now. If we can deliver like we just did, we should sweep the finals. Just do me a favor and stay away from the booze on Saturday, would you?"

"That seems reasonable."

"And watch your step around dangerous curbs."

"Sound words," Black agreed.

"Door knobs, too," Peter said dryly.

"I'll be the boy in the plastic bubble. Living in a Nerf world. I swear."

Rehearsal broke up, and Rooster didn't linger. Black made a point of standing outside the rehearsal room and watching him as he walked down the curving drive to where his car was parked at the front gates. Black debated following him on a pretense, but couldn't think of anything plausible and decided that it didn't matter. If Rooster was behind the sabotage attempts he was on notice, and if he wasn't, Black was wasting his time. He gave Ed a high five and finished his beer before walking back to the mansion as he dialed Roxie on his cell.

"Hey, boss. What's up?"

Black told her about the assault.

"But you're fine?" she asked.

"So far, so good. When you were digging on Rooster, did you find anything that you thought was unimportant that you left out of what you sent me?"

"Oh, you mean like he's the head of the 18th Street gang or something?"

"Yeah, like that."

"That would be a negative, chief. You know everything I do."

"Crap." Black thought for a moment and softened his tone. "How are things on your end?"

"I'm looking forward to my last day here. It's been like three months at the Hanoi Hilton. I kind of want to kill myself, but don't want to give the old bat the satisfaction."

"Come Monday, one way or another, consider yourself back at work."

"I'll believe that when I see it. What if you win? You're going to be busy with record deals and tours."

"Then I'll need an administrative assistant to manage things. Besides, since all you do is feed Mugsy between rounds of Grand Theft Auto, what's the difference?"

"Wow. Someone woke up with a hangover this morning."

"I wish. When are you planning to lower the boom on her?"

"Probably Saturday. I've already sweet-talked someone I hate into taking over for me."

"Short notice."

"I want to get paid on Friday. You don't know this woman. She'd totally stiff me if she thought I was leaving. I work for the Gorgon."

Black cleared his throat and spoke in a booming voice. "Release the Kraken!"

"It really freaks me out when you do that."

"It's the little things."

"Oh, and this is pretty cool. Alex is taking me to Mexico tomorrow night for dinner."

"How nice. Anyplace in particular?" he asked between clenched teeth.

"Ensenada. Apparently there's a really nice restaurant on the water just north of town."

"I thought he was still on tour."

"He'll be back for the finals on Saturday, and he's flying in the day before."

"Must be nice to have a private jet."

"Hey, you'll be in that life pretty soon as long as you don't cheese the last round."

"We're sounding good. I'm not worried."

"Bend in the Creek was great the last couple of shows."

"Our scores were better."

"I'm just saying. Wouldn't want anyone to get too cocky. Pride goeth and all."

"Always a delight, Roxie."

"When can I pick up Mugsy?"

"Win or lose, we're out of the mansion on Sunday. But that's okay. Sylvia and I can take him to the office. She's bringing my car in the morning."

"Cool. Is she going to the finals?"

"I think so."

"You haven't asked?"

Black paused. "I kind of suck, huh?"

"Better get busy. I'd have already dumped you."

"Good to know."

"You're welcome."

Black's next call was to Stan, who didn't have good news. "I questioned your chicken guy today."

"Rooster."

"Like I said."

"What did you think?"

"He was nervous, but most people are when I'm asking them questions. Bottom line is he has an alibi for the night Rick was killed. It checked out, which only rules him out as being there holding the needle."

"But if he hired somebody..."

"Exactly. Look, buddy, Rick's case is colder than a Kardashian divorce attorney. We're not getting anywhere, and I have probably thirty newer ones. Barring a sworn confession, this one ain't gonna get cleared. If Chicken Boy—"

"Rooster."

"Whatever. If he killed Rick, he's going to get away with it. That's the short version."

"I was afraid you'd say that."

"Sorry. But based on the beating you took, I'd stay locked in the mansion until the show starts. Along with everyone else in the band. Just to be safe."

"That occurred to me."

"I'll bet it did. Every time you lay eyes on Christina, my future ex-wife."

"I can introduce you once the show's finished. I'm sure she'd love to look at your sport jacket collection."

"Be still my beating heart."

"Thanks for sweating Rooster."

"You owe me a date with the hottie. Don't forget."

"I may have to drug her."

"Details."

Chapter 30

Roxie dabbed on a little more lip gloss and checked the time. The limo Alex was sending to take her across the border would be there any minute. She adjusted the red camisole and inspected herself in the mirror, noting how her black leather pants highlighted her slim hips and long legs, and the top displayed her tattoos in a flattering way, her arm ink accented by two inches of bangle bracelets on each wrist. After a final glance around her apartment, she dropped her cell phone and passport into a small purse and headed for the front door, taking care to turn off the lights as she left.

Downstairs a limo waited at the curb with a black-suited driver standing by its side, his hands folded in front of him as he watched her near. When she reached him, he nodded.

"Good evening."

"Hi."

He held open the door, and she climbed in. Once they were on the road, she leaned forward.

"How long will it take to get to the restaurant?"

"Three hours, if traffic permits. I was told your dinner reservation was at ten?"

"Yes. A late one."

"We'll be in the carpool lane all the way to the border, so we might make better time."

"I hope so."

"There's a screen and a control by your side if you want to watch movies. Several hundred of them on the disk. The same control works the sound system if you prefer music."

"Great."

"I'll put the privacy window up. The red button on the console is the intercom if you require anything. Will there be anything else?"

"No. You know how to get there?"

"I'm familiar with the restaurant."

Roxie thought for a second. "What's your name?"

"Jacobs."

She smiled to herself. Alex didn't do things in half measures. His concert in Arizona would be over by 8:00, and he'd be flying into Tijuana airport. They'd be staying at a beachfront villa down the coast and returning on Saturday for the show – the perfect spontaneous getaway in a romantic, exotic place.

Roxie had never been anywhere in Mexico besides Tijuana four years earlier with two of her bandmates, so she didn't know what to expect, but Alex had told her that the restaurant and villa were nothing like the border town. She was relieved; her memories of Mexico were of trash-clogged streets and junker cars spewing exhaust into the sky, with clumps of sketchy characters loitering outside the seedy bars, intent on preying upon drunken tourists.

She settled in as the limo rolled onto I-5 south, the freeway a sea of brake lights except for the car pool lane, which was moving at a rapid pace. The giddy sense of privilege, of being ensconced in luxury as she sped to Mexico, increased as she watched the rank and file sitting gridlocked in ugly commuter reality. She played with the remote control buttons, and a screen rose from the console at the front of the compartment. Within minutes she was watching *Team America* and laughing out loud.

The trip to San Diego seemed to take only moments, and before she knew it, the closing titles were drifting up the screen as the big car powered through Chula Vista, the border only scant miles away. She shut off the television and watched the glowing lights of the southernmost reaches of California glide by, and then they were at the crossing, all ugly glare and flashing warnings and armed border patrol agents.

The toll road to Ensenada was closed due to a landslide that had claimed half a mile of highway, and they wound up on the free road, which added considerable delay. By the time they reached the restaurant it was already 10:00, and Roxie hastily stepped from the car and into the velvet-walled lobby. The host showed her to a table in a private section of the restaurant, where she was alone, unobserved by the general dining public in the main room. A tuxedoed waiter brought her a margarita on the rocks, and she watched the waves crashing below her as she sipped at it, checking the time every few minutes.

After another quarter of an hour, a handsome thirty-something man in a blue suit approached the table.

"Roxie?" No trace of an accent.

Roxie set her empty margarita glass down. "Yes?"

"My name's Tony. I have to apologize. Alex is running really late. He asked me to come get you and take you to the villa. He's arranged for a private chef there."

"Really?"

"Yes, it's all taken care of. Again, sorry, but air traffic conspired against him this time. Can I get you another drink, or would you like me to pay the bill so you can get going?"

"Oh, wow, well, how long will he be?"

"Maybe another half hour or so." Tony smiled disarmingly and looked through the picture window at the surf, where the lights from the restaurant reflected off the surge.

"Might as well pay up. There's tequila at the villa, right?"

"Of course. A full bar."

Roxie rose, and Tony tossed a twenty-dollar bill on the table and nodded to the waiter. He led her outside, where a forest green SUV waited. Tony moved to open the rear door for her.

"Where's Jacobs?" she asked and froze when she saw the ugly muzzle of a snub-nose revolver in Tony's hand.

"Get in. Make a sound, I'll brain you. There's nobody around to help you, so it's a question of whether you want to get hurt or not," he snarled, the vestige of civility gone. "And worse comes to worst, I'll shoot you."

Roxie's eyes widened as she took in the weapon, and then Tony's powerful hand was on her arm, forcing her into the car. Another man sat on the rear bench seat, a pistol trained on her.

"Relax, princess. Don't make no trouble and you'll be fine," he snarled.

"What is this?" she demanded as Tony slammed the door and moved to the driver's seat.

"What does it look like? Lonely hearts club meeting," the man said.

The big engine revved, and they were out of the parking area in seconds and on the road south, the air thick with salt and exhaust. Tony caught Roxie's frightened glance in the rearview mirror. "Just do as we say and everything'll be okay. You understand?"

"Where's Alex?"

"You're not a smart one, are you? Guess they weren't handing out brains in the beauty line that day."

"He's not waiting for me, is he?"

"Here's how this is going to work. We're going to pull past a guard gate, where you're not going to make a peep. You do, they'll be scraping your brains off the window. Do you understand?"

Roxie nodded, the pressure from the unidentified man's gun in her ribs unmistakable. "Just don't hurt me."

"Just take it nice and easy. It'll be over before you know it."

"So this is a kidnapping?"

"Keep your piehole shut. *Capisce?*" the gunman hissed.

She didn't say anything. Soon they were pulling down a long drive alongside a large hotel. At the guarded barrier she did as instructed, and Tony gave the security man a salute and offered a few words of Spanish. The guard laughed and waved them through, and then they were pulling down a gentle rise toward a marina where at least a hundred yachts rocked at the docks in the darkness. Tony drove to the far end of the parking area, cloaked in gloom, and killed the engine.

"Put the tape over her mouth," he ordered as he held his gun on her. The other man unrolled a strip of duct tape and plastered it across her face. Roxie glared hatred at him, and Tony chuckled. "You're a handful, aren't you? Come on. Let's go."

The two men manhandled her out of the SUV and down a ramp to one of the shoreline security gates, where he swiped a card and pushed the steel door open. Halfway down the dock a fifty-eight-foot motor yacht brooded in the dark, the water in front of it silvered by the moon as it tugged at the dock lines. Tony stepped up a set of stairs and hopped aboard, then nodded to his companion. He pushed Roxie up, and Tony caught her as she almost went down, her feet slipping on the condensation.

The interior of the yacht was spacious, the salon rich red teak. Tony led her below to the aft stateroom and, with a swift gesture, ripped the tape off her mouth, leaving a pink welt in its wake.

"Ow. That hurt."

Tony ignored her. "These are the rules. No noise or it gets worse for you – much worse. No stupid escape or sabotage attempts, or I beat you senseless for fun. Just be a nice girl, keep quiet, and you'll get out of this fine. Try anything and it'll be your worst nightmare. My partner there would love a shot at you, if you know what I mean, so if you want to test me, there won't be any second warning, just pain and him, all night long." He paused to ensure it was sinking in. "This is for real. Do I need to knock out some teeth so you take me seriously?"

Roxie shook her head, clearly terrified.

"Good. There's a little bathroom in there. None of the windows open, so don't bother trying. And remember what I said – break one, you become a sex toy for big boy."

The door slammed behind Tony, and Roxie took in the dark surroundings. A platform bed occupied the center of the stateroom, and there were only two doors – the exit and the bathroom. She groped along the edge of the bed and felt for one of the small lamps mounted above it, but received nothing for her efforts but a click when she turned the switch. She felt inside of the fixture. No bulb. The other was the same story.

The bathroom was pitch black, but as her eyes adjusted, she could make out the commode and a sink wedged next to a shower stall. Dim light filtered in through the high, small window, and she remembered Tony's words about escape.

Roxie sat on the bed and cried as the boat gently rocked from the swell inside the protected harbor. The heavy nylon lines groaned softly over her muffled sobs as her dream getaway with Alex transformed into a trip to hell.

Up in the salon, Tony poured himself several fingers of Scotch over ice and sat in one of the two barrel chairs. "Toss her phone overboard, Bobby, and take a load off."

"You got it," Bobby agreed and slipped the iPhone out of Roxie's purse and moved up to the deck. Tony heard a muffled splash, and Bobby returned. "I hope there's beer."

"I'm sure of it."

Bobby went to the refrigerator and grunted. "*Dos* what? What happened to Bud?"

"Come on. Beer's beer."

Bobby reluctantly opened a bottle and lowered himself onto the couch that sat beneath one of the salon's windows.

"What time do we call this Black bozo?"

"The man said tomorrow at noon."

"Why wait?"

"Because it's after midnight, and the man wants him occupied tomorrow night. He's got to miss the show. Didn't I already explain this?"

"Why don't we just whack him? Why all the drama?" Bobby asked, then burped beer fumes.

"You're a pig."

Bobby burped again. "Oink."

"We whack him in the U.S. and that creates more problems. This way he just disappears."

"What about the girl? She's seen our faces."

"Doesn't matter. What happens in Mexico…"

"Then let me at her now."

"That isn't the deal. We're supposed to wait until we hear about whether this worked. We may need to put her on the phone to convince the guy. I don't want her in shock. Just hold your horses, all right?"

"Damned shame. She's a feisty-looking one, with that hair and them tats. I like 'em like that."

Down in the stateroom Roxie listened through the door, barely making out the words, but enough to understand that her hours were numbered. Shocked at the reality of her situation, she stood frozen, ear pressed against the slab of wood, as the captor named Bobby described exactly what he planned to do with her.

Eventually the discussion ended, and she stumbled back to the bed, already queasy from the rocking, the walls seeming to close in as her mind raced to formulate a plan to save herself before Bobby came for her.

Chapter 31

Ed's snores rumbled in the bedroom, Mugsy's softer drones a contretemps, making for a polyrhythmic moonlight sonata. Black rolled over, half asleep, wondering what had woken him. Something tugged at his awareness, but he tried to ignore it. Finally, he threw off the blanket and staggered to the bathroom, his eyes narrowed to slits in the faint light from the window. When he was done, he returned to bed, where the blinking red LED on his cell phone on the night table indicated he'd received a message. Black fumbled it to life and peered at the screen. He'd gotten one text from a number he didn't recognize.

Curiosity got the better of him, and he opened the message box. When he read the contents, he blinked rapidly, trying to clear his head, and then read carefully again. Fully alert, he got up and edged to where his pants and shirt were draped over the back of a chair and pulled them on before slipping out the door, barefoot, phone in hand.

The mansion was deathly quiet as he made his way down the stairs and outside to the pool deck. When he was far enough away from the house so he could talk without being overheard, he tapped a number in his speed dial. Stan's voice sounded even raspier than it had the other night.

"This better be good or I'm hanging up."

"I just got a text. I need your help," Black said.

"What? You can't read?"

"I'm serious. It's from Roxie. She's been kidnapped."

"Sure she has. Go sleep it off."

"I'm serious. The message says, 'Help, kidnapped in Ensenada, on a boat in harbor next to big hotel. Boat name *Downtime*. Roxie.' I don't think this is a hoax."

"What's she doing in Ensenada?" Stan demanded, sounding completely awake now in spite of it being three in the morning.

"She had a dinner date with that Alex guy from the show."

"In Mexico? Doesn't she know how dangerous it is down there?"

"What are we going to do?"

"Let me think for a minute."

"Do you have any contacts with the police south of the border?"

"Not really. They aren't very cooperative with us. Something about our government arranging for guns to make their way to the cartels, to be used against the local cops, rubbed them the wrong way."

"Then how are we going to save her?"

"I can try putting it through official channels. But they don't move that quickly, if at all." Stan paused. "You said she texted you?"

"Yes."

"You'd think the kidnappers would take her phone."

"Maybe they're not tech savvy?"

"They'd have to be brain dead. Did you try sending her a reply?"

"No."

"Why don't you? Verify it's really her. Ask her something only she would know."

"Okay. Hang on a second." Black typed in a fast question and pushed send. Twenty seconds later he got a response. "Dude, it's her."

"Ask her how many kidnappers."

Black did so, then read the answer out loud. "Only two that she knows of. But there could be others." Black heard Stan typing on his computer.

"She said it's a marina by a hotel?"

"Yeah. They were going to some restaurant on the coast, north of town. Why?"

"I'm on Google Earth, looking for marinas with a big hotel nearby. So far I only see one. Just a little north of the city. The main marina at the port is huge. Text her and ask her how big the marina is. How many boats."

Black did, and the response was immediate. "She guesses maybe a hundred. Mostly big."

"Bingo. That matches this one. Ask her what she's texting on."

Black tapped in his message and waited. His phone pinged and vibrated.

"Wrist phone her dragon lady gave her so she could always reach her." Black paused. "Really? I thought that was just in Dick Tracy or something. They have wrist phones?"

"You really don't get out much, do you? They're all the rage in some circles."

"Damn. She says to send help. She's in danger."

"Christ almighty. Fine. You're in Malibu, right?"

"Yeah."

"Do you have a car?"

"I'm not allowed to leave the house. And no, I don't have a car."

"Sounds like you better decide whether you want to save Roxie or obey your curfew."

"Screw it. I'll leave a note that I had a life or death emergency."

"I can be there in...give me an hour. I don't suppose you have your passport with you?"

"We'll have to stop by my place."

"There goes another hour. We're not going to be on the road till five or six at this rate. That won't put us into Ensenada until nine or ten. Depends on rush hour in Mexico."

"Do you have a plan?"

"You mean besides smuggling illegal firearms into Mexico and winging with an over-the-hill rocker to rescue his secretary?"

"Hey. Who's over the hill? I still have game."

"Sure you do, sport. I'll pick you up in an hour. What's the address?"

Chapter 32

Black was shivering from the chill at the bottom of the hill when Stan pulled up an hour and a half later in his 2011 Dodge Charger. Black was so used to seeing him in his undercover cruiser he had to do a double take at the apparition that seemed to float out of the fog.

"How the hell does anyone see out here?" Stan griped as Black got in.

"Beats me. Took you long enough, though."

"You try driving through pea soup. You're lucky I didn't wind up in the canyon."

Black pulled his door closed, and Stan eased the car forward. "It's only like this for a few miles, but it's rough going until we're out of it."

"I'd rather get there late than not at all."

"You heard anything more?"

"I got two more texts asking when we were going to rescue her."

"Have the kidnappers called?"

"Not yet. Assuming they call me at all."

"Why else would they have snatched her? Does she have family in town?"

"Not that I know of."

"There's your answer."

Black hesitated. "Maybe they want to get some cash out of Alex?"

"Possible. But frankly, right now, my money would be on him luring her across the border to facilitate a grab."

"Stan, the man's a star."

"Right. And everyone knows stars are never involved in anything shady. Just ask OJ."

"The last innocent man. You must be crabby."

"I don't do well on less than four hours of sleep."

"I hear you."

Black was in and out of his apartment in under five minutes with his passport in his back pocket and his Glock in his belt holster. Stan glanced at the gun as he got into the car.

"Possession of a firearm's a felony down there."

"Only if they catch you. Last time I was in TJ they didn't even stop the car."

"They aren't looking for much going south. Better hope it's our lucky day."

"You packing?"

"Of course. But not my service piece. An old spare. Untraceable."

"You old lawbreaker, you."

"Damn right."

The ride through Tijuana was uneventful, but the roads to Ensenada were clogged with traffic, the closure of the toll road causing massive congestion. By the time they made it to the marina, it was ten a.m., and it took a fifty-dollar bill and a story about meeting a friend at his boat to get them through the gate. They parked on the gravel lot adjacent to the docks, and Stan handed Black a pair of small binoculars.

"See if you can spot *Downtime*."

"I don't know… There are a lot of boats here."

"Better get started."

Stan opened his car door and got out, stretching his legs with a sigh.

Black glanced at him. "Where are you going?"

"I need to use the john. I'm guessing there's one up at the marina office."

"See if they have any coffee. I could use a gallon."

Ten minutes later Stan reappeared, accompanied by a short bald man with a swarthy complexion, who walked with him down to the nearest dock and unlocked the gate. Stan was gone for five minutes, and then the pair returned and repeated the performance at the next dock. Black was having a hard time seeing many of the transoms due to the angle, and was ready to get out of the car when Stan materialized by the rear fender.

"The boat's down on that dock," he said, motioning with his head. "About halfway down. Big sucker."

"You see any guards?"

"Nothing obvious."

"You have any thoughts on how to get aboard a boat in broad daylight without being shot to pieces by the kidnappers?"

"One thing at a time. Let's watch and wait. We might catch a break or see something we can use in our favor."

"So charging in guns blazing is out?"

"For now. But if we do that, you're going first."

"My turn for the bathroom run," Black said. "Didn't see any coffee?"

"The dock master said there's some in the hotel, but I didn't want to sidetrack him."

"How did you get him to show you around?"

"I told him I was thinking about moving my boat from Santa Monica and he got all flirty. Little peso signs blinking in his eyes."

Black trudged up the drive to the hotel, where he used the bathroom while waiting for one of the waiters in the downstairs restaurant to brew a pot of coffee. He bought two polystyrene cups of the rich dark roast and carried them past the large pool, where several couples were soaking up the late morning sun.

Two hours later they were no closer to saving Roxie than they had been when they arrived. Black had sent her another text message, and she confirmed that it was still only the two captors onboard. There were only a few people around, mostly local boat cleaners going about their chores. Black was almost ready to go back to the hotel for another bathroom break when *Downtime*'s cabin door opened and a dark-haired man wearing a dress shirt and suit slacks emerged. He stretched his arms over his head and glanced around before moving to the transom and hoisting himself onto the stairs. Stan and Black watched him stroll to the end of the dock and up the gangplank to the security door, which he pushed open.

Stan tapped Black's arm. "Get down. Duck."

Black slumped so he wasn't visible from the dock. They waited, holding their breath, and when they didn't hear an engine start, Stan peered over the dash.

"He's walking to the hotel. Probably to get lunch. This is our chance. You ready?"

"As ready as I'll ever be. But what exactly are we going to do?"

"I've been thinking. I know how to get us onboard without the other kidnapper getting wise. Or at least, buy us enough time to take him out."

"How?"

Stan watched a crew cleaning one of the nearby yachts, near the security gate, and turned to Black with a wan smile.

"How are your acting skills?"

"Are you kidding? For the last three months I've been playing a rock star."

"Good. We're going to need an Academy Award performance."

Chapter 33

Bobby absently picked at a scaly area on his beefy forearm. Every few minutes he stared at the aft stateroom door with lupine eyes, the thought of the young woman back there, defenseless, almost irresistible to him. They'd be making the call when Tony got back with sandwiches, and then, if all went well, the real fun would begin.

He stood and rubbed a calloused hand over his beard. They'd switched off three-hour shifts, but he hadn't been able to sleep. The woman's scent had drifted to his position on the couch like a taunt. He didn't understand why Tony was such a hardass, but he was senior to Bobby and as such, his word was law. They'd worked together on other jobs, mostly hits, and made a good team – Tony the brains, Bobby the brawn. Bobby had no problem with that arrangement and never gave it much thought. He was a good soldier, and his life with the family had treated him more than well, even when he'd been serving a hard nickel in San Quentin. Made guys had it easy in the joint, and he'd served three of his five like it was nothing, earning him the automatic respect of the elders when he got out. He'd never rolled on them, never said a word, and had taken the fall for the truck hijacking in silence. That had resulted in him being promoted to his current rank as a specialist, and he lived well – far better than anyone else he knew.

A commotion from the dock attracted his attention. He squinted through the blinds at two men, beer bottles in hand, eyeing the transom stairs. Bobby tried to make out what they were saying, but it was no good. He reflexively touched the Beretta in his shoulder holster and pulled on a hoodie to conceal its bulge before moving to the door and swinging it open.

The younger of the two, wearing a baseball cap, was halfway up the stairs.

"What the hell do you think you're doing?" Bobby snarled.

"Oh, shit." The man turned to his companion. "Dude, I think we've got the wrong boat."

"Damn right you do," Bobby said and then found himself staring down the barrel of Stan's pistol, the weapon steady as a rock as he trained it on the mobster's head.

"Nice and slow. Back up. Reach for your gun, and it'll be the last thing you ever do," Stan said conversationally. Black pulled his Glock from his belt and joined him in drawing a bead on Bobby's forehead.

"You have no idea who you're screwing with. Find somebody else to rob, and I'll chock this up to a misunderstanding. Guy's gotta make a living, and all. But you don't want a piece of this," Bobby said softly, his gray eyes unwavering as he stared Stan down.

"Back up and put your hands were I can see them. Last warning before I turn off your lights," Stan said as he cocked the hammer on the revolver.

Bobby slowly raised his hands and took two steps back.

Stan nodded and leaned toward Black. "Get on board. If he so much as moves, I'll blow his head off."

Black ascended the final step and hopped over the railing onto the deck. Bobby studied him like a mongoose eyes a cobra, seemingly unimpressed by Black's weapon.

"Back up against the far rail. Now," Black said.

Bobby gave him an ugly smirk and obeyed. "You two are dead."

Stan got on board and shrugged. "Everyone dies of something. Now, with two fingers, I want you to remove your gun and place it on the deck. I see you inching for the trigger, you get a one-way ticket to hell. Nice and easy. Black, get ready to shoot. He looks like he's feeling tricky."

Black nodded, his eyes never leaving Bobby's. "Nothing I'd rather do."

Bobby, seeming to move in slow motion, placed the weapon on the teak planks.

"Kick it over," Stan said.

The Beretta skidded across the deck. Stan scooped it up and pocketed it, then walked over to Bobby and slammed the butt of his revolver against the side of his head. Bobby went down, crumpling in slow motion, dazed but not out.

"That's for making me lose a night's sleep. Now get up and go inside. Slowly," Stan said. Bobby held a hand to his bleeding temple but didn't say anything, instead struggling to his feet. "Try to rush us and you're dead, so get that out of your pea brain. Now move."

Inside the salon, Stan pointed at the couch. "Sit."

Bobby collapsed on it, still dizzy from the blow.

"Where is she?"

"I don't know what you're talking about," Bobby said, his voice tight from the pain.

"Don't waste my time. We know your partner's going to be back any minute, so game's over. Last time – where is she?"

Bobby refused to answer. Stan nodded, and Black called out.

"Roxie?"

From the rear stateroom a small voice answered.

"Boss?"

Black nodded and moved to the door, down the stairs on the far side of the salon. He kicked the wooden wedge that had been jammed under the door to keep it from opening and twisted the knob. Roxie burst from the stateroom and hugged him so tight it took his breath away. Black held her close, her hair smelling like ambrosia against his face, and whispered to her, "It's okay. You're safe."

Stan, sensing that this would be the moment where Bobby would be likeliest to make his move, stepped back and gripped his pistol with both hands, assuming a modified Weaver stance to signal he was serious about punching the kidnapper's ticket. Bobby appreciated the professionalism, and his shoulders sagged as his interest in committing suicide appeared to wane.

Black released Roxie and studied her face. "Did they hurt you?"

She shook her head, tears of relief welling in her eyes. "Not yet. But that one was taking dibs on raping me after they called you."

Stan's face could have been carved out of granite as he moved to Bobby and pistol-whipped him unconscious. He wiped the blood off his gun butt with the man's hoodie and stepped back. Black caught his cold glare.

"What now?"

"Now we wait for the other one."

Chapter 34

Tony was whistling as he made his way back down the gangplank, a brown paper bag containing ham and cheese sandwiches in one hand, a cardboard tray with two cups of coffee in the other. He was getting ready to set the bag down and fiddle with the lock when one of the boat cleaners jogged toward him and opened the door. Tony nodded a curt thanks as the man held out his hand, obviously wanting a tip.

"*Gracias*," Tony said and brushed past him, having no intention of giving the man any money. He pretended not to understand the muttered curse and continued down the concrete dock to where *Downtime* was bobbing gently. He took careful steps up the stairs, mindful of the hot coffee in his hand, and dropped onto the deck, his balance perfect even after the long night.

The surprise on his face was genuine when he swung the cabin door wide and found himself confronting two armed men who looked like they knew how to use their weapons. He froze as the older of the pair moved toward him.

"Put the goodies on the deck by your side. Do it," Stan said.

"What is this?"

"A birthday party. Now shut up and put down the crap, and don't try to reach for your ankle holster. That's right. I can see it from here."

Black tilted his head to get a better look at Tony. "He means it. He gets grumpy when he's tired."

Tony slowly knelt, set the tray and bag on the teak planks, and then stood. "Now what?"

"Lie face down on the deck while my friend relieves you of temptation," Stan said.

Tony grudgingly lay down, the wood decking warm against his face, and Black took his gun. Stan approached the doorway and cleared his throat. "Now come into the boat. We're going to have a nice little chat, and if I'm feeling generous, you'll walk away from this alive."

Black stood by the transom, well away from Tony, training the kidnapper's weapon on him, having slipped his own gun back into his belt. Tony rose and stepped into the salon, an ugly expression on his handsome face. Stan motioned to the couch.

"Sit."

Black returned with the bag and coffee and set them on the counter. "Coffee smells great, and we're both starved. Thanks a million. Roxie? Come on up. Food's on." Black glowered at Tony as the aft stateroom door opened and Roxie joined them. "I'm guessing you didn't feed her or give her anything to drink. Call that a hunch."

Roxie shook her head. "Not a thing. Pricks."

Tony's face registered surprise. "Wait. You know her. You're...you're Black."

"Every day, Einstein. Now you can start by telling me why you kidnapped my friend."

"Screw you."

Stan moved into the kitchen and opened drawers, all the time watching Tony. In the bottom he found something promising – a short, aluminum baseball bat used to stun large fish.

"Not very accommodating, are you. Maybe after I break a kneecap, you'll reconsider," Stan said.

"Who are you?" Tony snarled.

Stan looked pensive. "I'm Roxie's friend, and I'm really annoyed you put me to this much trouble. Let's make this easy. I'm not going to warn you again. If you don't answer my questions, your left kneecap goes. After you come to, I'll go to work on the right. Eventually you'll talk. Roxie, sweetheart, you want to get some sun?"

"I heard them talking about beer," she said as she swung the refrigerator open. "Ah. Here we go. I'll close the door after me so nobody can hear the screams. That work for you?" she asked, grabbing her purse from the counter.

"Perfect."

The door slamming behind her sounded like a rifle shot. Stan held the bat up and considered it. "Keep your gun on him," he said to Black.

"You got it, boss."

"Your pal's going to need hospitalization for his head. It would be a pity if you couldn't walk by the time this is over. Who's going to help him? So here's question number one. Why kidnap Roxie?"

An internal struggle played across Tony's face. "To keep him from playing tonight," he said.

"Why?"

"Why do you think?"

Stan shook his head. "See, we were making progress, and now we're back to you bullshitting me. If I ask you a question, I want an answer, not another question. Get it? Why do you want him not to play?"

"So the other band wins."

Stan exchanged a glance with Black. "Why is that important to you? I can tell you're pro. Mobbed up, am I right? I can smell it on you."

Tony didn't say anything.

"Why does the mob want to stop my buddy from playing?"

"I don't know."

Without warning, Stan swung the bat and shattered the glass front of the microwave. "Remember what I said about not answering my questions?"

"Look, you can beat me senseless, but I still won't know."

"Who are you working for?"

"Santa."

"Very funny. You want the left or the right one gone first?"

"I mean it. They don't tell me that shit. They said snatch the bitch, keep her on ice, call numbnuts there and get him to Mexico. That's it."

Black shook his head. "I don't believe him. Who is it? Alex? Rooster? Come on. Talk."

"I can't tell you what I don't know. All I know is what they tell me."

Black glanced at his watch and then at Stan. "I need to get out of here. It's going to take a while to get back to L.A. Take out a kneecap and let's see if he sticks to his story."

Stan tossed Black a bundle of nylon rope. "Tie him up like his friend."

Black obliged, and within five minutes the mobster was trussed, immobile. Stan considered Black's handiwork and paused in front of Tony. "I'm going to leave you two to your fate. Notice that I'm not going to beat you to a pulp for exercise, even though I'm tempted. That's because I'm a kind-hearted soul. But if I ever see either of you again, I'll put a bullet in you."

Black nodded. "He's not kidding."

"You're dead. You know that, right?" Tony spat.

"See? That shows you're unclear on the principle. And here I was thinking I wouldn't open the sea cocks and sink this tub with you on board. That's the thanks I get." Stan moved to the hatch.

"No," Black said. "Come on. Let's go. The stink of this guy is making me sick."

"Grab his cell phone," Stan said and went into the aft stateroom for a moment before reappearing. "That wasn't hard. Hope you guys can swim. It'll take a good hour to sink. What's that you goombahs say? Sleeping with the fishes?"

Tony glared at him in silence.

As they walked up the dock, Roxie in the lead as the sun shimmered on the surface of the water, Black turned to Stan. "That wasn't a bad idea about sinking it, you know. But you didn't do it, did you?"

"I'd vote for sinking," Roxie interjected.

"That's not a surprise," Black affirmed.

Stan grinned. "I had a better idea. I stashed their guns under the pillows in the bedroom. We'll call the cops, they'll find them with their guns, and their problems will have just begun. I've heard you never want to see the inside of a Mexican jail. Want to bet that's no exaggeration?"

"You're an evil man, my friend," Black said.

"You don't know the half of it."

Chapter 35

Rooster locked his condo door and took the stairs down to the underground garage, a spring in his step. The day was shaping up to be a good one. He hadn't gotten any more angry calls once he'd delivered the bad news about Black's escape after the night club attack – Rooster had tried the best he could, but it hadn't worked out, so the problem would have to be solved by someone else. That wasn't his line of work, anyway, and it had been stupid to involve him overtly.

His BMW started with a purr, and he eyed the glowing dash dials with satisfaction before putting it in reverse and backing out of the stall. His only luxury other than his guitar collection, the sedan was all he really had to show for a forty-plus-year career and millions of records sold. The studio was a mountain of debt, with no prospects now that technology had rendered it obsolete. Most acts these days could record an album's worth of material for a fraction of what it used to cost, and big facilities like his had been one of the first casualties.

Traffic to the studio was light. He took his time – he had all afternoon before he had to be at the show for the finals. Maybe a long lunch to celebrate the end of the season. He could expense it to the program and nobody would blink, he knew. One of the perks.

He parked in the alley behind the studio and locked the car with a press of the key fob. Nobody would mess with his car. He was considered royalty in the neighborhood, above being screwed with by the predators. It didn't hurt that he had strong ties to the gang that ran these blocks, having helped several of the members cut rap tracks at a reduced rate. One hand washed the other. It was the way it had always been.

Two Caucasian men stepped from behind the dumpster near the mouth of the alley. Rooster immediately knew he was in trouble. They didn't say anything, just closed in on him fast. He tried to turn and run, but age and slick pavement conspired against him, and they reached him before he could make it far. The sharp spikes of pain from long blades plunging into him again and again were like white-hot needles, and when one of the men stabbed into the base of his neck and severed his spinal cord, it was almost a relief.

Rooster lay still, blood pooling around him, and the shorter of the two attackers removed his wallet and watch before turning and joining his partner at the alley mouth. By the time Rooster was discovered and identified it would be night, and the show would have gone on without him, the world continuing to revolve *sans* the bluesman, his musical legacy the only reminder of a life that had ended brutally on a strip of dank asphalt, an apparent victim of a mugging gone horribly wrong.

Chapter 36

Stan sighed in frustration as he sat in an endless line of cars snaking a solid mile from the border crossing. They'd only advanced a hundred yards in the last forty-five minutes. Legions of enterprising locals hawked Tweety Birds and bottles of questionable water to the captive audience in the chain of vehicles.

Black nervously checked the time. "At this rate I'm never going to make it. It's already two. The show starts at six. No way do we get through this in an hour."

"Sorry, buddy. Wish I had a helicopter. You're probably right, though. This seems more like a two-hour wait, minimum. Too bad we didn't take the turnoff to the Otay Mesa crossing. That might have been lighter."

"How far do you think we are from the border?" Roxie asked.

"The last sign said a mile. That was maybe a quarter mile ago," Stan said.

Black glared at the procession of vehicles in front of him. "I'm going to walk. I'll get a car on the other side."

"Probably want to leave your gun here, then. Just saying," Stan reminded him. Black took the belt holster off and handed it to Stan, who slipped it into his glove compartment. "The good news is I'm a cop, and the only ones checking anything at the border are Americans. I can talk my way through that if they decide to strip search me or something."

"I'm going with you," Roxie said.

Black shrugged. "You sure you can walk in those heels?"

"Watch me."

They set out, moving past a man displaying a multicolored blanket made in China, into a sea of controlled pandemonium of beggars holding babies, popsicle vendors burned brown by the sun, and children barely old enough to walk selling Chiclets. An old woman held up a small ceramic pipe crafted in an obscene depiction of female anatomy, and Roxie waved her off.

"You sure this is a good idea?" she asked.

"Do you have any better ones?"

"The limo thing didn't end well, so I suppose not."

"Tell me about that."

"The driver picked me up at my place and took me to a restaurant to meet Alex. He wasn't there. That Tony slimeball approached me after a few minutes and said he'd been delayed. Once they got me outside, they pulled guns. You know the rest."

Black marched along in silence. "Doesn't look so good for Alex, does it?"

"I don't know what to think right now."

"Roxie, I know you like him…"

"I can unlike him if he set me up to be raped and killed."

"Usually you don't get to the murder thing until after you're married," Black agreed.

"Which I totally understand."

Black wiped a bead of sweat off his face. "I'm sorry, Roxie."

"Don't be. You saved my life."

At the border they walked through immigration, the process lightning fast compared to the wait in the car. Once across they grabbed a taxi, and the driver grinned like he'd won the lottery when Black told him they needed to get to Los Angeles in record time.

Three hundred dollars and three and a half hours later, they pulled up outside the Verizon Theater in downtown Los Angeles with a little under fifteen minutes to spare. At the backstage entrance they had a short argument with the security team, and then Black and Roxie made it to the dressing area, where Christina and the band were frantic. When she saw him, she stormed toward him, anger etching ugly lines into her face.

"What the hell is this? Where have you been?" she hissed, eyeing Roxie like she was dirt.

"It's a long story. What's important is I'm here now. Did I miss anything?" Black asked.

"No. That's not going to fly. I want an explanation," Christina demanded.

Black nodded and moved to a more private area off the main hall. Roxie remained where she was standing, sensing that it probably wasn't a great time to butt in.

"I got a text last night. Roxie was kidnapped. I had to rescue her. In Mexico. Mission accomplished," he said simply.

"You expect me to believe that?"

"Christina – I haven't slept since three in the morning. I've been to hell and back and barely made it out of Mexico with my teeth. Believe it or not, everything's not always about you. But I will say this: somebody really doesn't want us to win. The whole thing was designed to keep me from playing. That's the truth. So direct your anger elsewhere. I'm not the enemy here. I'm on your side."

"What are you talking about? Someone kidnapped her–" Christina stabbed a finger in Roxie's direction "– to get you out of L.A.? That's nuts."

"I agree. But that's what happened. And I have a short list of suspects. Have you seen Rooster or Alex around?"

For the first time, Christina's angry composure wavered. "Why? You think they have something to do with this?"

"Roxie was in Mexico for a date with Alex. So yeah, I do. And I think Rooster set me up for a beating outside the club the other night. It was a small miracle I didn't break a finger. I think all of this is to keep Last Call from winning." Black allowed his words to sink in. "Again. Have you seen Alex or Rooster?"

She shook her head. "N...no. Rooster hasn't shown up yet. I don't think Alex has, either. But the judges should be here any second."

"All right. I'm here now. Let me get changed. Did somebody bring my guitar?"

"Of course. It's in the dressing room. First one on the right."

"I want to keep Roxie with me so we don't have another attempt. That okay with you?"

Christina nodded. "Sure."

"Great. Let's just focus on winning this, okay? We can deal with the rest after," Black said and turned to change in the dressing room. He stopped dead when he saw Roxie storming toward Alex, who'd just arrived.

"You! I want to talk to you!" she yelled, her voice radiating fury. Black rushed forward before she could take a swing at him and restrained her. Alex looked shocked and frightened – in keeping with a conspirator whose scheme had failed.

"Roxie! What are you doing here? Why weren't you at the restaurant?" he asked, his lower lip trembling.

"I was. Then your goons kidnapped me!"

"What are you talking about?" he demanded, and Black let go of Roxie and stepped forward.

"You heard her."

"Is this some kind of bad joke?" Alex asked.

"I'll say. You had a limo pick me up and take me to a foreign country so I could be kidnapped, you asshat. But it didn't work," Roxie fumed.

"I have no idea...look, I didn't do anything. I was at the restaurant twenty minutes after we were supposed to meet, and you weren't there. I figured you...I don't know what I figured. And you didn't answer your phone, so I thought maybe you were pissed off for some reason."

"Why didn't you ask Jacobs?"

"Who?" Alex said, looking more confused by the second.

"The driver you had pick me up," Roxie fired back.

Alex shrugged. "I don't know him. I didn't coordinate that."

Black put his hand on Roxie's shoulder and squeezed, signaling for her to stop. "Who did?"

"Sarah. I just told her about the restaurant, and she handled everything. I had concerts and a photo shoot and a bunch of other…"

A loud buzzer went off through the public address system, signaling that the show would begin in five minutes. Christina came running up. "We're out of time. Get changed, Black. We have to be onstage for the opening announcement and the introduction of the judges."

Black shook his head. "Where's Sarah?"

"I think she's out by the judge pods or something."

"Damn." Black turned to Alex and gave him a cold stare. "Alex, not a word about any of this. Do you understand? Not to anyone. Please. There's more going on here than you know, and you don't want to be involved."

"I…Roxie, I swear I didn't have anything to do with this…" Alex stammered.

"Alex. Focus. Don't talk to a soul, all right?" Black said.

"Sure. I mean…Roxie, you have to believe me…"

Roxie exhaled noisily. "Okay. After the show. Now don't you have someplace to be?"

Alex seemed to come out of his fog and glanced at his watch. "You're right. I'll come backstage after we're done. Wait for me. Please."

Black hurried to the dressing room and slipped on his rock attire – a pair of brown leather pants and a paisley long-sleeved shirt. A hairstylist ran a brush lightly through his hair, shaking her head. The makeup man patted on a layer of base and did a quick mascara job, making him look like an alcoholic barfly on a crying jag.

"Don't worry. You look great," Ed said, handing Black a beer. "You aren't stoned out of your mind on LSD or anything, are you?"

"I wish," Black said and toasted him. Peter came up and held out his hand.

"Christina told me what happened. That's frigging unbelievable."

Black shook it. "Yeah, I know. But for now, the best revenge will be to win this thing."

"Do you think one of the guys in Bend in the Creek could be behind this?"

"Anything's possible, but I don't think so. Those guys are just musicians, you know? This is high-level shit."

The stage manager pushed through the door, a headset on, and called out to the band. "We're going live in thirty seconds."

Chapter 37

Black could sense the size of the audience as he stood with the band behind a scrim on stage right, waiting for the announcer to introduce them. The air was charged, the buzz of anticipation coming off thousands of people seeming to crackle in the gloom. Holly and David were in place, center stage, and then a spotlight flashed on and they bathed in white light.

"Ladies and gentlemen, welcome to the finals for America's favorite talent contest, *Rock of Ages!*" Holly chirped, reading from the teleprompter's ghostly screen as she smiled. The crowd applauded, and the house band launched into several bars of up-tempo rock music, abruptly ending so the MCs could continue their intro.

Black listened as they did their bit, announcing the judges, who each took a bow and received their obligatory ovation. Then it was time for the setup, and David announced Last Call. The scrim rose as if by magic, exposing them as more lights flashed and cameras zoomed in, and the audience cheered the band like returning war heroes. Christina waved and blew kisses at the cavernous hall. The rest of the group waved too, knowing that every eye in the place was on their lead singer, and for good reason.

Next came Bend in the Creek, who likewise received a warm round of applause, and then it was time for Holly and David to vacate the stage and the special guest announcer, a popular television talk show host, to take over.

After a few lame jokes, he explained the rules: two songs per band, alternating, with the first slot going to the winner of a coin toss. Christina and the Bend in the Creek lead vocalist stepped forward into a neon-ringed circle, and a wonk from a prominent accounting firm made a big display of holding up a silver dollar, white-gloved hands like a mime's holding the highly polished coin. The host asked Christina to call it, and she chose heads. A snare drum roll built as the accountant tossed the coin into the air, and stopped when he caught it and placed it on the back of his hand. The camera zoomed in and the audience cheered. It was tails.

Bend in the Creek's equipment was set up on one side of the stage and Last Call's on the other. The band had two minutes to get situated, and then the host announced the first number – the elective song first, in this case Charlie Daniels' "The Devil Went Down to Georgia".

A strong choice, and one the group nailed. When they finished, Black knew he'd just witnessed a solid ten performance. The judges agreed, even if their votes were purely ceremonial – the phone-in audience would determine the winner of the event.

Last Call was announced next and delivered a surprisingly scorching rendition of "Like a Virgin", Christina milking it with every ounce of her considerable sex appeal even though the genre wasn't her forte. The crowd loved it, and again the judges handed out tens like condoms at a free clinic, leaving no doubt in anyone's minds that both groups were at the top of their game.

The house band played four songs while the bands changed outfits and freshened up, and then Bend in the Creek reappeared for their final song: "Roxanne" by the Police, a completely different style for the country-tinged group. They tackled the reggae rhythm with a down-home approach, making for an eclectic and surprising take on the classic.

Sarah materialized by Black's side while he was watching them, a scowl on her face. "Black, you were warned. You violated the curfew again and caused everyone a ton of trouble. That's unacceptable," she said, brandishing her clipboard like a weapon.

"I can guarantee you I've got the best reason you've ever heard."

"It doesn't matter. The rules are the rules, and you were warned. You're off the show."

"I don't care about the show, Sarah. But it's interesting that you've taken this moment to cut me out. Almost like you're trying to freak me out and throw my concentration."

"I don't care about your concentration. My orders are clear."

"Fine. But I'm playing this last song."

"No, you aren't."

Black leaned in to her. "Sarah, you stop me from playing, and the show's history. Do you understand? You won't be able to get a job cleaning toilets after this, and I'll be on every network by midnight describing how you deliberately screwed Christina at the last minute because of your hatred for her. And you'll have a lot of explaining to do for your role in the kidnapping. You want that?"

"Kidnapping? What are you talking about?"

"Do I seem particularly playful? A very close friend was kidnapped, and I had to save her. Wanna bet the news stations eat you alive when they hear about how you booted me after that?"

Bend in the Creek finished their song, and there were more tens as the crowd hooted and stomped. The singer waved and bowed in gratitude, and then it was Last Call's turn with "I Will Survive". Sarah seemed torn, for the first time he'd ever witnessed, and after a brief discussion on her radio, stomped off without another word. Christina caught Black's eye and he shrugged. She smiled and winked at him, and then it was show time.

From the very first notes it was obvious that Christina had the attention of everyone in the auditorium. She played the opening run on a grand piano at the side of the stage, a single pin spotlight on her, and began singing the verse, softly, as though sharing a secret with a close friend. Even though Black had heard the song a hundred times by now from the constant rehearsals, the hair on the nape of his neck stood on end, and he realized this was going to be a legendary performance. He'd had the same feeling with Nina back in the day, when they'd taken the dog-eat-dog Los Angeles club scene by storm, playing sold-out houses while A&R men frantically competed for them. Now, for the second time in his life, he was witnessing the making of a legend, and his heart rate accelerated as the crowd spontaneously burst into applause after the first verse, the wave of clapping so loud it almost drowned out the band.

When the song ended, Black's lead guitar wailing in time with Christina's final note, the audience exploded like a bomb had detonated. Black held his guitar aloft and flicked his pick into the crowd. Christina waved and did a mock curtsy, and Black could just make out Nina at the judge pods wiping her eyes as the judges rose to their feet in a standing ovation.

The applause seemed to last forever, even though it was probably no more than thirty seconds, and then it was time for the band to hear the judges' feedback. Even the normally taciturn BT Simms had nothing but superlatives, and Nina's final words would resonate long after she'd uttered them.

"I've just seen the future of music. I have no doubt you're going to be huge, and you deserve every bit of it. Bravo!"

Voting was closed half an hour after the final performance. With a theatrical flourish the accountant handed the host an envelope, which he opened, read, and then turned to the cameras.

"And the winner is…Last Call, with seventy-two percent of the votes!"

The judges filed onto the stage as the house band played the theme from *Rocky*, and everyone shook hands and slapped backs as the host delivered the closing lines that would end the telecast. The crowd cheered their new favorites, Bend in the Creek all but forgotten as Last Call was celebrated, lights playing over the clapping spectators as the cameras took it all in.

The following ten minutes were a blur of activity. Christina was swarmed by reporters while the show cameraman recorded the moment for posterity. Black stood with Peter and Ed by the side, largely ignored, and Roxie approached with a grim expression on her face.

"Did you hear? Rooster's dead."

The joy of triumph faded abruptly, and Black stepped away from the group and whispered to her, "What? How do you know?"

She pointed to where Stan was standing, just inside the backstage door, looking haggard and rumpled. Black moved to join him, and Stan shook his hand before murmuring to him in a low voice.

"Congratulations. You're a star. Sorry to be the bearer of bad news, but I guess Roxie told you."

"How did he die?"

Stan gave him a terse synopsis, and Black shook his head. "When did you get back?"

"About an hour ago. Took forever. I talked to the squad head, and he told me about Rooster's jacket landing on my desk. I caught the case because I'd been looking into him as a suspect in Rick's death."

"I thought you closed that."

"They're never closed if they aren't solved. Just dormant."

"So much for him being a suspect."

"Yeah, although he certainly could have been involved. But time of death was around noon, so it's unlikely he was the mastermind."

"What about Alex?"

"I'm going to question him."

"You should know something about Sarah. She tried to boot me at the last minute. I think if she hadn't thought there'd be a riot, she would have. I like her for it – she set up the whole date for Alex. The car, the restaurant, the villa...everything."

"What does she look like?"

"Tall, tailored suit, looks like she's got a stick up her ass."

"Is she here?"

"No, but she can't be far away."

"I'll look around for her." Stan paused. "Buddy, I saw that last song. You guys blew me away. Although it was mostly the singer. But you weren't bad, either."

Black was going to respond when Sylvia appeared at the backstage entry, where a bouncer was holding the crowd back. Black moved to him and gave him the okay. She ran to him and hugged him.

"You did it. You won! I'm so proud of you!"

"Thanks, honey. Yeah, I guess I did." He kissed her, wishing he wasn't wearing makeup.

Roxie joined them and cleared her throat. "Hey."

Black looked at her. "Hey."

"Does this mean you're going to be on the cover of *Teen Beat?* I'm kinda getting queasy thinking about it."

"I don't think so. Another generation's safe, for now."

"Have you guys talked about what's next?" Roxie asked, a hint of envy seeping into her tone.

Black shook his head and squeezed Sylvia's arm. "I don't think there is any next."

Roxie frowned. "What?"

"I've got to get out of this outfit. I think I'm allergic to leather pants. I'll tell you in a couple of minutes." He looked at Sylvia. "Will you excuse me?"

"Sure thing, rock star."

Roxie's frown deepened. "Now I really think I'm going to hurl."

Black was alone in the dressing room, where his street clothes had been hung neatly on a rack. He removed the leathers and the shirt and pulled on his customary cocktail shirt and slacks – the first clothes he'd gone for when he'd gotten dressed in the dark in the wee hours that morning. He felt better once he had them on, and studied his reflection in the mirror that ran along one wall. The makeup made him look ridiculous. He went into the bathroom, moistened a towel, and wiped as much of it off as he could. When he returned to the main room, he caught another glimpse of himself and made a mental note to get the damned hair extensions removed the next day.

A knock at the door pulled him back into the moment. Stan poked his head in and grunted.

"I'm about done," Black said.

"Good. The stage manager told me that Sarah just left the building and is headed for her car."

"What? Why? She'd normally stick around for hours…"

"I think we better find out, don't you?"

Black apologized to Sylvia and asked her to wait for him. "You can hang out with Roxie if you want. I shouldn't be too long."

"Right. Because she needs a babysitter. She's only nine, right?" Roxie said.

"That's not what I meant. I have to go. I'll be back in a few minutes," Black promised, and Sylvia nodded.

"It's okay. I'll just flirt with the road crew. Take your time," Sylvia said, glancing at a three-hundred-pound unshaven bear of a man with a foot of limp hair.

"I hate to intrude…" Stan said, and Black nodded.

"Which way did she go?"

"Through there," Stan called, already moving.

Chapter 38

Black and Stan found themselves in a private underground parking area, the gray concrete walls illuminated by overhead fluorescent lamps. They both heard the squeal of tires at the same time and saw a white Nissan Murano pulling up the ramp at the far end, headed for the exit.

"That's her car," Black said, recognizing it from the mansion. "Where are you parked?"

"Up on the street in a red zone. Come on. We can take the stairs and be at ground level by the time she makes it, if we're lucky."

They bolted up the steps, their footfalls echoing in the stairwell, and emerged through a steel service door just as they saw the Murano roll from the driveway, waiting for a break in traffic.

"Come on. I'm fifty yards down, on the left," Stan called, puffing from the unexpected exertion.

"You going to make it? You don't sound so good."

"Screw you. I'm just catching my second wind."

"You sound like the old boiler at my parents' house before it gave up the ghost."

"Thanks for the vote of confidence," Stan said as they jogged together to his car. Stan slid behind the wheel, and Black climbed into the passenger side and fastened his seatbelt. The engine started with a rumble, and Stan pulled from the curb, earning an angry honk from a green Infiniti that he cut off. "What the hell's wrong with people anymore?" Stan griped, the Murano taillights moving away from them in traffic.

"No common courtesy. I blame it on television. And rap music."

"And the Internet."

"Got that right. Not to mention cell phones." Black opened the glove compartment and removed his Glock. "I see you didn't get searched at the border."

"No, apparently old white guys aren't high on the list of smuggler profiles. I could have brought over a few kilos and paid for the gas with no problem."

"That's the entrepreneurial spirit that makes this country great."

Stan gunned the engine and surged past a VW. "I wonder where she's going? She's driving calmly for someone making a run for it."

"Guess we're going to find out."

They sat in silence for several minutes, and then Stan glanced at Black's profile. "So you gonna go on the road? Live *la vida loca?*"

"Nah. I mean, this was fun, and I can sure use my share of the money, but I realized at some point as I got serious about it that I didn't have the fire in me anymore. Maybe it's age, or maybe I proved my point by winning. But I can't see this as the life I want."

"Yeah, I can see being rich and famous wouldn't agree with you."

"Don't get me wrong. I mean, if they want me to play on the album, I'd definitely be up for that, but not the years of touring – and that's how most bands make their money these days. Selling T-shirts and concert tickets. It's a young man's game."

"Christ, you sound like my father. You're not that old. Forty's the new thirty, haven't you heard?"

"Maybe. But all I can think of is how I'll look like the guitar player for Mötley Crüe. You know, ten years older than the rest of them. Although I think Nikki was older than Tommy and Vince."

"Are you speaking in some sort of code?"

"I keep forgetting that you were listening to Elvis or whatever when I was in bands."

"The man wasn't called The King for no reason."

"Anyway, I had this vision of myself rubbing hemorrhoid cream on my ass while Ed was chasing groupies around the tour bus with a sword and a bottle of Jack, and I sort of realized that's not who I am anymore."

"Nothing wrong with Jack. Or with that Christina. She doesn't seem to mind you being…more mature. With age comes experience. That's my pitch, by the way, when I'm in the hot tub with her after you introduce me."

"There's a pretty visual."

"Focus on her, dumbass."

"Ah. Right."

The Murano made a left turn onto another large street, and Stan followed at a safe distance. Ten minutes later she pulled up outside of Simon's production offices and parked in front of the deserted building. Stan coasted to a stop behind the vehicle and killed the lights as she entered the lobby.

"Now what?" Black asked.

"We wait. I don't know what she's up to, but when she comes out, I'll corral her and question her."

A thought occurred to Black. "What if she's just running an errand?"

"At this hour?"

"I know. But hear me out. Does it seem like she's running for it?"

"Didn't I just say it doesn't?"

"Right. What if she's not?"

"I don't read you."

"What if Alex was lying about her setting everything up? I mean, I considered her as a suspect because of Rick, but what possible reason could she have for wanting to sabotage the show?"

"Could be she's doing that country singer and wanted him to win."

"I don't know. Seems thin."

"Look, this was your theory. I'm just following the lead you handed me. And you say she tried to keep you from playing. That's pretty suspicious."

"Good point."

Sarah returned carrying an armful of folders, and Stan opened his door. "Stay here." He walked toward her with his detective badge out. "Ms. Miller? Sarah Miller?"

Sarah slowed as he approached. "Yes?"

"I'm Detective Colt, with LAPD homicide. Can I have a moment of your time?"

"What, *now?*"

"Yes."

"Why? You said you were with homicide?"

"Correct. I just have a few questions."

"About what?" she asked suspiciously.

"A kidnapping," Stan said, watching her face.

"Homicide covers murders."

"They're related."

Black watched from the car as Stan conversed with Sarah, and after three minutes they walked together to the Murano, and he held the door open for her so she could put the paperwork on the passenger seat. Stan gave her a card, and when he returned to the car, he had a spring in his step.

"What happened?" Black asked as Stan got in.

"She was running an errand for her boss. You were right. But the good news is I think she likes older men."

"What's gotten into you lately?"

"It's those Viagra commercials. They get you thinking."

"So now what?"

"Back to the theater to interrogate Alex," Stan said.

"Wait. Tell me what she said. Exactly."

"That she set up the limo and the restaurant for Alex, just like he said. I told her I'd want to get a formal statement tomorrow morning, and she had no problem coming in. Said she'd be glad to help however she could. I think she's got the hots for me."

"Who wouldn't? I'm getting a little tingly being in the same car with you. But why interrogate Alex?"

"You have any better suggestions? Frankly, none of this makes any sense. Why would the mob be involved in kidnapping Roxie? That's been nagging at me all the way from the border. Something like that's not gonna be cheap, and they won't get involved for just anybody."

"All right. Sylvia's waiting for me, so I have to get back anyway."

"She's a cutie. Been so long since I saw her I almost forgot."

"Is that a reminder that we don't hang out much anymore?"

"Take it however you want," Stan said, putting the car in gear and giving it gas. "I still can't believe you're going to pass on being a rock god."

"The whole deity thing's not all it's cracked up to be."

"I'll have to remember that. But don't forget – you owe me an introduction to Christina."

"As if you'll ever let me."

"Squeaky wheel, baby, squeaky wheel."

Chapter 39

Roxie, Alex, and Sylvia were talking in the long hallway when Stan and Black got back to the theater. There was still a considerable crowd backstage, mostly crew and reporters finishing up their interviews with Christina. Stan led the way past the security guards, walked up to Alex and introduced himself, and asked him if he could have a few minutes of his time. Black was surprised at how smoothly he finessed the singer into an interrogation, how nonthreatening and almost friendly he appeared, and was reminded how good at his job Stan was.

As the two men walked away in search of someplace quiet, Roxie shook her head. "I don't think he's involved. Nobody's that good an actor."

"I think he's cute," Sylvia said. "I mean, hot young guy cute, not more mature guy cute, like you, Black."

"Nice save."

"Although I still can't get used to that hair."

"That makes two of us," Black agreed and turned to Roxie. "What did he say about the date? Did you grill him about it?"

"Yeah. He was totally worried about me. He'd never been to Ensenada before, and he kind of freaked out when I wasn't there. I believe him."

"Then how did he know about the restaurant? That's kind of weird."

"He got a recommendation from the producer."

Black's eyes narrowed. "Say that again."

"Are you going deaf in your golden years? He got a tip from that Samson guy."

"Simon. His name's Simon."

"That's right."

Gears meshed in Black's head, and he snapped his fingers. "Damn." He eyed Roxie. "Do you know what Simon looks like?"

"Sort of. I kind of remember him from the other shows. Totally fake Hollywood type."

"Have you seen him backstage tonight?"

"Nope."

Black spotted the stage manager and walked over. "Have you seen Simon? I need to talk to him. It's important."

"He left after the show."

"How long ago?"

The man shrugged. "I don't know. Maybe fifteen minutes."

"Damn." Black returned to Roxie. "You wouldn't happen to remember Simon's home address, would you?"

"Are you kidding me?"

"It's really important, Roxie."

"I could probably access my computer remotely and look it up."

"How?"

"If you can find me a computer."

Sylvia reached into her purse. "I have an iPhone."

Three minutes later Black had the address. He went in search of Stan and found him sitting in one of the unused dressing rooms with Alex.

"Can I see you for a minute?" Black asked.

Stan glared at him. "Kinda busy right now."

"It's important."

Stan sighed and stood. "Will you give me a second?"

Alex nodded. "Sure."

Stan joined Black at the door. "Better be good."

"It's Simon. The producer. Has to be. He's got money, clout...he's the only one that makes sense now."

"Uh-huh. And you know this...how?"

"He gave Alex the restaurant recommendation in Mexico."

"That's it?"

"It means he knew she'd be there. He could have asked Sarah how everything worked out in arranging things and found out when she'd arrive."

"He could have. But I'll need to question Sarah again to connect those dots. You're dead in the water if she says she never discussed it with him."

"Stan, he's gone. If he suspects we're onto him, he could be a flight risk. Kidnapping's serious shit. And we don't know what else he's into if he was trying to rig the show."

"Whoa. Just slow down. Even if it's true, I can't just go barging in with no–" Stan glanced at Alex "–real investigative authority. A producer's likely to get all lawyered up before he answers the door."

"And if he gets away?"

"That's a hypothetical built on a guess, my friend. I think you need some rest. Besides, if you're right and he didn't want your band to win, he's pretty screwed right now."

"Maybe he was trying to rig it for betting or something."

"Lot of maybes in all this. Seriously. Take a breather. It might look different after a good night's sleep."

Seeing he was getting nowhere, Black nodded, pulled the door closed after him, and returned to where Sylvia and Roxie were standing.

"Sylvia, did you drive my car tonight?"

"Yes. You wanted me to, remember?"

"I do. Roxie, could you give Sylvia a ride home if I'm not back in half an hour?"

"Where are you going?" Roxie asked.

"I need to check on something."

"Now?"

"Yup. No choice. Related to the kidnapping."

Roxie pursed her lips. "Fine. I can give her a lift."

Black kissed Sylvia. "Where's it parked?"

"In the main lot across the street from the Staples. Row B, about halfway down, under a light post," she said, handing him his keys.

"I'll be back, or I'll call you if I run into something unexpected," Black said to Sylvia, then glanced at Roxie. "Thanks. I appreciate it."

"No problem. You still have a credit from saving my life."

Simon's house was on the edge of Beverly Hills, in a good but not luxurious neighborhood. It took Black fifteen minutes to make it there, and when he pulled up a few homes down, he saw a car in the driveway – a late-model Mercedes. Black got out of the Cadillac and walked toward it. He was surprised to find the engine running. Senses alert, he moved to the home's front door, and after a moment's hesitation, pulled his Glock from the belt holster and chambered a round before trying the doorknob. It was unlocked.

The door creaked when he pushed it open, and he winced, cursing the old hinges. He stood, frozen at the threshold, weapon pointed down by his side. He debated going further into the house, but his instinct told him that would be a justifiable shooting if Simon felt like emptying a shotgun at him.

"Simon? It's Black. Are you here?" he called out. He heard a scrape from the rear of the house. "Simon? Your door's open. I'm worried. Are you all right?"

Having established what in his mind was a justifiable reason for entering, he called out one final time. "I'm coming in."

Another rustle and a creak from the recesses of the home. Black stepped across the threshold and took soft steps down the wooden hallway, ears straining as he made his way to the living room. It was nicely appointed, expensive furniture, obviously a bachelor pad. He moved into the formal dining room and then down the hall to the first of the ground-floor doors. He swung the nearest one open to find himself looking into a closet. The next was a small guest bedroom. Past the stairway, he arrived at the final door – at the back of the house.

Black twisted the knob, weapon at the ready, and abruptly pushed it open while standing to the side in case gunfire exploded from within.

Nothing. Just a breeze.

From the open window of the small office.

"Damn," Black cursed as he swung around and ran back to the front door.

By the time he reached it, Simon's car was gone. Black's gaze swung down the street, but it was too late.

Simon had disappeared.

Chapter 40

Mugsy rolled over so Ed could rub his distended belly while Black finished packing his things. It was Sunday, the cameramen were gone, and everyone had to be out by midday so the cleaning crew could ready it for return to the owner. Mugsy's purring sounded like a lawn mower, and Black smiled as he zipped his bag closed.

"I'm gonna miss the little guy," Ed said.

"He seems to like you. That's rare."

Ed nodded. "You talk to Christina?"

"Yeah. She's not thrilled, but hey. It is what it is."

"I don't get it, man. Don't you want to go on the road, at least for a while?"

"Twenty years ago I would have killed to. Ten ago I would have probably given everything I had to do it. Now? I don't know. This was more than enough for me. Although I think you guys are going to be mega, and you totally deserve it."

"You got us there."

"Nah. You can have your pick of the litter now. Serious guitar players who can take you to the next level. They'll be lining up around the block."

Ed grinned at Mugsy. "You're probably right. Still, it kind of sucks. We had something, you know?"

Black nodded. "That we did." He moved to the cat carrier and opened the door. "Want to put him in this thing?"

"Sure." Ed hoisted Mugsy and carried him to the crate. Mugsy didn't struggle, which amazed Black.

"You've really got a way with him. You should be a vet. Or a lion tamer," Black said.

"For now I'll stick to drumming."

Peter and Christina were sitting on the couch when Black and Ed came downstairs. They rose when they saw Black, and Peter extended his hand. Black shook it wordlessly and then faced Christina, who was filling out her official salmon Mugsy tank top admirably.

"There you are. You got a minute, Black?"

"Sure."

"Let's go out by the pool. Might as well enjoy the last of it before we leave."

Black set his bag and guitar down by the wall. "Lead the way."

They settled in on the lounge chairs in the warm sun. The mild breeze carried with it the smell of the sand and sea from the nearby beach. Christina sighed contentedly and closed her eyes.

"You sure you won't reconsider?" she asked softly.

"It wasn't meant to be. My part's over. Time to find fresh meat that can go the distance."

"You were pretty fresh last night."

"Maybe so, but I couldn't do that two hundred nights a year, and that's what it'll take. Year after year. It's exciting, but it's also a grind, and I don't have it in me. I'm old enough to know that."

"Have you thought about what we discussed?" Christina and Peter had floated the idea of Black doing some songwriting with them.

"Yeah. That actually sounds great. I like playing with you guys, so that could work. And it'll force me to keep on the guitar, which is never a bad thing. I hadn't realized how much I missed it until now, so that was an unexpected bonus to all this."

She turned her face toward him. "I guess our unfinished business is going to stay unfinished, though, huh? With your girlfriend back in the mix?"

"Some things were never meant to be. I'm sorry, Christina."

She closed her eyes and rested her head against the cushion.

"So am I."

Chapter 41

The exotic car dealership "Little" Sal Capelloni used as his business office was empty except for six bodyguards posing as help and one genuine salesman, who was sitting, bored, reading a magazine at his desk, the glittering Ferraris and Lamborghinis on the floor attracting no buyers at ten o'clock on a Monday morning.

The front door chimed as Stan pushed through and walked casually to the rear office. Two of the bodyguards moved to block his way. He stopped and held up his badge.

"I need to speak to your boss."

The heavier-set of the pair fixed Stan with an impassive stare. "What for?"

"What for is that a homicide detective wants to talk to him and doesn't have to tell you squat."

The office door behind them opened, and Sal's head popped out. "Boys. No problem. What can I help you with, Detective...?"

"Colt. Stan Colt. I think this would be better in private."

Sal nodded. "Suit yourself. You packing?"

"Of course."

"Leave the heat with one of them."

"Not a chance. You want to have this conversation here or down at the station?"

Sal sighed. "Fine. Come in. Have a seat."

Stan entered the office and closed the door behind him. Sal sat behind his desk and waited for Stan to make the first move. Sal's face resembled nothing to Stan so much as a ham with two olives for eyes. He pulled up a chair and lowered himself into it.

"I had a run-in with some fellas down Mexico way on Saturday. In Ensenada," Stan began, watching Sal's expression for any hint of reaction.

"Yeah? What's that got to do with me?"

"They were goombahs."

"I have no idea what you're talking about."

"Two made guys, far as I can tell, kidnapped a young woman who's a friend of mine."

Sal's eyes narrowed. "Sounds like that was a bad idea."

"One of the worst in history."

Sal nodded. "We agree on that."

"Let me tell you a story. You don't have to comment."

"I love stories." Sal hesitated. "For the record, you wearing a wire?"

"No."

"Just asking. No offense."

"None taken. This story's about a reality TV show an extremely close buddy of mine was on. A music show. The producer was rigging it so he could control who won. But something happened this season. My friend wouldn't play ball. I'm thinking that producer reached out to his friends – maybe they're business associates, maybe he owes them money – I don't know, and I really don't care. My guess is they decided to help him out. At first it's just strong-arm stuff, but my buddy doesn't buckle, and it escalates into the kidnapping of his lady friend." Stan paused, waiting for Sal to say something. He might as well have been talking to the wall. "That's where I get involved. I've got a couple of homicide cases on my desk that look to be connected. Then I get a call from my buddy, and he needs help rescuing his friend. So I help. The two guys wind up taking a fall in Mexico on gun charges. One of them's pretty badly beaten up."

"Is this going to be a movie, or TV? Or are you pitching me?"

"I'm here to tell you that my buddy means a lot to me, and if there's any more trouble for him, I'll take it personally. As in my entire department and all my colleagues will make it their life's mission to come down hard. A nice, calm status quo will go to hell, and it'll be the full-court press to go after everything I know about – and I know a lot. I'm talking feds, IRS, you name it. Big-time trouble."

"Sounds like a threat."

"I don't threaten. I warn. But I'm also a reasonable guy. I have no need to go to war if nothing happens to my friend or those around him. I'm still going to work the homicides to the best of my abilities, but I have no real interest in a Mexican kidnapping. But I could get real interested if I hear even a peep of trouble from my buddy. At that point I'd get interested like it happened to my brother, you know?"

"If I had any idea what you were talking about, I'd advise whoever was foolish enough to get involved in this to wash his hands and let bygones be bygones. Too bad I don't know anyone like that."

Stan stood.

Sal cleared his throat. "What happened to the producer?"

"Dunno. He disappeared. There are warrants out for him in connection to my cases, but so far he hasn't surfaced."

"Sounds like a smart guy. If he was involved in anything, that is."

"I have a long memory. If he reappears, I'll take him down."

"As I would expect." Sal cracked a pained smile. "I don't suppose you want to buy a Maserati for yourself? Or maybe for your wife? Mistress?"

"Not today."

"That's a shame. The car business ain't what it used to be. Recession and all."

"Things are tough all over."

"That's what I hear."

Stan moved to the door and opened it. The two guards were hulking immediately outside, looking dangerous. Stan ignored them, his message delivered, and walked across the showroom floor, leaving Sal's door open.

When Stan left the building, Sal sighed as he picked up the phone.

Chapter 42

A mild surf lapped at the mocha-colored beach south of Jaco, Costa Rica, on the Pacific side. The sun glinted off the surface of the azure sea as puffs of clouds drifted lazily across the sky. Across the shore road several small homes perched precariously on the bluff, tin roofs reflecting bright blue, washboard façades weathered by the ocean breeze.

Simon stirred from his position on the sand and turned to his young companion, her dark skin glowing with taut vitality, her pert breasts jutting skyward in defiance of gravity, her ebony hair spread out against her towel like an inky halo. Simon took in the afterthought of a bikini bottom that barely concealed her charms and smiled wolfishly, savoring the faint scent of coconut oil rising to meet him from her dozing form.

"Maria, go up and get us some cold *cervezas* from the house, *sí?*"

The woman cracked one eye open. "*Amor*, I was sleeping."

"I'm thirsty."

She moaned deep in her throat and sat up. Simon had met her in the capital, San Jose, where she was earning her keep as a paid escort to visiting gentlemen in search of a walk on the wild side. Simon had waved sufficient money around to coax her into spending two weeks with him on the coast, where he was renting a bungalow.

"You want a snack, too?" she asked, her voice professionally interested in his needs.

"No, just the beer. Bring the cooler. It's next to the refrigerator. Put some ice in, too."

Maria stood and secured her bikini top. After a glance down the deserted beach, she padded up the sand, animating the tattoo of a scorpion on her shoulder as she moved.

A minute later a shadow fell across Simon's face, and he opened his eyes. A man wearing khaki slacks and a tangerine resort shirt stood blocking the sun, the silenced barrel of the small-caliber pistol pointed at Simon's head.

"Simon, I presume," he said, his voice flat.

"What...no. Wait. This is a mistake."

"Sure it is."

"I had to leave town and let the heat blow over. They were right behind me. But I was planning to send you money..."

Even to Simon's ear, his words sounded hollow.

"I'll bet."

Three seagulls flapped into the sky down the strand, the muffled pops from the gun startling them aloft. The gunman studied Simon's corpse in silence before sliding his weapon into the waist of his trousers and pulling his shirt over it. He turned to face the jungle across the road and trudged back to where his car was parked behind a grove of trees, out of sight from the few hillside dwellings, the license plate obscured with mud.

When Maria returned from the house, her scream echoed off the water like the shrill cry of a wounded animal. In the near distance a lone pelican skimmed six feet above the surf line, riding an updraft off the water, its form distorted by the heat waves rising off the beach, its endless quest for sustenance untroubled by the human drama playing out on the sprawling stretch of baking tropical sand.

Chapter 43

Black trudged up the stairs to his office, the hall's musty smell strangely reassuring. When he came to the door, he could still see the faint outline of the cheap lettering that had adorned it before the move, and noted that Mugsy's cat door was still working. He pushed it open and came face to face with Roxie, who was unpacking a box of office supplies.

"Good morning, Roxie."

"Morning, boss."

"How does it feel to be back in the old digs?"

"Like having to wear the same underwear again the third day in a row."

"It was for the best. I never want to have to worry about making a huge rent payment again."

"It wasn't luck that nobody had leased this pit. Who in their right mind would want it?"

"It's not that bad."

"That's like saying VD isn't that bad."

He looked around. "Where's the Mugster?"

"Hiding under my desk."

Black glanced at the base and nodded. "How are sales going?"

"Mugsy Inc. is still going strong. Although now he's off the air, it'll probably slow."

"Still. It's got to be throwing a ton of cash."

"After taxes, we're seeing a few grand a day."

"A day! Hell, I'm going home. Why work?"

"Exactly. Probably cuts into your drinking time."

"Damn right it does." He smiled. "Anyone call?"

"Stan said he'd be by. And a couple of new clients Bobby referred."

Black's face registered surprise. "Really? You aren't bullshitting me?"

"It's totally true. I put the numbers on your desk."

"That's awesome. Between the Mugsy money and the twenty-five grand from the show, we're fat again. I'm going to go buy a new computer."

"You don't know how to work your old one."

"Exactly. Did Stan say what he wanted?"

"Probably to talk about the case. I told him I pieced together what I think Simon was doing. He had a disguised interest in a songwriting company that his management company controls. It wasn't obvious: that management company, from the outside, appears clean, but if you look at the ownership, you find a shell company in Delaware that his production company owns. It's convoluted, but once you know what to look for…"

Black nodded slowly. "So Bend in the Creek was effectively signed to him. He wanted them to win so he could pocket most of the songwriting money."

"And I'll bet the management company has the rights to the merchandising."

"What about last year? Alex? Do the same companies own the rights to his stuff?"

"No. I'm way ahead of you. But Alex is still getting taken to the cleaners. A different company owns his rights. A bunch of guys with Italian last names are the shareholders."

"Ah. So it starts fitting together. There's the mob connection."

"Yeah. My guess is he did those guys a favor last season, and this year decided to pocket the real money himself."

"But he had to be making bank off the show."

"You'd think. But his car's leased, he's got a second mortgage on his house, and not a lot in his personal account."

"I'm not going to ask how you know that," Black said.

"That's probably best."

Black moved toward his office door. "At least it doesn't smell like a sewage treatment plant in here from Mugsy yet."

"How can you bag on a cat that's paying the rent?"

"I know. Talk about turnaround."

"Maybe we should call it Mugsy Investigations. He's got the name recognition now."

"It would mean new business cards. And you'd have to remember to answer the phone correctly."

"Oh. Right."

Black turned to Roxie. "How'd it turn out with Alex?"

"Okay. I mean, he's still walking on eggshells because of the kidnapping thing, but all in all...he's back in Denver today for a show."

"It's going to be tough to maintain a long-distance romance."

"Where there's a will."

"That's the spirit. How did telling the old lady you weren't going to be working for her anymore go?"

"She called me an ungrateful whore and demanded her wrist phone back."

"So it went well."

"As expected." She studied him. "When are you getting those extensions removed?"

"This afternoon. Why?"

"Oh, nothing. It's just with that suit and the hair...it's even douchier than usual."

"Is that even a word?"

"Douchiesque. Douchier. Whatever. If the douche fits."

"I missed your compliments."

Black entered his office, hung his jacket on the door, and moved to his desk. He glanced at the two message slips. "Roxie, there's no name on one of the messages."

"Crap."

"Do you remember who it was?"

"No. Just call and find out."

Black sighed and looked through the grimy window at the street below. On a whim, he pulled up YouTube, searched for *Rock of Ages*, and found the final show. Wavering for a moment at his decision to leave the band, he clicked on the clip and watched his swan song with a racing heart.

By the end of it, his resolve was back.

For once he'd done the right thing.

Maybe not for everyone.

But absolutely for him.

<<<<>>>>

About the Author

A *Wall Street Journal* and *The Times* featured author, Russell Blake lives full time on the Pacific coast of Mexico. He is the acclaimed author of many thrillers, including the Assassin series, the JET series, and the BLACK series. He has also co-authored *The Eye of Heaven* with Clive Cussler for Penguin Books.

"Capt." Russell enjoys writing, fishing, playing with his dogs, collecting and sampling tequila, and waging an ongoing battle against world domination by clowns.

☼

Visit RussellBlake.com for updates
or subscribe to: RussellBlake.com/contact/mailing-list

Co-authored with Clive Cussler

THE EYE OF HEAVEN

Thrillers by Russell Blake

FATAL EXCHANGE

THE GERONIMO BREACH

ZERO SUM

THE DELPHI CHRONICLE TRILOGY

THE VOYNICH CYPHER

SILVER JUSTICE

UPON A PALE HORSE

The Assassin Series by Russell Blake

KING OF SWORDS

NIGHT OF THE ASSASSIN

RETURN OF THE ASSASSIN

REVENGE OF THE ASSASSIN

BLOOD OF THE ASSASSIN

REQUIEM FOR THE ASSASSIN

The JET Series by Russell Blake

JET

JET II – BETRAYAL

JET III – VENGEANCE

JET IV – RECKONING

JET V – LEGACY

JET VI – JUSTICE

JET VII – SANCTUARY

JET – OPS FILES (prequel)

The BLACK Series by Russell Blake

BLACK

BLACK IS BACK

BLACK IS THE NEW BLACK

BLACK TO REALITY

Non Fiction by Russell Blake

AN ANGEL WITH FUR

HOW TO SELL A GAZILLION EBOOKS

(while drunk, high or incarcerated)

CPSIA information can be obtained at www.ICGtesting.com
Printed in the USA
LVOW11s0700150215

427084LV00003B/179/P